"Nothing in my life,* nothing,*" Jillian stressed, "is the same anymore."

She'd thought Ben would understand. He'd seemed so understanding of everything else.

"I even look different. The Kendrick women are tall and blond and poised and self-confident, but I'm short, brunette, and so…not."

Reaching out, Ben grabbed her wrist. "Trust me," he insisted, as his eyes shifted from her mouth to the skin exposed by the vee of her top. "The last thing you ever need to worry about is how you compare to your half sisters."

Beneath his fingers, Jillian felt her pulse give a betraying little leap. Too aware of his big body, she took a step back, turned away.

"You don't need to humor me, Ben. That's not what I want from you."

When she met his glance, his smile was gone.

"I'm not humoring you, Jillian. I meant exactly what I said." His blue eyes narrowed as he cautiously searched her face. "Now that you've mentioned it, what *do* you want from me?"

Dear Reader,

The bulletin board above my desk is a mess. The green bamboo backing that I thought looked better than plain cork is barely visible. It's covered with reminders, schedules and little bits of inspiration. That inspiration includes an 8x10 of an incredibly hunky guy—the hero for my work in progress—and dozens of quotes. Some of those quotations make me smile. Most make me think. One inspired this story.

"Life is change. Growth is optional.
Choose wisely."
—Attributed to Karen Kaiser Clark

We know we can't always control what happens to us. And sometimes it takes us a while to realize that our response to a situation is as important as the change itself. Change can be difficult. Growth can be a struggle. That's why my first response to a crisis is to head for anything chocolate…and take it from there.

Love,

Christine

THE RELUCTANT HEIRESS

CHRISTINE FLYNN

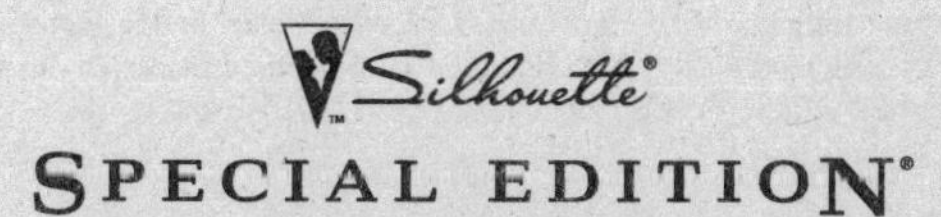

Published by Silhouette Books
America's Publisher of Contemporary Romance

If you purchased this book without a cover you should be aware that this book is stolen property. It was reported as "unsold and destroyed" to the publisher, and neither the author nor the publisher has received any payment for this "stripped book."

ISBN-13: 978-0-373-24835-3
ISBN-10: 0-373-24835-0

THE RELUCTANT HEIRESS

Copyright © 2007 by Christine Flynn

All rights reserved. Except for use in any review, the reproduction or utilization of this work in whole or in part in any form by any electronic, mechanical or other means, now known or hereafter invented, including xerography, photocopying and recording, or in any information storage or retrieval system, is forbidden without the written permission of the editorial office, Silhouette Books, 233 Broadway, New York, NY 10279 U.S.A.

This is a work of fiction. Names, characters, places and incidents are either the product of the author's imagination or are used fictitiously, and any resemblance to actual persons, living or dead, business establishments, events or locales is entirely coincidental.

This edition published by arrangement with Harlequin Books S.A.

® and TM are trademarks of Harlequin Books S.A., used under license. Trademarks indicated with ® are registered in the United States Patent and Trademark Office, the Canadian Trade Marks Office and in other countries.

Visit Silhouette Books at www.eHarlequin.com

Printed in U.S.A.

Books by Christine Flynn

Silhouette Special Edition

Remember the Dreams #254
Silence the Shadows #465
Renegade #566
Walk upon the Wind #612
Out of the Mist #657
The Healing Touch #693
Beyond the Night #747
Luke's Child #788
Lonely Knight #826
Daughter of the Bride #889
When Morning Comes #922
Jake's Mountain #945
A Father's Wish #962
**Logan's Bride* #995
**The Rebel's Bride* #1034
**The Black Sheep's Bride* #1053
Her Child's Father #1151
Hannah and the Hellion #1184
From House Calls to Husband #1203
**Finally His Bride* #1240
The Home Love Built #1275
Dr. Mom and the Millionaire #1304
The Baby Quilt #1327
Another Man's Children #1420
Royal Protocol #1471
Suddenly Family #1504
Four Days, Five Nights #1566
†*The Housekeeper's Daughter* #1612
†*Hot August Nights* #1618
†*Her Prodigal Prince Charming* #1624
§*Trading Secrets* #1678
§*The Sugar House* #1690
§*Confessions of a Small-Town Girl* #1701
‡*The City Girl and the Country Doctor* #1790
†*Falling for the Heiress* #1816
†*The Reluctant Heiress* #1835

*The Whitaker Brides
†The Kendricks of Camelot
§Going Home
‡Talk of the Neighborhood

CHRISTINE FLYNN

admits to being interested in just about everything, which is why she considers herself fortunate to have turned her interest in writing into a career. She feels that a writer gets to explore it all and, to her, exploring relationships—especially the intense, bittersweet or even lighthearted relationships between men and women—is fascinating.

Prologue

Jillian Hadley always waited until September to make her New Year's resolutions. Where the rest of the world planned new beginnings on January first, she waited for the start of the new school year to compile her annual list of the faults she would fix, habits she would break and objectives she would pursue.

She wasn't rebelling against convention, though she definitely marched to her own drummer. She wasn't asserting herself, either. The little quirk affected no one but herself. The independent streak she'd been raised to protect simply found the timing more logical. A new school year was a fresh start in itself. January came in the middle of it.

As had become her habit, she'd turned on the television in the living room for company the minute she'd walked into the cozy little duplex she called home. Accompanied by a persuasive male voice promising her better gas mileage, she lugged the luggage she'd taken on her trip into her bedroom, flipped on the overhead light to illuminate the purely feminine space and tossed her suitcase and carry-on bag onto her white eyelet-covered bed.

Only once in her eight years of teaching had she returned to Thomas Jefferson Elementary without her usual, lengthy list of items geared toward self-improvement. That had been last year; her very own personal year from hell. It had actually been closer to eighteen months, but there were details she preferred to overlook about that time as she unzipped her suitcase and started to unpack.

Within three months, her mom had become seriously ill, her now ex-fiancé had informed her that he had no intention of marrying her and her mom had died. It seemed as if bad news had simply been heaped on worse to the point where numbness had become a constant state of being. She hadn't even realized how much of a fog she'd drifted in until the pain and numbness had finally, mercifully begun to dull over the past summer.

She lifted a slightly squashed, pale-pink orchid lei from atop a stack of shorts and tank tops. As of now, as of that very moment, she was declaring that horrible time officially over. Done. Finished. The loss of her mom, she would feel forever. Beth Hadley had been her friend, her champion and the strongest woman she'd ever known. Eric Chandler, she had long since concluded, she could easily survive without.

It was her awareness of how completely she was over the man she'd once thought she would grow old with—and the realization that her biological clock hadn't stopped running just because the rest of her life had gone on hold—that led straight to her first resolution.

This year, she decided, hanging the lei over a post of her four-poster bed, if Coach Gunderson asked her out again, she would go. He was a nice guy. A little bald, but nice. And heaven knew how hard it was to find a decent guy anymore. One that wasn't married, involved or gay, anyway. She would also avoid the doughnuts in the teachers' lounge, learn to play the guitar she'd bought four years ago, and seriously consider getting her long, impossibly curly hair straightened. If she was feeling particularly adventurous, she might also get the unmanageable mass cut and dyed some color other than the uninspiring shade of plain old dark brown that it was.

The reemerged optimist in her could practically feel all manner of change coming on. Her vacation—a major, much-needed splurge—was now officially over. Other than the lei and a bunch of little paper drink umbrellas, all she had left of those ten days on Maui was a hibiscus-print sarong she'd probably never wear, the postcards and photo books she'd brought back to share with her students and the great tan she'd acquired because she'd kept forgetting to reapply sunscreen.

It didn't matter that her vacation was now nothing but a memory. She felt none of the letdown she would have experienced even a few weeks ago at returning to her ordinary, rather predictable life. Even tired from eleven hours in the air, three plane changes and interminable waits in airports, she found herself looking forward to the new school year, to meeting her new students, to putting her resolutions to work. She didn't even mind that before she could go to bed, she needed to do laundry so she could wash the top she wanted to wear to school tomorrow.

In the interests of time, she dumped the remaining contents of the suitcase into her laundry basket and headed for the washer and dryer behind the louvered doors in her kitchen. Thinking she should check the messages on her blinking answering machine, she'd just passed the assortment of herbs and a fern she'd left in water in her sink when the disembodied male voice on the evening news brought her to a halt.

With her heart beating a little too rapidly, she turned to the television opposite the sofa dividing the area in half.

"...affair early in my marriage. That affair took place more than thirty years ago and resulted in a daughter I didn't know I had until she approached me after her mother's death last year. The photographs taken by Bradley Ashworth were of that meeting. As you know, Bradley was married to my youngest daughter, Tess. When Tess told him she wanted a divorce to escape his mental and physical abuse, he told her I was having an affair and used those photographs to blackmail her into silence."

On the screen, a distinguished-looking, silver-haired gentleman spoke in solemn tones from behind a bank of microphones. His sharp gray eyes peered intently toward his audience of millions.

With her pulse beating in her ears, Jillian tried to concentrate on the man's words. He was saying that to protect her family's relationships and reputation, his daughter Tess had allowed the world to believe what Ashworth had claimed; that she had left him because she'd become bored with marriage and wanted other men.

Jillian remembered the scandal that had erupted when the beautiful Tess Kendrick had taken her young son and left the country last year. At the time, Jillian had thought the woman the epitome of spoiled self-indulgence. Because of the relentless media coverage, so had everyone else. Beyond that recollection, though, little else about the woman and what was being said to clear her name computed just then.

The entire nation knew the man on the screen. The powerful former senator was one of the richest men in the country. As a young man, he had charmed a princess into giving up a kingdom to marry him and he, his glamorous wife and their four pampered and privileged offspring had been treated by the press as America's royalty ever since.

Jillian had grown up with the media stories about their fairy-tale lives right along with everyone else. In high school, she and her girlfriends had devoured everything printed about the family, especially the girls. Ashley had been younger than Jillian by only a couple of years. Tess, by maybe two more. They had worn designer clothes and ball gowns. They'd attended the best private schools, had bodyguards, servants, staff. They'd spent summers in their royal grandmother's tiny European kingdom of Luzandria. Their older brothers were gorgeous. The girls themselves had grown up to be as stunning as their mother, the elegant ash blonde the cameras now revealed to be sitting supportively at William Kendrick's side.

Jillian's heartbeats turned to sickening thuds. Her mom had been the only person she knew who seemed to ignore everything about the Kendricks and their celebrity. She'd never heard her comment on any of the magazine or news articles about any member of their family. If Jillian brought them to her attention with some publication's picture of the girls all decked out for a charity ball or riding horses on their fabulous estate in Camelot, Virginia, her only remark would be a seemingly preoccupied "how nice," or something equally innocuous before changing the subject entirely.

Jillian had simply thought that the lives of the rich and famous held no interest at all for her very practical, hardworking mom. At least, she had until two days before her mom had died.

That was when she'd finally told Jillian who her father was.

She was the illegitimate daughter the man on the screen was talking about. And he had promised he would tell no one she existed.

His somber image gave way to a reporter who looked properly grave himself as he proceeded to recap what William had just said about Tess Kendrick having been abused by her ex-husband, then blackmailed into silence with supposedly incriminating pictures of William and an unidentified woman.

It barely registered to Jillian that she had been mistaken for William's lover. She barely even noticed that her name hadn't been mentioned. All that mattered was that William Kendrick had just broken his word to her.

The basket of laundry had slid from her arms, bits of pale neutrals and pastels now scattered over beige carpet. She had met him only once. Grief, resentment and a whole host of bitter and unidentified emotions had driven her to seek him out a few weeks after her mom's death. As ambivalent as she had felt about him, and because she'd had no desire to become tabloid fodder herself, she'd made it unquestionably clear that she didn't want their relationship made public. As quickly as he had agreed, she'd felt certain he hadn't wanted that, either, if for no other reason than to avoid the scandal such news would create. He had promised her—*promised*—that he would tell no one other than his wife that she existed.

She pressed her fingers to her mouth, realized she was shaking. She wasn't sure if she felt sick, furious or numb as the newscaster began to speculate about who—and where—the daughter from his affair might be. All she knew for certain was that her mother had never stopped loving William

Kendrick. The admission had come with nearly her dying breath. Yet, as much as Jillian loved and respected the woman who had held her head high and raised her illegitimate daughter alone, Jillian couldn't imagine ever feeling anything remotely resembling affection for the man who had fathered her. Because her mother had shied from involvement with any other man, she suspected that he had hurt her badly. And now he had betrayed Jillian herself.

The change she'd felt coming on minutes ago no longer seemed welcome at all. As she watched the image on the screen cut to archive footage of Tess and Bradley, then to William as a young senator to capitalize on the dual scandals coming to light, what she'd felt now was more like the beginning of a nightmare.

Chapter One

Ben Garrett did his best work under pressure. He thrived on challenges, deadlines and delivering the impossible. Obstacles were nothing more than hurdles to be jumped, shifted or removed as he saw fit. But the part of the game he loved best was developing strategies to alter or influence the public's perception, and he always played the game to win.

His clients paid him handsomely to see that he did.

The hard muscles of his athletic frame shifted beneath his tailored three-piece suit as he moved from the unanswered front door to the side gate of the modest beige duplex in the working-class suburb Hayden, Pennsylvania. The toylike, earth-green Volkswagen he recognized as Jillian Hadley's sat parked under the carport that belonged to her unit. It was a good bet that she was around there somewhere.

Ben's specialty was media relations for The Garrett

Group's high-profile clients; Washington, D.C.'s movers and shakers, and the rich and famous—or infamous—who wanted their images enhanced, subdued or altered completely. In the fifteen years since he'd earned his MBA from Yale, he'd also earned a reputation in those rarefied circles as *the* expert at damage control. That ability was why his father, the senior partner in their prestigious public relations firm, and William Kendrick, his father's close friend and a longtime client, had both insisted that he handle Miss Hadley himself.

The good news was that he would get to her before the press descended on her like vultures on carrion. The bad news was that the information he'd been given about William's newly disclosed daughter left him little to work with. All he knew about Jillian Hadley was that she taught grade school, that her sole meeting with William had not gone well and that no one had been able to reach her to warn her about yesterday's press conference. What concerned him most, though, what concerned them all for that matter, was that she was a potential powder keg in the scandal that had broken twenty-four hours ago.

There hadn't been a newspaper, television station or radio talk show in the country that hadn't jumped on the stories about William's youngest daughter, Tess, being blackmailed by her ex-husband, and about William's newly revealed affair and offspring. The gossip had gone international at the speed of light. The *London Daily Star* had announced the Crisis in Camelot in bold type on its front page. Headlines in Paris, Rome and on the Internet had leaned toward the theme of Tess paying for the sins of her father and speculation about whether his unnamed daughter had been paid for her silence.

Since no one had any idea what Jillian might say, it was Ben's job to keep the powder keg she represented from blowing. Part of his job, anyway. William had also been adamant that she be protected from the media for her own sake as much as to protect him and his family from any potentially damaging comments she might make.

He reached a small side gate in the white picket fence surrounding the backyard. Letting himself through, he strode past the neat, profusely blooming flowerbed at the side of the house. He had allotted himself twenty-four hours to accomplish his goal with Miss Hadley. As he absently checked the date and time on his Rolex, he hoped fervently that this aspect of the "affair situation," as it was being referred to in the office, would go as smoothly as the press conference he'd arranged and scripted yesterday. He was in the middle of a little family crisis of his own.

He rounded the corner of the tidy little yard that looked much like the small yards on either side of it. Fruit trees and flower beds took up most of the space both sides of the duplex apparently shared. The bulk of his attention, though, settled on the slender brunette standing barefoot in the grass by a redwood picnic table.

He recognized her delicate cameo-like profile from the photos of her he'd seen yesterday. And her hair. The long, wild curls tumbled past her shoulders in a cloud of unrestrained dark silk.

In the space of seconds his glance shifted over her gentle curves. The white tank top and the khaki knee-length skirt she wore were the antithesis of the corporate, chic and designer attire worn by most the women in his sphere, the sophisticated Kendrick women included. If she was wearing makeup, he couldn't tell. As she sensed his presence and glanced toward him, she simply looked tanned, healthy and far younger than the thirty-three years he knew her to be.

Still assessing her, he felt himself frown. He hadn't expected her to appear so…natural. He didn't expect how cheated he felt, either, when the smile of greeting that curved her lush mouth and lit her beautiful dark eyes died at the sight of him.

From that soft smile, she'd clearly expected him to be someone she knew. At the very least, she hadn't expected to be faced with a total stranger.

Not wanting to alarm her by getting close enough to offer his hand, he stopped near the opposite end of the table and motioned toward the house.

"I rang your doorbell but no one answered," he told her, explaining his presence in her backyard. "I'm Ben Garrett, Miss Hadley. William Kendrick's public relations manager."

Jillian's heart gave an unfamiliar little lurch as the lean hunk of dark-haired, blue-eyed perfection in the expensively tailored suit gave her an easygoing smile. The rich, deep tones of his voice held equal notes of reserve and friendliness. So did the strong, decidedly handsome lines of his face. The combination might have struck her as rather remarkable to achieve had she considered it. As it was, she was too busy dealing with dismay at his presence to worry about his effect on her pulse.

"William said someone was coming when he called this morning." William Kendrick had actually called her twice before that. So had his secretary. Theirs had been four of the messages waiting for her last night on her answering machine. "I'm sorry he didn't reach you in time."

One dark eyebrow slowly arched. "In time?"

"To tell you that coming here was unnecessary."

She looked back to the rocks and twigs she'd gathered for her classroom's new terrarium and began placing them in a plastic bag. The kids wouldn't return to school for a few days.

This week was for teacher preparation. Yet, rather than class sizes and curriculums, it seemed every conversation she'd had or overheard had included gossip about William Kendrick's mystery daughter and the affair tainting what had been long regarded as his and Katherine Kendrick's perfect marriage. Sympathy had leaned heavily toward the wronged party, the beautiful Katherine. After all, her husband had cheated on her. Worse, he'd had a child by that other woman.

That woman was her mother.

Jillian had stayed as far from those conversations as she could and tried to tune out what she couldn't help overhear. When Carrie Teague, her teaching partner for the past two years, had noticed her lack of participation in the discussions and asked point-blank what she thought about the scandals, Jillian had offered the excuse of being too jet-lagged to care about anything but school and sleep. That comment had, mercifully, led to questions about her vacation and the uncomfortable subject had been dropped. Temporarily, anyway.

From the messages Jillian had listened to last night, she now knew that William had made an honest effort to reach her before his broadcast, to explain what he felt he had to do. Deep down, she supposed she even understood that he'd done the only thing he could do to protect and to clear the name of his real daughter, as she thought of Tess. She had also been infinitely relieved to learn when William had called that morning that he hadn't divulged her name or anything about her to the press. None of that changed her opinion of him, though. Her other reasons for feeling so resentful toward him remained firmly in place.

In an ideal world, she would never even have heard the Kendrick name. And Ben Garrett wouldn't be standing in her backyard messing with her heart rate.

He hadn't offered anything remotely resembling a goodbye. He'd done nothing but remain with his size-elevens planted firmly on the lawn studying her as a scientist might some intriguing, or unexpected, specimen he needed to identify and catalogue.

"Actually, I'm afraid my presence is necessary. Or will be."

His too-thorough scrutiny unnerved her. Preferring that he didn't notice how her hands were shaking, she left the sack on the table and crossed her arms. "You said you're in public relations?"

"I am."

"Then, honestly," she insisted, "we really don't have anything to discuss. I don't deal with the public. Not in the sense you do. William said no one knows who I am," she said, not knowing what else to call the man she refused to refer to as "my father." "I'm perfectly happy to remain anonymous. The Kendricks have their lives. I have mine. I'd prefer it remain that way."

Her gaze remained direct and uncompromising. Like her words, that expression spoke more of conviction than challenge. It was her body language that told him how valiantly she was trying to hide how upset she was with William and what he'd done.

It also seemed as obvious as the uneasy way her glance finally flicked from his that she lacked either the sophistication or the practice to effectively pull off that feat. Anxiety had her hugging her arms tightly enough to leave white marks on her skin.

It relieved him to know she wanted to remain unknown. She wouldn't get her wish, but that desire meant she wasn't interested in running out to sell her story, whatever it was, to the highest bidder. That desire, however, also gave him a new concern. All she would have to do is repeat in public what she'd just told him and the press would be all over her preference to have nothing to do with the Kendricks. As persistent as the media tended to be, they'd hound her into the ground trying to find out why.

Rubbing the side of his nose, he considered how best to help her face how complicated her life was about to get. "Things aren't quite that simple, Miss Hadley. William didn't tell the press who you are," he confirmed, deciding to simply lay it all out. "But you won't be able to avoid them. I figure you have somewhere between a couple of hours and a couple of days before reporters show up here."

Her expression held infinite patience as she cocked her head. "If he didn't tell anyone who I am, then how will they find me?"

"One of William's attorneys learned this morning that a tabloid paid an undisclosed source a small fortune for copies of the photographs. The ones William refused to describe or show during his press conference," he explained. "One of those pictures contains a shot of the two of you in what looks like an embrace..."

Confusion entered her tone. "There was no 'embrace.' He might have tried to put his arm around—"

"Another shows you in what looks like an argument," he continued without pause. "Both show the two of you beside a Volkswagen with Pennsylvania plates. William said the car was yours.

"The tabloid probably already knows who you are," he warned. "And any news editor who gets his hands on those photos will use his contacts to run those plates just like William's attorney did."

Confusion gave way to uneasy comprehension. "Is that how you found me?"

He shook his head, stepped closer. "We already knew you lived in Hayden. You'd told William," he reminded her. "Locating you was just a matter of plugging your name and town into the Internet."

"I'm on the Internet?"

"Just about everyone is," he assured her. "Anyway," he continued, more interested in making his point than in her apparent ignorance of what could be obtained for five bucks from the right search site, "the attorney ran your plates just to see what anyone else running them would come up with.

"What they'll get is your name and address and the name of the lien holder on your little Beetle out there. Once they know who and where you are and you're recognized as the woman in those photos, your anonymity will be history."

Ben's first impression of the woman he'd been sent to guide and protect was that she was the sort of person who went through life flying under the radar. Considering her and her modest surroundings, she appeared to be a quietly attractive woman of average means, one whose life was as relatively uncomplicated as she appeared to be herself. She didn't want the world to know her. She didn't want notoriety or fame. From what she'd rather emphatically made clear to him, all she wanted was whatever it was she had now.

It wasn't his fault her life was about to be upended. Yet, something about the way she struggled to mask her apprehension as she searched his face brought an unexpected twinge of sympathy. And guilt. She was looking to him for help. Just not the kind he was prepared to offer.

"The pictures were sold?" Looking as if she absolutely did not want to believe what she'd heard, she lifted her hand, pushed her fingers through the wild tangle of her incredible hair. "Who else had access to them?"

Her motions drew the soft cotton of her tank top taut below the fullness of her breasts. Ben felt his breath stall. He was already more aware than he wanted to be of the litheness of her feminine body, the delicacy of her shoulder blades, the long length of her shapely legs. He preferred women who looked refined, sophisticated, sleek. Standing barefoot in the grass with the soft, golden skin of her slender limbs exposed and her thick curls uncontrolled, she looked more like a young earth mother. He could easily see her wandering down a beach or through the woods with a dozen little kids in tow.

Still, there was no denying the quick tightening low in his gut as he met the anxiety in her eyes once more. As cynical as he'd become, the sympathy he felt for her was disconcerting enough. The last thing he wanted was the reminder of just how long he'd gone without a woman.

"Tess Kendrick's ex-husband. Bradley Ashworth," he said, burying his responses to her the way he did anything else he didn't want to think about. "We suspect he sold them in retaliation for William exposing him as the louse he is."

A little panic on her part wouldn't have surprised him. At the very least, he expected a little more cooperation.

"They might know who I am," she conceded, "but I don't have to talk to them."

"That's not going to stop them from invading your life. That's why I'm here," he emphasized, needing her to grasp the gravity of the situation. "My job is to help you with the media that's going to descend the minute they discover your identity." And to put the proper spin on what you say, he admitted to himself. If she knew that, though, she'd only want to get rid of him that much faster. "They will arrive," he assured her. "If not today, then tomorrow for certain. As difficult as it may be to accept, you can't avoid any of this."

The woman clearly had no idea how vulnerable she was. Hoping he didn't sound impatient with her, he deliberately gentled his tone.

"William wants you to know he's not about to leave you to the wolves. And that's exactly what you'll think has happened once your phone starts ringing with requests for statements and interviews." He slowly shook his head. "This really isn't something you want to try to handle alone."

For a moment Jillian said nothing. She found it disconcerting enough to be face-to-face with one of her famous father's associates. But Ben Garrett was unsettling in his own right. The man was confident to a fault, incredibly persuasive in his arguments and utterly convinced of his certainty of what was about to happen. Yet, even more disturbing than his absolute insistence was the physical impact of his presence.

He possessed the same compelling aura of authority and influence she'd sensed in William when she'd met him, only in a more elemental and infinitely more disquieting way. He stood nearly ten feet from her, yet she could almost feel the energy that radiated from him like a force field. That raw power sensitized her nerves, tugged hard at something low in her belly.

She didn't doubt for an instant that he was a man accustomed to achieving exactly what he set out to accomplish. He was the alpha other men envied and women turned stupid for—just as her mother had done with William. But turning stupid over a total stranger wasn't on her list of back-to-school resolutions. Nor was she about to have a stranger tell her what she should do. Especially one she strongly suspected wanted only to cover William's tracks.

Feeling a definite need for the situation in general and this unnerving man in particular to go away, she adopted the end-of-discussion tone she used when a student was being particularly obtuse.

"Mr. Garrett," she began, "please tell your client I appreciate his concern, but I can manage on my own. If I can handle thirty second-graders on a sugar high after a class birthday party, I can probably deal with a few reporters."

"It'll be more than a few."

"Then, I'll handle however many there are," she insisted, only to immediately soften her tone. "I'm sorry you had to come all this way for nothing. I'm sure you're very qualified to do whatever it is you do, but I don't want anything from William. Not even his help.

"No offense to you," she concluded, because she didn't believe in shooting the messenger—even if the messenger was part of the reason her stomach was jumping.

She'd seen something that looked suspiciously like sympathy in his disturbing blue eyes moments ago. She caught a glimpse of it again before he glanced away. She just couldn't tell if it was real or calculated.

She never should have gone to see William, she thought, reaching to stuff the last of the stones and twigs into the bag. Loss and anger had pushed her. That alone should have told her seeking him out would be a mistake.

The chirping of birds joined the rustle of plastic as Ben prepared to argue his position. The woman really had no concept of what she was about to face. He'd seen seasoned politicians and corporate heads cave under the media's badgering, and he had no clear idea of what she would say or do when the press found her. But pressing his point didn't seem like such a good idea just then. Jillian Hadley might be as naive as a newborn about what was to come, but there was a sense of independence about her—or maybe it was simply stubbornness—that told him pushing too hard would only push her farther away. He needed her cooperation. He wouldn't get it by badgering her.

With his first efforts frustrated, Ben prepared to retreat. He wasn't admitting defeat by any means. He would simply let time work in his favor.

Reaching inside his jacket, he pulled out a pen and one of his business cards. Using the table beside him, he wrote his cell phone number on the back of the card. Two steps later he held it out to her.

The breeze shifted. As it did, it caught her scent, something elusive, faintly exotic and far more sensual than he would have expected a woman who worked with small children to wear.

A muscle in his jaw jerked.

"Call me when you change your mind."

"That's not going to happen," Jillian assured him, but took the card anyway. Anything to get him on his way. "But thank you."

With a nod of his dark head, he murmured, "You're welcome," and turned to stride back the way he'd come.

Not until he'd disappeared around the side of the house did Jillian realize she'd been holding her breath. Realizing it now, it escaped in a rush as she stuffed his card in her skirt pocket and grabbed her sack.

Considering the amount of doom he'd predicted, she hadn't expected him to give up and go so easily. Just glad that he had, she hurried toward her back door with her chest feeling far too tight and a sense of foreboding fast on her heels. If the press did find her, the next few days could be a little unsettling. But she had weathered upsetting days before.

For months after her mom had been diagnosed and she'd lost both her mom and Eric, she'd felt as if she'd been in a total, stomach-dropping free fall. Nothing about her world had felt the same. Not even the parts that had kept her from feeling as if she had nothing to latch on to, nothing to keep her life from spinning completely out of control. Now that she'd finally gotten her feet back under her, and the dark cloud that had hung over her head had lifted, she was not about to let her life get messed up again. Especially not by William Kendrick.

She could handle this, she assured herself over the squeak of her back screen door as she pulled it open. And she could handle it on her own. She did not need Ben Garrett.

Or so she thought before she found herself rather desperately needing to seek his advice less than twelve hours later.

Chapter Two

In the five minutes since Jillian had scrambled from her car into her duplex, her telephone had barely stopped ringing. It rang now as she paced behind the low moss-green sofa dividing her normally tranquil living room from her kitchen and dining area. Her teacher's copies of the textbooks she would be using that year lay scattered over the sofa's cushions. She'd dumped them there on her way across the room to yank closed the drapes.

Opposite the sofa, the offending instrument summoned her from the end table between two barrel chairs. In between, sat the coffee table holding a trio of lime-scented candles, the latcst cooking magazines and *Cosmo,* and the faucet knob that had come off in the shower that morning.

She had intended to mention the broken knob to her landlady when she returned from school that afternoon. Her phone conversation a minute ago with Irene White, however, had not been about the plumbing.

Holding Ben's business card between two fingers, she nervously flicked it with her thumb.

Had she known anyone else who would know what to do, she would call them and beg for help. She just couldn't think of a single person who'd had any experience being followed by a pack of rabid reporters.

She paced back past the phone, nerves jumping. It was no longer possible to believe she could somehow escape recognition, or that she could handle the press alone. Hoping that the matter would simply go away had been a total waste of energy. So had been praying for a miracle. The "matter" had arrived. It was literally on her doorstep—and the only person she knew with the expertise to deal with it was the six feet of disturbing, urban masculinity that William Kendrick had sent to deal with her.

Hating the position she felt forced into, she snatched up the phone seconds after it stopped ringing and punched in the cell phone number Ben had written on the back of his card. She was staring at his handwriting, thinking that the bold, confident strokes suited his personality perfectly when he answered on the third ring.

"Ben Garrett."

She would have recognized the deep, authoritative tones of his voice even if he hadn't identified himself. Pacing to the window facing the street, she peeked between the heavy beige drapes she'd closed only minutes ago.

"It's Jillian. I have a…situation."

Over a faint crackle in the connection, he calmly asked, "What's going on?"

"Do you want to know what's going on now? Or what's been going on all day?"

"You choose."

"In that case," she replied, more irritated at William by the minute for putting her in this position, "a gray SUV followed me to school this morning. I thought I was just being paranoid when I first saw it because of what you'd said yesterday about the press showing up, but there was a black car behind it. It followed me, too."

She found it impossible to remain still. Nerves had her turning from the drapes to pace around the coffee table. "They both parked outside the school and both were still there when I left. In between, one of the teachers told me after lunch that a reporter was in the school office asking personal questions about me. He apparently had a picture of me and William.

"The principal asked him to leave," she continued, feeling her grip on calm slip, "but there were more guys with telephoto lenses on their cameras hanging over the schoolyard fence when I left. I think most of them followed me home. I know the first two guys did. They're out front with the reporters who were waiting for me when I got here."

The muffled honk of a horn filtered over the phone line. A moment later a brushing noise made her think he must be in his car and had just switched his phone to his other ear.

"What did you say to them?"

"I didn't say anything."

"Nothing?"

"Not a word." She couldn't even recall all the queries that had been hurled at her as she'd darted from her little Beetle to the door of her carport. All she'd cared about just then was that none of the half-dozen people thrusting microphones toward her had managed to block her way to her side door.

"Look," she continued, having paced back to peek between the drapes again. There were now television cables on her front lawn. "I have a dozen strangers outside my door, my phone has been ringing since the minute I got here, and Mrs. White is threatening to call the police because her mums are getting trampled. She tends those plants as if they were her children."

"Who's Mrs. White?"

"My landlady. She lives in the other half of this duplex." Her disquiet compounded itself. A woman with a camera crew just crossed the street to knock on Hal Pederson's door. Hal worked graveyard shift at the grocery warehouse and slept from two o'clock in the afternoon until ten. He wouldn't appreciate being awakened after having just gone to sleep.

The two news vans at the curb in front of her house had been there when she arrived. A third van pulled up, the satellite dish on its roof already rotating to seek the strongest signal.

"CBS just got here," she told him, identifying the logo on the side of the vehicle as someone knocked on her front door. "And there's a woman with a microphone at the house across the street. It's one thing to have them outside my door, but now they're disturbing my neighbors. Should I call the police?" she asked him, her distress mounting as the knock repeated. "Or would that just make this all worse?"

"I'll call. The police can't stop the press from talking to your neighbors, but they'll get them off of their lawns. And yours. I'm on my way," he told her. "Don't open the door until I get there. I'll come around back."

The line went dead before she could do much more than open her mouth. She'd been about to ask how long he would be. The address on his card indicated his office was in Washington, D.C.

Thinking it could be nearly three hours before he arrived, she hung up the phone—only for it to start ringing again.

She didn't recognize the name on the caller ID. But then, except for Mrs. White's, she hadn't recognized the names or numbers of any of the other people who'd called since she'd come home, either.

Feeling besieged, needing an ally, she thought about calling Stacy Fisher. It was Stacy who'd talked her into blowing some of the money she was saving to buy a house on the week with her in Hawaii.

"You need to do something fun for yourself," her ever-adventurous—and only single—friend had insisted. "You can buy a house when you're married. You need to lie on a beach and drink mai tais while some buff, bronzed hunk rubs suntan lotion on your back."

The beach and the mai tais had materialized. So had the hunks, actually. Jillian hadn't been as receptive to them as Stacy had, though. She preferred men who could converse without staring at her chest or feeling compelled to impress her with what kind of cars they drove and how well their stocks had performed last quarter. Or without using the words *dude*, *righteous* and *gnarly*.

Stacy had said she just needed more practice. She'd been stuck in the Eric rut so long before she'd had the good sense to dump him, that she'd forgotten about the frog-kissing a woman had to do.

She hadn't talked to Stacy since they'd returned from Hawaii a couple of days ago, so the fearless, bubbly blonde she'd known since college had no idea what was going on. Still, Jillian knew she could always count on her for solid, no-nonsense advice. Stacy, who now taught seventh grade at a middle school on the other side of town, had once taught in the inner city where lock-downs and crowd control had been as common as chalk dust. Her advice on how to handle the intruders outside her door would probably be to turn a hose on them, so she'd be no help there. But being the people person she was, she could give her a little practical perspective on how to deal with her colleagues at school.

That morning, talk about the Kendrick scandals had pretty much been an echo of yesterday. Gina Wasserman, the librarian, had claimed, again, that there was no way she could have sat in front of a camera and listened to her husband tell the world he'd been unfaithful to her. "Katherine had to be devastated," she'd insisted, speaking of the man's wife as if she were her dearest friend, "but she showed such class."

"Unlike whoever that other woman was," had sniffed the grand dame of fifth grade, Yvonne Bliss. "She knew he was married. She knew he had a family. What did she think? He was going to leave Katherine Kendrick for her?"

According to Carrie Teague, Jillian's outspoken teaching partner, some women simply didn't think in those situations. They were attracted to the power. What Carrie had been more interested in was how much his "secret daughter," as the press had started calling her, had been paid to keep quiet. The married mother of two was absolutely certain it must have been a fortune.

The gossip had changed tone, however, after the reporter had shown up. Thanks to Yvonne, who'd been in the office at the time and who also happened to be the biggest gossip in the school, news of his presence and his photograph had spread through the halls like an annual virus.

Once word was out about Jillian's identity, some staff had practically tripped over themselves explaining that they'd never have said what they had if they'd known they were talking about her and her mother. Others had chosen a speculative silence. Or outright skepticism.

Ted Gunderson, the built and balding coach who'd smiled broadly every time he'd seen her the past couple of days had walked up to her in the hall with his hands on his hips and a frown on his face.

"You're not really his daughter, are you?" he'd asked.

Since there was no denying what certain lawyers, reporters and a tabloid already knew, she'd reluctantly admitted that she was.

His only response had been to consider her with an even deeper frown—before he'd turned and walked away.

So much for him asking her out.

There had been a few others who'd jokingly asked her not to forget them now that she was famous. Yvonne had glared at her as if she had been the one to come between William and her much-admired Katherine. Carrie, who in the two years Jillian had taught with her had rarely had an unspoken thought, had decided it was obvious that Jillian hadn't been paid off since she was still working and living in her duplex. She'd also wanted to know if she was coming into money now and what she planned to do with it and if she would share.

The phone stopped ringing. Desperately needing a friendly ear, she grabbed it before it could start again and punched in Stacy's number.

Hearing her friend's recorded voice when her answering machine picked up, she blew a breath and punched the off button.

The phone immediately started to ring again. Not recognizing that incoming call, either, she reached behind the table and unplugged the line from the wall jack.

She'd just slipped the now mercifully silent instrument back onto its base when voices from outside penetrated the walls and another knock rattled her front door.

The only way she could think to block the intrusive sounds

was to turn on the television in the entertainment unit, raise its volume and escape into her bedroom.

With the sounds outside finally muffled, she headed down the short hall behind the living room wall and turned into her room.

The drapes she'd opened that morning framed a view of the flower-filled yard Mrs. White so lovingly tended—and a tea-saucer-size black photo lens pressed to the outside of the multipaned glass.

Her heart jerked as adrenaline surged. All she could see of the man holding the camera were his bony fingers and a head of wiry red hair. Behind him approached a mountain of muscle with no neck wearing a dark ball cap.

The camera flashed even as she grabbed the door handle and jumped back into the hall. The door slammed so hard it rattled. The bones in her body seemed to rattle, too, when her back hit the wall behind her.

Moments ago she'd felt under siege. With the privacy of her home invaded, she felt violated and vulnerable. A total stranger had been photographing the room where she slept, the room that was, to her, the most personal.

She had always felt safe in her home, rented though it was. And as physically secure as she was likely to feel anywhere. Hayden was a relatively quiet town. Her little corner of it was quieter still. But just then all she felt was surrounded. And angry. And trapped.

The blinds were open in the kitchen, too.

Remembering that, she hurried from the hall, her footsteps pounding along with her heart. When she'd closed the drapes in the living room, her only concern had been with what had been going on out front. Obviously, fences and gates meant nothing to the press Ben had described as "persistent."

She apparently needed to pay more attention to his assessments.

Her kitchen was a small, efficient ell of white counters and appliances that held her considerable collection of cookbooks and cooking gadgets. Ceramic canisters painted with ivy sat beneath a rack crowded with spices and herbs. When she couldn't sleep, she baked. Cookies, cakes, lasagnas. Everyone at the school knew when she'd had a bad night, too, since they were the beneficiaries of her insomnia.

She'd done pretty well sleepwise lately. At least, she had before William had made his little announcement.

She dropped the blinds over the sink and was calling herself six kinds of idiot for having ever sought out William Kendrick when a hard knock on her back door almost sent her back into the little hall.

It was only the muffled voice that shouldn't have sounded so welcome that stopped her.

"Jillian, it's Ben."

Relief that he'd arrived canceled any concern about how anxious she appeared to him when she ripped back the chain and yanked open the door.

He looked much as he had yesterday as he slipped inside, glancing over his shoulder as he did. Tall, confident and more attractive than a man had a right to be. He even wore the same beautifully cut navy suit that so perfectly fit his lean, broad-shouldered frame. The shirt and tie were different, though. Crisp white had given way to a light blue that picked up the flecks of silver in his deep-blue eyes.

He could have been built like a tire and had eyes like a rabbit for all she cared. Now that he was there, she just wanted him to tell her how to get her privacy back.

A faint tension radiated from his body as he slipped the

chain back in place and glanced at her. That tension seemed to snake toward her, through her. Disconcerted by the oddly intimate sensation, uneasy enough already, she moved farther from the door. And him.

"You didn't go back to Washington."

"It seemed more practical to stay in Hayden." Dismissing the fact that he'd obviously known he would be back, he flicked an assessing glance over her uneasy features. "I was already on my way over here with your other bodyguard when you called."

"Other bodyguard?" She had bodyguards?

"You have two. One of them is the man you saw following you in the gray SUV this morning. Steve Schroeder. Big guy. Blond. Blue ball cap. The other just got in." The dark slashes of his eyebrows merged. "Didn't you get my message?"

As rattled as she'd been when she'd arrived home, she'd totally ignored the blinking light on her answering machine. "I haven't checked my messages yet."

"I left you one at seven-thirty this morning."

At seven-thirty she would have been getting ready for school. They were on late schedule this week. "I must have been in the shower."

She had bodyguards. The thought seemed inconceivable to her.

"The police should be here soon," he continued, taking in the impeccably neat space. His glance landed on the one object in the room that didn't look almost painfully ordered; the refrigerator she used for a bulletin board. The front and what was exposed of the sides were covered with postcards, pictures of children and magnets holding up reminders to herself to do whatever it was she apparently knew she'd forget without a note.

"Mr. Garrett…"

"Ben."

"Ben," she conceded, as anxious to distract him from his perusal of what she thought important as she was to get his advice, "how do I get rid of them? You said yesterday that you were here to stop them from invading my life. That's what they're doing, so…please," she said, stepping back to clear his path to the front door, "stop them."

He remained right where he was, partway between her round white dining table with its vase of bright-yellow sunflowers and the back of the sofa that cut the open area in half.

"What I said is that my job is to help you with them. And I will," he assured her over the voices of a television talk show. "We just need to talk first."

"About what?"

"About what you want to say to them."

"I don't want to say anything to them. I want them to go away!"

His forehead pleated as he motioned to the entertainment center. "Can we turn that down?"

She turned on her heel. She had the distinct feeling that this would have all been easier if she'd let him help her yesterday. No doubt he'd had something preemptive in mind. But it was clearly too late to beat anyone to the punch. Just as clear, from the level way he regarded her after she'd hit Mute on the remote control and turned back to him, was that he would be a gentleman and not point that out.

Grudgingly grateful for that courtesy, she watched his focus shift from the V of the pale coral T-shirt she wore with brown linen capris to the closed drapes by the barrel chairs.

She supposed she should ask him if he wanted to sit. As agitated as she felt, she much preferred to stand herself.

"The best way to get rid of reporters is to give them what they want," he advised, before she could make the offer. "What they want are answers to their questions. Or a statement. If you'd like, I can help you write one."

"I don't have anything to say. How I feel about William Kendrick is private. What happened between William and me is private. So is what happened between him and my mother.

"I don't even know that much about what went on with them," she admitted. "What little I do know I'm certainly not going to share with rest of the world. I don't want my mom's name dragged through the dirt. And it will be," she insisted as the sense of urgency she felt identified itself. "My mother was the 'other woman.'"

She had no idea what to make of the way Ben's eyes narrowed on her. In some ways he reminded her of a predator calculating his prey, biding his time until a weakness or lack of guard betrayed itself. She didn't doubt for a moment that behind that sharp, intelligent gaze, he was processing everything she'd said and figuring out the perfect way to get around it, or use it to his advantage.

Turning from those unnerving prospects, she closed her eyes and snagged her hair back with both hands. She'd barely considered just how unmerciful the public might be when she felt the weight of his hands settle on her shoulders.

Without a word, he aimed her toward one of the slat-backed chairs at the table, pulled it out and turned her around.

He had felt her stiffen the moment he'd touched her. Dismissing the odd disappointment he felt at that, he nudged her down to the seat. More conscious than he should be of how fragile her bones felt beneath his fingers, of the softness of her hair brushing his hands, he deliberately drew away.

He'd caught her fresh, provocative scent the moment he'd

come up behind her. He could have sworn he caught a whiff of coconut in there, too. In her hair, maybe. From her shampoo.

Uncomfortably aware of the effects she seemed to have on his body, he pulled out the chair next to her, swung it around to face her and sat down himself. Leaning forward, he clasped his hands between his knees.

"Jillian," he said, practically leaking the patient control he prided himself on maintaining, "if it's your mother you're concerned about, you'll have far more control over how the public views her if you speak about her first. The same goes for how you will be perceived yourself. Public perception is very much about first impressions. You can get by with a 'no comment' today, but you'll be better off in the long run to come up with some tidbit for the press before they put their own slant on your silence. And they will. I promise you that."

He'd promised yesterday that the press would find her.

She held the certainty in his eyes only long enough to feel her stomach knot. She needed time. Time to digest what he'd said. Time to decide what she could possibly say to defend her mom when she knew in her heart that the only defense her mother had for sleeping with a married man was that she'd loved him. And that was no defense at all.

The thought of talking to the press made her positively queasy.

"They'll go away if I just say 'no comment'?"

"You'll have to give them a little more than that," he conceded. "You'll have to tell them you'll be available for an interview tomorrow. Or that you'll give them a statement then," he added, holding up his hand to stop her when she started to protest. "If they know they don't have a chance of getting anything today, the big guys will go home."

"The big guys?'

"The networks and their affiliates. They're the ones out there with news vans and camera crews. They might leave a reporter behind to see if he can catch you leaving, but the stations will probably send their crews on to other stories. It's hard to say what the newspaper reporters will do. It depends on how close they are to deadline and what else they need to turn in." His mouth momentarily thinned. "The paparazzi won't go anywhere. I don't know how many are out there, but you have at least one that's been on your tail since this morning."

"The guy in the black sedan," she concluded. The one with the wiry red hair who'd been photographing her bedroom.

Ben gave a confirming nod. "Schroeder…the guard who took up his post about midnight," he clarified, "spotted him when you left for school this morning.

"There will be more," he told her, utter certainty in the calm tones of his voice. "The first pictures of you will be worth a small fortune, so you can count on paparazzi doing everything short of dropping down your chimney to get those shots."

He could have told her it would be worse if she was reclusive. The harder a target tried to escape the prying lenses of the cameras and the fewer pictures there were to sell, the more valuable the target became. From the way her soft-brown eyes held his, he had the feeling he didn't need to mention that inescapable fact. She'd already figured it out.

She couldn't seem to stay still. Chair legs scraped against beige linoleum as she rose to move away. From him. From the situation.

"So," she said, seeming to weigh all she'd just heard, "if I do that…if I tell them I'll give them a statement tomorrow, the news crews will stop bothering my neighbors?"

"Unfortunately, no. They want information about you, and your neighbors are the logical first source."

"But the police..."

"All the police can do is cite them if they park illegally or ticket someone for trespassing if someone in the neighborhood phones in a specific complaint. Worse comes to worst, they can probably block off your street to all but residents if you wind up with a crowd out there. But right now, there's nothing to stop a reporter from using a walkway to approach a front door and knock on it." He looked from where she stood beside him to the gold watch on his wrist. "I'll talk to them when they get here. It shouldn't be too long now."

The knocking on her door had stopped about the time Ben had arrived. She wondered now if her bodyguards were responsible for that. The man she'd noticed coming up behind the paparazzo at her bedroom window must have been one of them.

"How long do you think it will be before I can leave without being followed?"

Rising, he gave a shrug of his broad shoulders. "Weeks. Months, possibly. It depends on how interested the public becomes in you."

"I have to live with this for months?"

"Or longer."

It seemed as clear as the distress in her eyes that his conclusion wasn't what she'd wanted to hear. Equally clear was that the slightly chaotic circumstances provided the perfect opportunity for him to accomplish one of the judiciously unmentioned goals on his agenda. He'd known yesterday that he hadn't had a snowball's chance in the Sahara of talking her into a meeting with William. Not only had she barely tolerated the sound of the man's name, she'd been dead certain she could handle the press on her own. With that naive assumption put to rest, he could use her concern for her neighbors and her clear desire for privacy to his advantage.

"They can't follow you if they don't know where you are," he pointed out. "Once they figure out that you're not here, your street will get a whole lot quieter, too.

"If you'll go pack a bag, I can have you away from all this in no time. There's a room reserved for you at the Four Seasons in Washington," he continued, fairly certain she'd see the wisdom in leaving. "William would very much like to talk to you.

"We thought you would be more comfortable in neutral territory," he explained when she visibly stiffened. "He didn't want to impose himself on you by showing up unannounced at your door, and we were both certain you wouldn't want to meet on his turf. Washington is about halfway for both of you. We can be there in a little over an hour."

Jillian said nothing. She didn't even ask how he planned to cut the drive time to D.C. in half. Despite his and William's apparent consideration for her comfort, she didn't care at all for being manipulated and maneuvered. As her defenses toward William rose even higher, she had every intention of letting his very practiced and professional cohort know that, too.

"I'm not talking with William." Ever again, she thought. "Feel free to pass that on, too. And I'm not leaving Hayden," she informed him, her agitation rising. "I have school tomorrow and a principal who will not be happy with me if I'm not where I'm supposed to be. Even if I didn't love my job, I have an obligation to it, the other teachers and to my students. That job is all that kept me sane after my engagement got canceled and my mom died and I'm not about to blow off my responsibilities to it."

Ben's eyebrows bolted into a single slash.

"Your engagement?" The information was news to Ben. It also raised a definite sense of caution and about a dozen red flags. "Who called it off?"

Totally confused by his concern, she said, "I did."

"Was the breakup amicable or ugly?"

"What possible difference does that make?"

"I need to know if there's anything potentially embarrassing your ex-fiancé might say. Or show," he emphasized as she frowned at him. "The press is sure to track him down once they learn about him. And they will," he assured her. "If he doesn't come forward himself, someone you know will mention him."

Uncertainty clouded her face as Jillian cocked her head. "Show?"

Ben didn't even blink. "Nude photographs or videos. Letters or e-mails that detail anything erotic or kinky. Is he in possession of anything you wouldn't want anyone else to see?"

"Of course not!" Jillian was dumbfounded. "The split hurt, but I can't imagine that Eric would say anything to embarrass either one of us. And recording our lovemaking was definitely not something we were into. As for kinky, I don't even like to make love with the light on." Coloring to the roots of her hair, she took a step back, threw up her hands. "I can't believe I'm having this conversation."

Wishing to end it, she turned away.

"Did you know this Eric well enough to be sure he hadn't taken pictures of you without you being aware of it?"

The question stopped her cold. Turning back, she faced the man who seemed to have no qualm at all invading the very depths of her privacy. The paparazzi had nothing on him.

"Incriminating photos of unsuspecting partners wind up on the Internet all the time, Jillian. Especially when revenge is involved. Most especially," he emphasized, "when a person is the item de jour for the press because the tabloids pay so well for anything remotely sensational."

His eyes remained hard on hers. From the way he refused to look from her face, it seemed almost as if he was forcing himself not to let his glance move down her body.

He lasted about six seconds before his eyes drifted downward anyway.

Not caring to imagine what he might be considering about her just then, she tried to ignore the knot his presence put in her stomach and turned to pick up the books she'd dumped on the sofa. She had always liked order. In her surroundings. Especially in her life. She didn't always get it. There had been times when she hadn't even came close. But she could at least control the state of her possessions.

Gathering the books in her arms, she set them in two neat stacks on her coffee table.

"Eric would never do such a thing," she insisted, straightening the already perfectly aligned trio of citrus-green candles. She added the faucet knob to the top of one stack. "He's not a criminal sort of louse like Tess Kendrick's ex-husband. He's just the run-of-the-mill sort. Asking me to marry him had just been a way to keep me around.

"He kept balking at setting a wedding date," she explained, if for no other reason than to divert him from her so not adventurous sex life. "So I finally asked if he ever intended to marry me. He said he didn't know. What he did know was that he didn't want the kids that were so important to me. That's when I broke up with him. He strung me along, but I can't see him trying to hurt me in any other way. There's nothing for him to seek revenge for."

"You're certain."

She reached to straighten one of the half-dozen throw pillows on the sofa. His skepticism stopped her short.

The man didn't seem to be hearing her at all.

"I'm quite certain." He wasn't just not listening to what she said, he wasn't accepting it. She doubted he had any idea how much he'd just revealed about himself. "But if that's the sort of faith you have in people, then I really feel sorry for the woman in your life."

"I'm divorced. That gives me a certain insight into just how little a person can truly know about someone else's character."

There was no mistaking the bitterness in his tone. That quiet hostility fairly coated his words, tightening them right along with the lean, chiseled line of his jaw.

It seemed she wasn't the only one who'd come away scarred from a relationship. But she felt ready to move on, to leave the past and its hurts behind. Ben, apparently, did not. She'd glimpsed more than his bitterness. She'd seen pain. And loss.

Wondering if he simply hadn't had time to heal, if maybe his hurts had been more recent, she watched him deliberately look away. It seemed he knew what he'd so inadvertently exposed and wasn't about to reveal anything more.

Yet he already had. There wasn't a doubt in her mind that all the subterfuge and maneuvering he must encounter in his work played pure havoc with his faith in people, too.

"I'm sorry." The unexpected twinge of pity she felt for him softened her voice. "I guess I operate from a different level of trust than necessity dictates to you."

He had been thinking the same thing about her, and wondering if she had any idea how dangerous such naïveté could be. She didn't seem to have a clue what some people would do for a buck, or that infamous fifteen minutes of fame. His ex-wife had gone for both.

"Let's just say I have a hard time giving people the benefit of the doubt."

"You have a gift for understatement."

"Thank you."

The muscle in his jaw tensed once more. He had forcibly blocked the mental images of her driving some guy wild in bed. He worked now to do the same with the defenses that had slammed into place at the sympathy still in her eyes. That sympathy was misplaced. The wounds meant nothing to him now. The scars had hardened, and so had he.

"So," he continued, preferring her baggage to his own, "can you think of anyone else who might know anything incriminating about you?" Despite his skepticism, he felt somewhat appeased by what he'd just heard. It didn't sound as if her ex-fiancé had a specific reason to rush forward with an exposé of her past, their relationship or whatever it was he might care to share in an interview. That didn't mean there wasn't someone else out there with some detrimental little detail he should be aware of. "Another lover? The disgruntled parent of a student?"

Disbelief flashed in her eyes. "There's nothing incriminating for anyone to know! What kind of person do you think I am? Do you think I have some torrid past that will come to light and embarrass your client? Are you afraid the…"

"Jillian, I'm just—"

"…world is going to hold him responsible…"

"It's not like that."

"…for something I've done that might not reflect well on him?"

"Will you listen?"

"I have been! And so far I haven't heard—"

"I didn't mean to insult you!"

The room suddenly went quiet. In that deafening stillness, Ben pushed his fingers through his hair, then jammed his hands on his hips. His negotiating skills were usually far superior to this.

"I didn't," he repeated quietly. "And I'm sorry that I obviously have. I'm only asking these questions because it'll be easier to help you if there are no surprises." He was growing more certain by the moment that what a person saw with her was exactly what he got. The realization caught him a little off guard. He hadn't thought that such unprotected openness existed in any human past the age of twelve. "I really am sorry. Okay?"

If the wary way she watched him was any indication, she wasn't overly anxious to accept his regret. She really wasn't, however, like any of the women he knew. Rather than make him stand there and squirm, repeat himself or otherwise grovel, she gave a small, cautious nod.

"Okay," she conceded, sounding as guarded as he felt. "I'll accept your apology…but only if you stop worrying about what some reporter might dig up, and tell me how I'm going to get to school tomorrow without being followed."

"That's not going to happen. You will be followed. But we'll get to that in a minute." Having almost blown his welcome, what he needed to focus on was her resolve to not budge from her house. That refusal was keeping him from taking her to meet with William. It was also threatening to cut into the time he'd promised his grandfather he'd spend with him.

"You said you hadn't listened to any of your messages." Wanting her to appreciate how much worse things would be before they got better, he motioned to the blinking answering machine by the oddly silent phone. He would have bet his box seats at the symphony that the thing would have been ringing right off its base. Or so he was thinking before he noticed that the phone was unplugged. "I think we should listen to them now."

Chapter Three

Checking the messages on her answering machine just then seemed pointless to Jillian. She knew from what she'd seen on her caller ID and from what she'd heard before she'd turned down the speaker volume so she couldn't hear what was being recorded, that at least some of the calls had been from the local newspaper. Since Ben seemed to think listening to them was important, though, and since he was arguably more experienced than she with the logistics of such situations, she punched the play-messages bar on the phone base and crossed her arms over the knot in her stomach.

An electronic voice told her she had fourteen messages. As she moved from the phone, Ben pulled a small notebook and pen from his inside jacket pocket, sat down in one of the barrel chairs and propped one ankle on his opposite knee.

The first three calls were hang-ups. The next began with a female voice efficient in tone and broad on vowels.

"Ms. Hadley, this is Karen Mabry, Nina Tyler's assistant with *Good Morning, USA*." The woman named the major television network in New York that produced the nationwide newscast-cum-talk show. "We'd like to interview you tomorrow on our program and will make whatever accommodations you need to get here. If tomorrow is a problem for you, we'll work with you to get a more compatible date. Please call me at 1-800-555-6000 when you receive this message. I look forward to hearing from you."

Jillian looked toward Ben. She listened to *GM, USA,* as it was known to its viewers, nearly every morning while she got ready for the day. Nina Tyler and her cohost were as familiar to most of the general public as sports figures and rock stars. Yet Ben didn't appear at all impressed or disturbed by the show's interest in her. His features revealed nothing as he wrote down the woman's name and number and listened to the beep that preceded the next message.

The next call was from the assistant of a nationally known afternoon-talk-show host who wanted the same thing: an on-air interview.

The call after that was from a major television journalist wanting her for a special.

A publisher wanted to talk to her about a possible book deal before she talked to anyone else.

Vanity Fair wanted an exclusive.

In between there were more hang-ups and the calls from the newspapers she heard when she'd first come in. Nina Tyler's assistant from *GM, USA* left another message.

Jillian had sunk to the sofa between messages from the journalist and the publisher.

She now blinked at the primary colors spelling out *Fun*

With Math on the textbook atop the stack on her coffee table. Her life, it seemed, had just officially turned surreal.

Afraid to wonder how much more bizarre things could get, she watched Ben go back through his notes and add a mark by Nina's name. He still didn't look especially concerned about what he'd heard. If anything, she had the feeling that the messages were pretty much what he'd expected them to be.

Looking as if he'd written nothing more interesting than a grocery list, he tucked his gold pen back inside his jacket.

Beyond the walls of the duplex more vehicles arrived. She could hear the muffled sounds of their engines, of their doors being slammed. Voices raised and lowered outside her door. Unnerved by the continuing onslaught of press, she watched Ben turn his dark head toward her.

She was again looking to him for help.

Ben realized that the moment his eyes met the subdued panic in hers. He would have regarded that as a point in his favor, too, had the vulnerability he could also see not totally knocked the wind from the thought.

He was accustomed to dealing with people far more experienced with the cutthroat aspects of life in the corporate, political or media world. In her sphere, she was undoubtedly perfectly capable of holding her own. More than capable, he imagined, considering what she did for a living. Dealing with a brood of other people's children while trying to funnel knowledge and discipline into their active little minds wasn't a job for the weak or fainthearted. In his world, though, she was the proverbial lamb among wolves.

The odd and unfamiliar sympathy he'd felt for her yesterday was back. Still, he told himself it was only practicality pushing him when he decided not to ask what she wanted to do about the calls. He already suspected that the only way she knew to cope in such unfamiliar territory was to dig in her heels the way she had when she'd refused to leave. If she got to feeling too overwhelmed, she might dig in so deep that he'd never get her out of there.

Tugging at the knees of his slacks, notebook in hand, he crouched in front of her.

"You don't need to worry about these messages right now. You have enough to deal with today." Paper crackled as he ripped off the pages he'd written on. "Do you want these, or should I keep them?"

"I don't want them."

He gave her a nod. Folding the pages in half, more aware than he wanted to be of the effect of her soft scent on certain of his nerves, he tucked them and the notebook back into his jacket pocket.

"You do need to do something about the reporters outside, though," he reminded her. "If you don't want to tell them yourself that you'll give them a statement tomorrow, I can take care of that for you."

Would you? she thought. "I'd appreciate that," she said.

With a faint smile for the relief she'd done her best to play down, he planted his hands on his knees. "Be glad to."

"What are you going to say?" she asked as he rose.

"They're going to want to know who I am. I'll identify myself and tell them I'm with a media relations firm. They'll want to know the name of the firm and who hired me. You or William. I'll tell them that no questions will be answered today, but that you'll have a statement for them by this time tomorrow." He arched one dark eyebrow. "Is that okay with you?"

He clearly had all the bases covered. Terribly grateful for that, she gave him a nod and watched him head for the door.

Voices rose the moment he opened it.

Part of her wanted nothing at all to do with the circus out front. Another part needed to see for herself what the man who'd just closed the door behind him would do. Hurrying to the window, she edged the drape open a scant inch. She couldn't see Ben, but she knew he'd stayed on the porch. Every set of eyes, all the cameras and a forest of microphones were aimed in that direction.

The police had arrived. Two officers in the city's blue uniforms wove their way toward her door, waving reporters off the lawn and back onto the cracked sidewalk. They, too, seemed to be listening to the man who'd just taken command of the situation.

She couldn't hear Ben, but she had to assume that he echoed what he'd told her he would say. Even if it hadn't been evident from the way half the microphones withdrew that he'd just said no questions would be answered that evening, it was in his client's best interests not to put words in her mouth about the situation. It would be too easy for her to publicly call him on them.

A frown pulled at her forehead. It wasn't like her to think a person would deliberately betray her. It wasn't like her not to give someone the benefit of the doubt. She had been deceived, let down and disappointed. Few women who had been around for over thirty years hadn't. Yet, despite the scars and the hurts, despite the setbacks and disappointments in her own life, she wanted to believe that people were basically decent and true to their word. It would be too hard to go through life cynical and distrusting of everyone as Ben seemed to be.

At the moment, though, she had to admit that she couldn't bring herself to trust the man who'd just entered her field of vision. Not where his motives were concerned, anyway. She knew where his loyalty rested, and despite his claim that he'd been sent to help, that loyalty wasn't to her.

Mrs. White had come out. Feeling like a voyeur, she watched the seventy-something widow in the flower print muumuu work her way to the police officers as Ben and two men, each the size of Humvee's, approached them himself. Cameras flashing, her short, rather round little landlady tipped back her curly white head and, talking a mile a minute, wagged her finger in the general direction of the mums lining the walkway.

The men with Ben had spread their massive arms to help the officers edge back the crowd when someone spotted her in the slit of the drape. With everyone turning toward her front window, she all but jumped back and sank to the sofa to wait.

"Your bodyguards are both staying tonight," Ben told her. "They'll keep an eye on your place, front and back, and chase off anyone who gets too close. These are their cell phone numbers in case you hear something you want them to check out."

The men he'd introduced to her as Steve Schroeder and Moses Jackson had just checked her doors and windows and let themselves out. Both worked for Bennington's, the exclusive personal security company the Kendricks had relied on for years for their own security needs. Both men were dressed in T-shirts and jeans to blend into the working-class neighborhood. And both assured her that they would see she was not disturbed that evening.

Ben placed a sheet of paper from his notepad next to the phone base on her end table. From beyond the windows came the sharp reports of car doors closing, the muffled hums of engines starting up.

"The police said this address will be on the patrol list tonight," he continued, reiterating what the officers had told her themselves. "They'll give a description of Jackson and Schroeder to the next shift, so whoever is patrolling will know they belong out there. I'll have Schroeder take you to school in morning. What time do you need to leave here?"

It seemed to Jillian that she should feel relieved as the sounds of cars and vans begin to fade. The reporters were leaving. The bulk of them, anyway. She had two very large men watching out for her. She had the expertise of a ruthlessly efficient, undoubtedly very expensive publicist who seemed to think of everything, including arranging transportation for her so she could get to school. Yet, relief simply wasn't there. She was no longer being hounded, harassed or pursued. She was now, however, a prisoner in her own home.

"I need to be there by eight." Shoving her fingers through her hair, she swallowed the pride she feared would only come back to bite her, anyway. "Ten to will be fine."

This time yesterday she would have flatly refused the offer of a driver. The bodyguards, too, for that matter. She wanted nothing from William. The past few hours, though, had taught her that her pride provided lousy protection from reporters, and even worse security. She might not want William to do her any favors, but she wouldn't be in this position if it weren't for him. Accepting a ride to and from school tomorrow and some muscle to keep the press at bay seemed only practical.

Then there was Ben. She didn't want anything from him, either. She didn't want to want anything, anyway. But at that moment, she honestly didn't know what she would have done without him.

The moment he'd walked in, the growing panic she'd felt had actually lessened. It had all reasserted itself, but just knowing he could handle the ropes she'd probably hang herself with was huge.

"Thank you," she murmured. "I know you're just doing your job, but I appreciate you taking care of…everything."

"Not a problem. Can you think of anything else you need tonight?"

"Just the ability to make myself invisible," she muttered. "Either that or a transporter."

"A transporter?"

"You know. One of those things that scrambles your molecules and moves you at light speed from one place to another." She wouldn't need a driver then.

"I thought a woman did that with the twitch of her nose."

She met the hint of a smile in his eyes. "We obviously hang out with different types and age groups." She tipped her head, gave a small shrug. "Since I don't imagine you have an invisibility cloak or transporter with you, I guess your work here is done for now."

The small smile she offered was guarded, a faint shadow of the sunshine-bright expression he'd glimpsed in the brief seconds yesterday before she'd realized who he was.

He should have felt relieved to get any smile from her at all. And he might have, had it not been for the strain behind it. Even with her lush mouth curved at the corners and a glint of light revealing the flecks of bronze and gold in her deep-brown eyes, she looked defeated somehow. Defeated, and a little lost.

He pulled his glance, his brow furrowing. "Is there anyone you want here with you tonight? A relative? A girlfriend?"

She shook her head, her mop of soft-looking curls swaying against her shoulders. The lock she'd pushed behind her ear sprang free to brush her cheek. "I'm my only family. And I'm not sure I'd be good company for any of my friends tonight." She might try to reach Stacy again later. But she really didn't feel like spending the whole evening talking about what she'd rather not think about at all. "I'm fine."

The hell she was, he thought. "Then I'll let Schroeder know what time to be at your door."

"Thanks," she murmured.

"You're welcome," he murmured back, and nudged the hair from her cheek.

His fingertips grazed her skin as he tucked the long curl behind her ear. The softness of it had barely registered when he realized that the motion had curved his hand at the side of her face—and that she had gone as still as he had himself.

His eyes caught hers. He had just breached a professional line he would never have crossed had he thought for a second about what he was doing. But he hadn't thought, and that wasn't like him at all.

Feeling the warmth of her skin penetrate his palm, he slowly pulled back his hand. As he did, she touched her fingertips to her cheek as if to hold in that small, unexpected contact.

It took a lot to unnerve him. What he had just done certainly had. But the thought that she might actually be feeling as lost as she looked just then unnerved him even more.

"I'll meet you here after school tomorrow." He had thought about asking if she wanted to work on her statement for the press. Shoving his hands into his pockets, he decided she'd dealt with enough for now. Not comfortable with how bad he felt for her, distance seemed like a better idea, anyway. "We can work on your statement then."

Jillian quickly lowered her hand, gave him a nod. Judging

from the six feet of silent space he'd put between them, what he'd just done had caught him as off guard as it had her.

She curled her fingers into her palm, thinking of the unexpected tenderness in his touch, hoping he didn't realize how the simple gesture had affected her. "I'd rather you figure out a way for me to avoid having to give one."

"I'll call if I come up with anything." Taking another step back, he gave her a guarded smile. "In the meantime, I'll see you here about four."

She'd barely given him a nod before he let himself out the front door.

Almost immediately, she heard a car door slam. Then another. Reporters were no doubt scrambling to see if they couldn't get something from him after all.

The room suddenly seemed too quiet. Automatically she moved to the remote control for the television, raised the volume on *Dr. Phil.* She would lose herself in someone else's problems for a while. Then, she'd go through her closet and sort out the stickers she'd stashed there, the ones for all the holidays and those that said *Good Job!* and *Much Improved!* Anything to avoid wondering why she hadn't felt so alone until he'd touched her, or why she hadn't pulled back first herself.

By eleven o'clock the next morning, her only thoughts of Ben were to wonder what influence he had with the National Guard. Thomas Jefferson Elementary school was a zoo. Isolated in the library, Jillian hadn't been aware of the worst of it until Jan Nguyn, one of the third-grade teachers, rushed in to tell her that Roland, one of the janitors, had just chased a guy with a camera out of the girls' room in Hall C. And that a reporter was wandering around Hall D looking for her.

Within seconds of that breathless announcement, Jillian heard the school secretary page her to the principal's office.

Dr. Geraldine Webster was the principal who'd hired Jillian fresh from student teaching eight years ago. Considering what Jillian had heard from other teachers in other schools, the sixtyish PhD with the stylish gray bob and a penchant for pantsuits and brightly rimmed bifocals was a teacher's dream. She championed her staff to the school board. She went to battle for them when necessary, commiserated with them when her hands were tied and truly seemed to hear their complaints and suggestions. She was fair and forthright and with few exceptions, most notably, Yvonne Bliss, the staff thought she could walk on water.

It was because Jillian knew the woman to be as rational as she was reasonable that she didn't bother to point out that the mob scene of reporters and paparazzi in the schoolyard was hardly her fault. As she entered the woman's office with its walls of filing cabinets, diplomas, certificates and commendations, she felt certain Dr. Webster already knew that.

"Dr. Webster," she began, coming up behind one of the visitors' chairs facing the principal's file-stacked desk, "I just heard about the paparazzo and the reporter." She'd all but run to the woman's office after making sure the hall she'd had to use was clear. "I'm so sorry this is happening."

"I am, too, Miss Hadley." Concern added a few more creases to the woman's rounded face. "As chaotic as it is here, I can only imagine what the situation has been like for you at home.

"Of course, I've called the police," she continued. "Coach Gunderson is looking for the reporter now and will ask him to leave the building or face arrest. Roland said he thinks he can identify the man he chased out. Apparently, he has rather distinctive red hair. But even if he's arrested for trespassing, he is only one part of the problem. I've had teachers tell me reporters have practically accosted them in the parking lot. I'm sure they would have been followed were we not keeping the doors so they could only be opened from the inside. As it is, three reporters came here wanting a copy of your employee file." She gave a snort of disbelief. "As if I'm going to hand over confidential information just because someone flashes a badge identifying them as press.

"I asked them to leave," she continued. Despite her displeasure with how easily her normally quiet little school had been invaded, she still looked most sympathetic. "Roland is checking all of the doors to see which one they came through and will lock it so no one else can get in. I've asked the police to arrest anyone on the property who isn't here on official school business."

The law didn't allow anyone inside the school without permission. Except for special events, even parents had to be cleared by the office to access any area where students might be. It didn't matter that the students wouldn't be there until classes began the coming week. Rules were rules, especially where school security was concerned. Even though the kids weren't there, the disruption to the other teachers clearly couldn't be tolerated.

"Which brings me to why I asked you here. Please," she said, walking around the front of her desk to lean against it, "sit down."

Jillian would have much preferred to stand. At the request from her principal, however, she lowered herself into one of the chairs. Dr. Webster took the one beside her.

"Miss Hadley. Jillian," she amended, personal concern slipping into her voice. "You know that it's always been my policy not to pry into the personal life of a staff member as long as a person's personal life didn't call her integrity into question or affect her effectiveness as a teacher. I'm not going to pry now, either," she assured her. "Your situation is…unique…to stay the least. I can only imagine the changes you're dealing with right now."

"None of which will affect my ability to teach," Jillian insisted. "Except for that," she said, motioning beyond the office walls, "nothing has changed.

"I hate all of this, Dr. Webster. I never dreamed anything like this would happen, and the last thing I want is all that out there. I just need time to figure out what I can say that will get them to back off."

"I'm afraid there isn't anything you can say. And your life *has* changed," she pointed out mildly, "whether you can see that now or not.

"I understand that you need time," she assured her. "But I don't have time to give you. This isn't a situation that will resolve itself anytime soon. I have four hundred students and a staff I need to think about. I have schedules that need to be maintained. First and foremost, I have an environment that I have to make sure is as secure as possible for all concerned. This building is old. It's open and accessible to anyone who thinks his purpose is more important than ours and our rules."

Genuine distress flashed through her eyes.

"We could address the immediate problem of security with city police on the grounds for a few days. But that's only a temporary fix. We can't have the students' routine disrupted by reporters and cameras, so anything long-term would have to be with private security. Even if there was money in the budget for such an expense, that isn't the sort of environment we want for our students."

She kept saying "we." That could only mean she'd already conferred with the school district's superintendent.

"I need you to take a leave of absence," she finally said.

For a moment, Jillian found it hard to breathe. "For how long?" she all but whispered.

"At least this school year. As I said, this situation won't resolve itself quickly. I've requested interviewees to fill your position. I'm sorry, Jillian. You either take the leave or I'll have to let you go."

Jillian had ridden to school in the back of the gray SUV with the tinted windows that had followed her there yesterday morning. Schroeder, who epitomized the blond version of the strong, silent type, had delivered her to the main door while his equally watchful and silent colleague, Jackson, who'd followed them in his sedan, escorted her inside. Behind them had trailed the swarm of paparazzi who'd lined her sidewalk to snap pictures of her as she'd ducked into the SUV.

Now that same caravan along with an assortment of vehicles belonging to the reporters and paparazzi who'd been waiting at the school jockeyed for position behind Schroeder as he drove the SUV from the parking lot.

Jillian wasn't with him. She sat in the backseat of the car being driven by the stalwart Jackson, feeling a little sick and lot angry while she waited for Ben to answer his cell phone. With everyone scrambling to follow the vehicle they'd seen her arrive in, they paid little attention to the dark sedan taking the driveway behind the Dumpsters.

"Schroeder will lead them around long enough for me to get you safely inside your home, Miss Hadley. I'll have you there in five minutes."

She thanked the man she'd yet to see crack a smile. Not

that she felt anywhere near like smiling herself. As upset as she was, she didn't even bother to marvel at how effortlessly the two men had coordinated her escape. All she cared about was that Ben had just answered.

"I was just put on leave," she said without greeting, "because I'm William Kendrick's daughter. My principal doesn't think the public's interest in me is going to die down anytime soon so she's replacing me. She said my presence is a disruption and a security risk to the students because of all the press and paparazzi, and the school district can't allow the chaos my situation is already causing. Do you have any idea how incredibly unfair and just plain wrong it is that I am now without a job because that man happens to be my father?"

"Jillian. Calm down. What happened?"

"I don't *want* to calm down." The very request offended her. "And I just *told* you what happened. If it weren't for William, there wouldn't have been reporters all over the school or a paparazzo lying in wait in the girls' restroom. I don't know if the creep was just hiding in there or planning to get a picture of me when I walked in, but teachers don't even use the students' restrooms. We have our own in the teachers' lounge!"

She couldn't believe she'd just explained that. But then, she couldn't believe she didn't have her job anymore, either.

She knew she sounded every bit as upset as she felt. She didn't care. She grasped hard at her anger. She wanted to hold on to it, embrace it, as Stacy would say, because being angry felt infinitely safer than the awful, directionless sensation clawing inside her chest.

"Jillian." Once more, Ben spoke her name with infuriating calm. "I'll meet you at your place. Schroeder said Jackson should have you there in a couple of minutes."

Her glance flew to the back of Jackson's closely cropped black hair. It appeared that he and his blond counterpart didn't just provide protection for her. Their job was to report her whereabouts and whatever happened to her back to her babysitter.

She had no clue how she felt about that, but being upset about it seemed to be in order, too. Feeling as if she'd just been sealed inside a large glass bubble, she snapped her cell phone shut, closed her eyes and tried hard to think of where she could go to escape what was happening.

The void inside her felt almost as horrible and hollow as it had following the loss of her mom. She felt nearly as empty and even more uncertain about what to do next. But when she'd lost her mom she'd had her job and her friends to fall back on. Now her job was history, and the people she worked with, who constituted the majority of her friends, were either upset with her because they were being badgered by the press or asking the same questions she didn't want to answer and many she simply couldn't.

She was not about to bare that much of herself to the man whose sole purpose in her life was to manage her. All she wanted was for him to understand what William had just cost her.

Or so she was thinking when Jackson parked across the street from her house. He couldn't pull into her drive. It was blocked by the first of the more astute members of the press who'd figured out that the SUV had merely been a decoy and made a beeline for her home. With more vehicles arriving, neighbors poked their heads out their doors to gawk.

Jackson had already asked her to have her key ready. Opening her door, he held out his arm to fend off a particularly aggressive female reporter rushing toward her. The brunette with the enviably straight and shining hair thrust a microphone in Jillian's face the moment she stepped from the car.

"Ms. Hadley, how long have you known you're William Kendrick's daughter?"

Ignoring her, head down, Jillian started across the street. Another microphone appeared, this one held by a masculine hand.

"How does it feel to be William Kendrick's daughter, Ms. Hadley?"

With the slam of car doors and the pounding of footsteps on pavement, more reporters hurried toward them. Cameras flashed. Someone yelled for someone else to "fix the sound feed!"

Bodies crushed toward her as she hurried forward.

From behind her came Jackson's stern, "Move aside. Let her pass."

"Where did he and your mother meet?" the first reporter asked as the group moved forward.

"Did he pay child support?" came another voice.

"Did he pay your tuition to the University of Pennsylvania?"

"Did he and your mother continue to see each other before she died last year?"

They already knew so much about her. They knew where she'd gone to school. They knew when her mom had passed away.

She wasn't sure if she felt invaded or assaulted as a deep-seated sense of self-preservation took over and she spun on her heel. She made eye contact only with the woman with the straight hair and bright white teeth, but spoke to them all. "The answer to most of your questions is no. I have no relationship with Mr. Kendrick at all." Ben had said that the only way to get rid of them was to give them what they wanted. Which was basically something to report. He hadn't said she needed to be particularly verbose about it. "I appreciate that people are interested in whatever goes on in his life, but he's in a better position than I am to answer your questions." Ducking her head again, she aimed herself for her front door. "I have nothing else to say."

"Miss Hadley…"

The questions continued as the media competed with one another to be heard. More intrusive questions came at her about whether or not her mother had been married herself at the time of the affair, about how long the affair had lasted, about how Jillian had felt living as she had when the Kendricks had so much.

They made it sound as if she'd been raised in poverty when, in fact, her mom had seen that she had everything she needed. She had everything she needed now. Except a job. Obviously that bit of news hadn't yet leaked from the school or they would be demanding details about that, too.

Overwhelmed, she stepped over a television cable and continued up her sidewalk, people parting like the Red Sea. She knew her bodyguard was behind her. She could hear him telling everyone to let her through. For a moment she even thought it was him taking her arm. Something about that protective grip, though, had her glancing up.

It was Ben ushering her up the steps. Torn between relief at his presence and fury that his presence was even necessary, she said nothing as they hurried inside and her bodyguard blocked her door.

"The street out there will be clear in about a minute and a half." Ben crossed the dim living room, heading for a table lamp. She'd left her drapes closed. The thought of strangers peeking in her windows taking pictures gave her the creeps. "That's about how long it will take the news crews to get their equipment back in their vehicles and make the scramble for their stations. They'll want to get the first words from your mouth on the next broadcast."

The lamp clicked on. In that pool of bright light, she watched his glance skim over the narrow cream T-shirt she wore with a simple beige skirt, down the length of her bare legs to the espadrilles that exposed her pale-coral toenails. She rarely wore anything dressy. Some women adored silk, cashmere and pashmina. Her favorite fabrics were cotton and fleece. He, however, apparently lived in suits. The one he wore today was a tailored charcoal that made his shoulders look a yard wide.

"All things considered," he continued, walking toward her, "you did very well out there."

Her response was a glare. "You'll pardon me if I'm not terribly grateful for that reassurance. William Kendrick was the curse of my mother's existence. It seems he's now mine, as well."

His expression turned placating. "This can all be managed, Jillian. It's just a matter of—"

"Finding the proper spin?" she completed for him. "Excuse me, but he's cost me my privacy and my job. Teaching isn't just work to me. It's my life. My friends are teachers. What I do after school and on weekends and during the summer revolves around them and the school activities that I'm…I was…involved in. My principal doesn't even want me to help tutor. Our PE coach doesn't want me to help out at games. Aside from the fact that my job and my social life have been royally screwed, I've also just lost my income."

She should never have let Stacy talk her into going to Hawaii. The airfare alone would have paid half a month's rent. "I have no idea how you can spin any of that to be anything other than exactly what it is."

Her phone began to ring. In no mood for a repeat of yesterday, she motioned toward it. "You answer it," she muttered, and headed for her bedroom. She was either going to cry or hit something. The last thing she wanted was to embarrass herself or be charged with assault.

Ben slowly pushed his hands into his pockets as he watched her disappear. A quick glance at the caller ID told him she'd just made the wires. "AP, New York" glowed in digital green.

He'd heard the questions that had been fired at her. The personal questions about her mother's marital status at the time of the affair and how long the affair had lasted. He'd seen the consternation in her profile and caught the quick pinch of her brow when another insensitive reporter asked how she felt having grown up with so little when the Kendricks had so much.

He had no idea what her childhood had been like. All he really knew was that she cared deeply about how her mother would be perceived, and that the questions raised about her mother's ethics and morals had to hurt.

His jaw worked as he blew a breath and studied the shine on his shoes.

He knew exactly what it was like to care about a relative who was being judged unfairly. Or, at least, without the benefit of her—or his—side being heard or considered. His dad had decided that Pops, his own father, was no longer thinking soundly and was doing all that he could to have Ben's grandfather give up the very things that had always mattered most to the older man. But Pops had Ben on his side. Considering everything Jillian had just unloaded on him, he wasn't sure his client had left her with much of anyone.

Except him.

He should have resented that, he thought. Or played it to his advantage. Yet at the thought, he could have sworn he felt something inside him crack and shift. He knew his first loyalty was to William. He knew he should be cashing in on how upset Jillian was by suggesting she meet with her father now and express her grievances directly to him herself.

As he turned off the phone's ringer and headed in the direction she'd gone, he realized he simply couldn't bring himself to add more stress to what had already been piled on her. He knew exactly what it was like for a person to have his life summarily destroyed by someone else, to have everything he'd believed in and counted on torn right from his grasp. It didn't matter that he'd experienced that destruction at the hands of someone who'd promised to love, honor and cherish rather than someone he barely even knew. The impact was pretty much the same.

The little hallway was barely big enough to turn around in. One door led into a bathroom that still held the scents of her soap and shampoo. The other opened to a room that reminded him of spring.

A thick white duvet covered her queen-size brass bed. Pale-green and yellow throw pillows echoed the colors in the white framed posters of tulips lining one wall.

A black suitcase sat on the butter-colored throw she'd pulled partway from the foot of the bed. She had her back to him as she reached into one of the long drawers of her dresser.

Jillian knew he was there. She could feel him. The sensation made no sense to her. It wasn't a prickle at the back of her neck, or anything like the feeling of being watched. It was more of a pull, like the invisible tug of gravity.

Preferring to ignore the sensation, she added a couple of T-shirts to the capris and jeans already in her suitcase. Turning back, she pulled open another drawer.

"Where are you going?" he asked, sounding as casual as he looked leaning against her doorjamb.

"Yesterday, you suggested a hotel as a place to escape. I'll find one I can afford. Someplace obscure. And quiet," she decided, throwing in a sweatshirt. "Someplace away from phones and people, where I can think."

"That's reasonable."

"Don't placate me."

"I'm not. I think it's a good idea. That room at the Four Seasons is being held for you. It has excellent security. Diplomats stay there," he pointed out, wanting her to know just how secure and undisturbed she would be. "It's quiet and you can leave instructions for all your calls to be held. No one even has to know you're there, unless you tell them."

"I'm not going to let William pay for anything for me." She could only imagine what a suite in a hotel like that must cost. A thousand dollars a night wouldn't be out of the realm of possibility. "Other than for the bodyguards," she qualified on her way back to the dresser again. "I hate that I need them. But I want them to make sure I'm not followed."

He watched her turn again. But it wasn't the agitation in her movements or the high color her anger put in her cheeks that held his attention. It was the lingerie she held in her hands, the bits of delicate pastel lace that were far more provocative than what he'd thought she would wear.

The image of her with that frankly feminine underwear exposing her hips and the long, tanned length of her legs, burned itself into his brain as she headed back toward the suitcase. As upset as she was, she didn't seem to notice that she'd dropped a bra.

He was trying hard not to imagine that particular scrap of lace on her, failing miserably, when she threw what she held into her suitcase and headed past him to her closet.

"You said I'd be able to protect my mom's reputation

best by telling people about her myself. The problem is that I don't know what to say that can change what she did." She grabbed running shoes and a pair of sandals. "I don't know what happened between her and William. I don't know if he pursued her until she caved in or if she threw herself at him. I don't even know how long the relationship lasted. All I know is that she loved and feared him until the day she died.

"That sounds pathetic even to me," she admitted, grabbing a jacket from a hanger. "I can only imagine how it would sound to everyone else."

The jacket landed in a heap on her bed.

"She'd only sound more pathetic if I tell everyone that she would never let herself get involved with another man. She raised me by herself because her parents wouldn't have anything to do with a daughter who'd had an illegitimate child. I know how her parents felt because she took me to see them when I was eight."

The shoes were shoved into the suitcase's inside pockets. Turning, she walked up to him, waited for him to unblock the door, then headed into her bathroom, continuing as if she'd only paused for breath.

"I'd been asking why I didn't have a dad and grandparents and aunts and uncle like the other kids. At that point Mom avoided questions about my father the way she always did, but she explained that I didn't have aunts and uncles because she was an only child. She told me that I had grandparents, though. I think she decided for my sake that I needed to meet them so I'd know for sure that I did have other family. That was when she told me it was time they saw what a wonderful granddaughter they had.

"We came back that same day," she said, stuffing moisturizer and mascara into a bright-pink makeup bag. "My mother cried all the way home. I don't remember what all they said, but we never even went inside their house. We just stood on the porch with Mom holding my hand. They barely looked at me and they told Mom she was the biggest disappointment of their lives.

"My mother didn't deserve that," she fumed. "My mother was anything but a disappointment. She was the kindest, strongest person I've ever known." Her voice threatened to crack as she whipped back the shower curtain. She grabbed shampoo, conditioner, body wash. "She doesn't deserve what people are thinking about her now, either."

She whirled around, pinned him with all the hurt and anger in her eyes.

"Yvonne Bliss didn't even know my mother and the Kendricks' marriage remained intact, but she called her a homewrecker and a tramp."

Ben hadn't a clue who Yvonne Bliss was. He knew only that what the woman had said cut Jillian to the core. "She said that to your face?"

"She said it to everyone in the teachers' lounge. She didn't know at the time that she was talking about my mom, but that detail doesn't change her opinion. The point is that no one is going to consider that Beth Hadley was simply a young, decent woman who'd made the mistake of falling in love with the wrong man. She's going to be vilified, and Katherine will be lauded a saint for sticking with William. No matter what I or anyone else who knew my mom says about how wonderful she was, it won't matter. She was William's mistress. They'll know her only as 'the other woman.'"

She moved past him, her arms loaded with toiletries, her distress practically vibrating around her.

Turning back to the doorway of her bedroom, Ben watched her stuff aerosol cans and bottles into the plastic pockets inside the suitcase.

She had said last night that she didn't want to talk to the world about her mother's relationship with William. He'd known then how fiercely she'd felt about protecting the memory of her mother. Yet it was only now that he began to realize the toll knowledge of that relationship had taken on Jillian herself.

Then there was what had just happened with her job.

Guilt jerked hard. He could have warned her about what would happen with her teaching position. Could have, but had deliberately chosen not to. As adamant as she'd been about going it on her own, he'd thought it would work more in his favor to let her find out on her own how badly she would need her father's help.

The bra she'd dropped still lay on the floor. Busy stuffing and zipping pockets, she hadn't seemed to notice it.

Ben walked over, picked it up. He didn't know too many people as genuinely protective of those they cared about as she seemed to be. His father certainly wasn't. With few exceptions, the Kendricks included, his clients weren't. It was his experience that most people would sell out their own mothers if it would serve their purpose somehow. But all she wanted was to protect the memory of hers—and find a little peace and quiet while she figured out where to go from where she was.

He couldn't deny the sense of responsibility he felt to help her find the space she was looking for. It was simply there, underscoring the guilt that he hadn't expected to feel, either. After all, he'd just been doing his job.

He didn't question the decision he'd just made. He knew only that she was out of her depth and that she would totally sink her mother's reputation without help. "I need to make a couple of calls," he told her. "Then we'll leave."

She turned, frowning. "I don't know where I'm going yet."

"I do."

"I'm not going to Washington."

"I'm not asking you to. Just trust me," he insisted, lifting his hand toward her. Her bra dangled by one scalloped strap from his finger. "Okay?"

The look she gave him said that trusting him was never going to happen. Seeing what he held, however, seemed to temporarily rob her of the ability to say so out loud.

The sheer garment with its lace trim and tiny center bow looked all the more feminine for the sheer masculinity of the hand—and the man—holding it. More disconcerted than she cared to admit by the level way he watched her, Jillian snatched it away and turned back to her task.

"Look," Ben said, unwillingly intrigued by the color he glimpsed in her cheeks. "You don't have to trust me completely. Just meet me halfway. I promised my grandfather that I'd see him this weekend. If you aren't somewhere where I know you're not being harassed or feeling caged in, I'll have to call him and cancel. I don't want to disappoint him like that. Sunday is his eighty-first birthday."

Jillian felt a bit of the fight drain right out of her. She had deliberately tried not to think of Ben in any context beyond his life creating, maintaining or cleaning up the images of the infamous, the famous or those wanting to be. She'd also done her level best to ignore the way he could alter her heart rate with little more than the lift of an eyebrow or the brush of his hand.

Yet, even as upset as she was, as uncertain as she was feeling, she couldn't help the way her guard slipped at the mention of his grandfather.

He didn't want to disappoint the older man.

Despite Ben's apparent aversion to romantic relationships, his family evidently mattered very much to him.

With the bra tucked in with the others in the suitcase, she glanced to where he stood, waiting, behind her.

The circumstances she found herself in were not his fault, she reminded herself. He was not the one who'd just dismantled pretty much any sense of security she'd possessed. That didn't make her less aware of the job he'd been sent to do. It did, however, remove a paper-thin layer of her resistance to his suggestion.

"Where is the place you have in mind?"

"Maryland. On Chesapeake Bay. One phone call and a room will be ready for you."

"Will it cost me much?"

"No," he promised. "It won't."

She really had no idea where else to go to hide out from the press. Hating how little she did know about how to handle her life at the moment, she drew a deep breath and murmured, "Okay."

His response was the nod of his dark head before he turned, pulled out his cell phone and started punching numbers on his way back to her living room.

It seemed she was going to Maryland. In her desire to escape, what she didn't ask was how he would get her there.

Chapter Four

The municipal airport on the outskirts of Hayden divided factories from farmland and served private planes and crop dusters with its single runway. Since the nearest commercial airport was in Pittsburgh and Hayden Municipal was miles from anywhere she ever needed to go, Jillian had never been there herself.

As Schroeder whipped the SUV through the open gate in the chain-link fence and bypassed the small terminal, she truly wished she had no reason to be there now.

She couldn't believe how quickly everything seemed to be happening. By two o'clock Ben had made several calls on his cell phone while she'd finished packing and added water and her houseplants to her kitchen sink so they wouldn't dry out. One of those calls had apparently been to the airport's security people whose single vehicle and one police car closed ranks at the gate behind the SUV and the sedan behind it. The maneuver effectively halted the stream of reporters and paparazzi Schroeder hadn't managed to lose at one of several red lights on his way through town. It stopped them from immediately entering the airport property, anyway. It did nothing to keep them from battling for position along the chain-link fence.

Another call must have been to whoever a person contacted to get a private jet.

Schroeder ignored the parking area and tiny rental-car kiosk. Aiming for the small white jet on the runway apron, he drove past a row of hangars and propellered airplanes and came to a halt beside what looked like a white bullet with six oval side windows. Its twin engines were already running. The door behind the cockpit windows stood open, the short stairway lowered.

Right behind the SUV came Ben in the rental car he had been driving between the motel and her duplex. Looking behind her, she saw that Jackson, in the black sedan, had left his car at the kiosk and was now jogging toward them.

Before she could open the door herself, it was opened for her. The smell of heat and jet fuel hit her nostrils. The sound of slamming car doors joined the high-pitched whine of two tons of thrust straining to be unleashed. Beneath that deafening roar she heard Schroeder yell to Jackson that he'd meet him in a minute and dropped two overnight bags on the tarmac. Theirs, apparently.

The choreography involved in simply getting her out of town suddenly struck her. Even as she realized they were turning in the other two rental cars, she saw a man in a captain's uniform bounce down the stairs and hold out his hand to Ben. It was then that she noticed that Ben was carrying an overnight bag and briefcase.

He obviously had known he would get her to come with him somehow. They hadn't made any stops anywhere for him to have picked up his things.

The disquieting sense of having been maneuvered had barely registered when a well-tended, middle-aged woman wearing a white blouse and black slacks appeared at the top of the four short stairs. The pilot was already back inside with her suitcase. Carrying his own, Ben took her arm with his free hand and hustled her up the stairs himself.

"Welcome aboard, Mr. Garrett. Miss Hadley," the attendant said, apparently already familiar with who she was.

"Rita, take care of Miss Hadley, will you? Rita will get you whatever you need," he said to Jillian as the attendant stowed all the bags in what looked like a little closet behind her. "We'll go as soon as Jackson and Schroeder get back."

"Miss Hadley? You'll probably be most comfortable there." Rita gave her a pleasant smile as she put her hand on one of the two middle seats in the plane. "The seat belt is the same you're familiar with in commercial craft. If you'll make yourself comfortable, I'll get you something to drink as soon as we're airborne."

Ben had poked his head into the cockpit. With his attention on his conversation with the pilot seated in front of a technophile's fantasy of LEDs and electronics, she glanced down the eighteen-foot length of the plane's beautifully appointed interior.

A narrow center aisle divided six cream-colored, tufted leather seats. Behind them, a floor-to-ceiling galley gleamed with lacquered cherry wood and stainless steel. That same rich wood and shining metal provided accents along the interior walls and formed a diamond-shaped medallion above a leather jump seat.

She'd seen pictures of planes like this in magazines and in movies. She'd just never imagined she would ever be in one herself. She'd never even flown first class.

It occurred to her vaguely that it had to cost a fortune to use something like this. Unless William owned it outright, she thought. In which case, it had to cost a fortune to buy.

Taking the indicated seat, she buckled herself into a cocoon of butter-soft leather. Out the oval window beside her, she saw her two bodyguards jogging back toward the plane. They no sooner emerged through the door than the mechanical sounds of stairs being retracted and the door closing joined the murmur of voices from the cockpit requesting clearance.

Jackson and Schroeder, their dark T-shirts clinging to their massive muscles, took the seats behind her. Preoccupation shadowing his lean features, Ben took the one directly in front.

She suddenly wanted him to be more specific about where they were going. He'd said Chesapeake Bay, but the bay, with its thousands of miles of shoreline, was huge. With her anxiety level already in the stratospheric range, she didn't ask, though. The alternative to going wherever he was taking her was to subject herself to the press she could see lined up like vultures along the chain-link fence.

Paparazzi had jumped that barrier. Two policemen motioned them back. One had his nightstick drawn, apparently to keep them from approaching restricted areas. Flashes of cameras winked up and down the line. Considering that it was broad daylight and the fence was a couple hundred yards away, the use of the strobes made no sense to her at all. But then, little made sense at the moment.

Don't think. Just breathe, she told herself. So that was what she did while the plane started to taxi, then took off at a stomach-dropping angle to arc over billowing steam from tall chimneys and a patchwork of grain fields before leveling out to climb higher still. She simply sat there, breathing, and focusing on the fact that she had actually left the press behind.

Rita appeared at her elbow. The soft-spoken woman asked if she could bring her something to drink. Even as she did, Ben unfastened his seat belt and headed back to the cockpit.

"Miss Hadley?" the woman repeated. "Coffee? Soda? A cocktail?"

Quickly looking from Ben's broad shoulders, feeling uneasy with whatever it was that had so much of his attention, she thanked the woman and asked for water. Had it been later in the day, she would have opted for something with more clout. Something tall and strong and guaranteed to take the edge off her nerves.

Rita wanted to know if she wanted still water or sparkling. Within seconds it seemed, she reappeared with sparkling mineral water and a slice of lime in a crystal goblet and told her they would be having salad and paninis for lunch. She understood the caterer she'd called to have them delivered to the plane was the best in Hayden. She then wanted to know if she would like a magazine and named the news and business publications they had on board. Or, she told her, she had picked up a copy of *Vogue* for herself which Jillian was also welcome to read.

The woman treated her as if she possessed royal blood.

Feeling her smile of thanks falter at the thought, she told the attendant that she didn't really need anything else and turned back to the window. William Kendrick's other children actually did have regal lineage. Their grandmother was a queen. She had no idea if the royal consort had been a king or a prince, but that made their extended family on the maternal side princesses, duchesses, dukes, lords and ladies. She was not only his illegitimate daughter; in his family, she would undoubtedly be considered totally… common.

She could only imagine what was being said about her in their rarified midst, or what fears might have been raised by her very existence. The fact that she was currently being handled by William's personal public relations manager spoke volumes about how acute those fears must be.

The plane made a stop in Baltimore to drop off Schroeder and Jackson. According to Ben, she wouldn't need security where they were going, but both men would be available to her when she left. It was then that she finally did ask their destination.

"Taylor's Cove," he told her, which told her exactly nothing.

Because he was so obviously avoiding her, she asked no further questions as he went back to visit with the pilot while they waited to top off their fuel tank and to get clearance for takeoff.

It was after six o'clock before the plane set down on a small landing strip that made the airport in Hayden look like LaGuardia. Even the approach had an entirely different feel to it. From the air, Jillian had seen rocky shoreline and a thin ribbon of road winding through thick trees. She noticed a few rather large, totally secluded homes tucked back in the woods or overlooking inlets. Any one of those structures looked big enough to be a hotel. A very small, very private, very exclusive hotel and not at all the type she could afford.

The scent of salty air filled her lungs the moment she stepped off the plane. Snatching her hair back from the breeze, she quickly took her wheeled suitcase from Ben as the plane's stairs were retracted behind them. Dragging the bag behind her, she could hear the jet's engine change pitch as it turned to taxi into takeoff position.

"Over there," Ben said, pointing to a silver SUV waiting off to one side of the otherwise empty landing strip. "That's our ride."

She wasn't sure why, but the feeling of having been maneuvered compounded itself.

"What's the name of this hotel?" she asked, seeing what looked like a little old lady in the driver's seat.

"It's not exactly a hotel."

Hesitation shaded her voice. "What exactly is it?"

"A house."

"Whose?"

"Does it matter?"

She started to tell him it most definitely did. Instead, stopping in her tracks, she called to his back, "Is he there?"

Ben seemed to hesitate himself. When he looked back over his shoulder at her, though, she had the sense that it had just taken him a second to figure out who she was talking about.

"I promise you. William is not there. No one is." He cocked his head toward the SUV and the woman emerging from the driver's side. "Come on. We'll be there in a few minutes. We'll talk then." He turned away. "Mrs. Bingham," he called.

His voice held a smile for the raw-boned woman wearing a plaid cotton shirt and jeans. Her pearl-gray hair had been skimmed back tightly from her creased face and hung to the middle of her back. Deep lines fanned from the corners of sharp hazel eyes. She had the look of someone who'd spent her life working outdoors, in her garden perhaps, though there was a hardiness about her that spoke of heavier work.

"Thanks for picking us up on such short notice. This is

Miss Hadley," he continued, heading for the back of the vehicle to load their luggage. "Jillian, Mrs. Bingham."

Reserve marked the weathered-looking woman's expression.

"I'm the housekeeper." Behind her silver-rimmed bifocals, her sharp glance darted over the short-sleeved cream T-shirt and dark-beige skirt Jillian still wore. An instant later, as if having expected someone less...ordinary, reserve softened to practicality.

"It's starting to cool off a bit in the evenings now. You brought a sweater, I hope."

In the few minutes it took to drive a mile, Jillian caught glimpses of narrow roads cut into the trees, open fields with tiny run-down houses and, finally, the rocky shoreline she'd seen from the air. In the distance, easily twenty miles away, the eastern shore of the bay formed a thin dark line on the horizon.

The shoreline disappeared entirely as the two-lane road veered to the right. Lined by trees once more, she was wondering if the road ended in Taylor's Cove itself when Ben turned into a narrow opening in the oak trees on the left.

Crushed shells crunched beneath the tires. Moments later they were on pavement that led into a secluded inlet sheltering an exquisite Cape Cod-style estate.

Ben had seemed preoccupied, almost...restless, she thought, ever since they'd left Hayden. That same preoccupation marked his profile now as he parked beside a well-used pickup truck near the imposing structure's front door and carried their bags inside the foyer.

Edgy herself, and not at all sure what to expect, Jillian watched him set down the bags at the foot of a white, angled staircase.

To her right, the expansive living room windows exposed a million-dollar view of the bay. The living room itself seemed to blend with the fading blues of the water and the sky. Even the whites and grays of the billowing clouds were captured in the summery tones of the beautifully upholstered furniture. A three-foot-tall sculpture of a crane occupied the center of the coffee table. Above the stone fireplace filling one wall, hung a huge oil painting of a clipper ship under full sail. A beautifully detailed schooner filled the length of a long console table.

Her glance darted past Ben to where the open, high-ceilinged space held a dining table overlooking a patio and that same view. She couldn't see all of what looked like a cook's dream of a kitchen. She glimpsed only a white granite-topped island, the end of a matching counter and white bead-board cabinets.

"Mrs. Bingham," he said, skimming a glance past her to the woman who accompanied her in. "Would you please show Miss Hadley her room while I make a couple of calls?"

He looked back to Jillian, offered a hint of a smile. "I only need five minutes," he told her. "Come on out to the patio when you're through."

Mrs. Bingham grabbed the handle of her suitcase. Sounding as if she had every intention of facilitating his request for privacy, the sturdy woman started up the stairs, her clogs soundless on the navy print runner. "This way, please."

The suspicion nagging at her began to grow as Jillian spared a quick look to her left. A library occupied the end of the hall. Or maybe it was an office. Floor-to-ceiling books covered the wall behind a polished oak desk that matched the gleaming hardwood floors

Mrs. Bingham had already reached the landing leading to the next flight up. Realizing she was waiting for her, Jillian somewhat reluctantly started up the stairs herself.

Two minutes later she felt more certain than ever that Ben had totally ignored what she'd said about not wanting anything from William. This house, with its beautiful carpets, antiques and accessories, had cost a fortune to buy and furnish. No detail had been overlooked. She hadn't been given a tour of the upstairs. The only rooms she'd been shown were those she was expected to use; a white-and-blue bedroom with a sitting room, balcony and another endless view. A bathroom of white granite, complete with French milled soaps, Egyptian cotton towels and a tub large enough to float a fishing boat. But what she'd glimpsed of the two rooms she'd passed proved them to be just as well appointed.

Considering what she'd heard Mrs. Bingham say to Ben on the way there about having brought in groceries and freshened the rooms, it seemed the house wasn't being lived in on a regular basis. If she had to guess what this place was, her money would be on a vacation home. For a very wealthy family.

Mrs. Bingham had led her back down to the living room. With her hands fisted at her waist, the woman who'd said little that wasn't necessary glanced around the rooms as if checking for something she might have missed.

"I need to be getting home," she announced. "So, unless you can think of anything else you might need, that's what I'll be doing."

"I can't think of a thing." Except to find out what's going on, she thought. "But thank you. Very much."

"You're most welcome. Enjoy your stay."

With that, she stuck her head out the open French door leading to the patio, called something to Ben, then headed for the entry credenza where she'd left her pocketbook.

She'd barely left, apparently heading for the truck out front, when Ben walked in and shrugged off his jacket.

She'd had no idea that he wore suspenders. She'd never seen him without his jacket on before. Without it, though, the rather old-fashioned yet trendy accessory made her even more aware of the breadth of his shoulders, and the sophistication he wore like a second skin.

He'd already removed his tie. Tossing his jacket over a side chair at the dining table, he slipped a gold cuff link from one sleeve.

"Sorry about that. The calls," he clarified, his expression oddly cautious. "I had a small fire to put out at the office or I would have shown you around myself."

She couldn't help the coolness in her tone. It was simply there, civility etched with ice. "May I ask you something?"

Beneath crisp white cotton, his broad shoulders lifted in a shrug. "Go ahead."

"What don't you understand about me wanting to take as little as possible from William? This is one of the Kendricks' vacation homes, isn't it? You're putting me up under his roof."

There was no question in her voice. There was nothing but conclusion, and the offense she clearly felt at him for having taken advantage of her need to escape her home.

Ben's glance swept the rigid line of her body. He'd been wrestling with the wisdom of bringing her here ever since he'd slowed down long enough to think about it. He'd had no idea what her reaction might be to him bringing her onto his turf. He had not, however, expected the one he got.

"I understand your position completely," he murmured, flattered that she thought the place worthy of a Kendrick. "This doesn't belong to William." Having offered that assurance, he braced himself. "It's mine."

She blinked at his level expression. Pique seemed to give way to pause.

"Yours?"

"Mine," he repeated.

The delicate lines of her eyebrows merged. "And the plane?"

"That belongs to the Garrett Group. Since I'm a partner in the firm, it's partly mine, too. I didn't know when we'd be leaving, so I kept it available. The crew was on call at the motel where we'd been staying."

He released a mental breath. She didn't look upset. She merely looked confused. Confusion, he could handle.

Jillian watched him roll up his sleeve as he moved to the other end of the white granite island with its tall glass apothecary jar filled with seashells and a bowl of fresh fruit. She had been so certain the plane belonged to William. At the very least, she'd thought it had been leased by him. And this incredible house…

"Mrs. Bingham comes in once a month to keep things up, or more often if I ask her to," he said, cutting into her thoughts as he deliberately changed the subject. "She'll shop, but she never cooks. Unless you can cook yourself, you're at the mercy of whatever Charlene is serving at The Crab House a half mile up the road, or whatever I can grill."

He pulled open a drawer, took out a phone book thinner than most hardback novels and tossed it onto the counter. "Taylor's Cove is just a fishing village, so Charlene's is pretty much it for here. There are other restaurants in Beckley, ten miles the other direction. And delivery pizza," he added, nodding to the book as if that was the option he preferred. "How is your room?"

"It's—" fabulous, she thought "—lovely," she said. Now, thoroughly confused, she watched him remove the link from his other cuff. Her brow knitted as she glanced back up. "But I thought you were taking me to a hotel." Someplace…impersonal, she thought. "Why did you bring me here?"

"Because it's the only place I could think of where you'd have the seclusion you wanted while you decide what you want to do about the press requests. And about your father. And, probably, about your life."

The link joined the other in his slacks pocket. As he rolled the cuff back onto his sleeve, his voice seemed to drop.

"It's also less than a mile from Pops's place."

"Pops?"

"My grandfather."

The one having the birthday this weekend. Remembering that, she drew a breath that brought the faint scents of lemon oil and floor wax and tried to quell the thread of panic running through nearly every thought. Of everything going on around her, the need to celebrate a birthday seemed totally incongruous.

Ben's reminder of the scope of what she needed to consider had done little to assist her effort. She'd felt as if everything was spinning out of control even before she'd been uprooted and dropped…where? she wondered. She didn't even know quite where on the map she was.

Desperately needing everything to slow down, she focused on the only solid, stable element in her life at the moment.

Ben.

He was there for her whether she wanted him to be or not. He was also allowing her to encroach on his personal space to accommodate her need for some space of her own. Granted, bringing her there served a purpose for him, too. But considering what that purpose was, she could hardly find fault with him for it.

"I'm sorry," she murmured. Moments ago she'd thought for certain that he had no consideration at all for her. Now she couldn't help feeling castigated—and touched—by his thoughtfulness. "I never intended to impose on you. I didn't mean to be difficult by refusing William's accommodations for me. I just don't want to be obligated to him," she hurried to explain, "and now here I am, obligated to you."

She pushed her fingers through her hair.

"I'm sorry," she said again, because she hadn't intended to sound ungrateful for the shelter he was offering her. "I'm just so used to taking care of myself. You have no idea how much I hate that I can't seem to manage that at the moment."

Actually, Ben thought, he had a rather excellent idea of how she felt about nearly everything. There was no way anyone could doubt her frustration with her circumstances, or deny how completely she'd understated the impact the events of the past few days had had on her. The strain of it all robbed the light from her eyes, etched tension in her forehead where she absently rubbed her temple. She looked tired and worried. And scared.

He knew she had every right to feel that way. And she should. But as she stood there looking lost, trying desperately not to, he found that he wanted to tell her he was sorry, too. He wanted to tell her that this would all be over soon and promise her that her life would get back to normal. But it wasn't his place to promise her anything, and she would probably never know "normal" again. She was just too busy dealing with each moment right now to realize how totally her life would change.

As closely as he guarded the control of his own life, he couldn't seem to help how bad he felt for her.

Realizing how unguarded that feeling had become, and how close he was to moving her hand away and easing her into his arms, he took a step back. The last thing he wanted was for her to think he'd brought her there to take advantage of her.

"First, you're not obligated to me." He wanted that out of the way up front. "And you don't need to apologize. I know none of this is easy. But it will get better," he assured, because he could at least offer her that much. "At least it will once we've decided on a plan of attack."

Jillian stepped back herself, snaked her arms around her waist. It alarmed her to realize how badly she'd wanted him to reach for her while he spoke the assurances she desperately needed to hear. Even now, she wanted him to hold her while he told her again that he understood, and that something about this little nightmare would soon get better. If he held her, even for a few moments, then maybe she wouldn't feel as isolated as she truly was.

The way he'd moved from her, though, made it clear he wasn't offering her anything but shelter. And while she truly appreciated that, she'd never in her life felt quite as alone as she did just then.

Determined to keep that feeling to herself, along with the confusion she now felt toward Ben on top of everything else, she sought escape in the view from the windows overlooking the bay. Moving toward them, aware of him watching her, she looked out on the deep lawn that stretched toward a gray strip of shore that disappeared into the water. A weather-grayed dock extended past the gently lapping waves.

The sun had set behind them, muting colors, turning everything the graying shades of twilight.

As lovely as it all was, escape and the serenity of Ben's surroundings were lost to her just then. He said she needed a plan of attack. She already knew that. She'd already considered calling the lawyers her mom had freelanced for and the handful of friends that had made up her mom's social circle and asking them to vouch for her character. Just the thought had made it feel as if her mom was on trial—which, in effect, she was. In the court of public opinion, anyway. But who knew what the media would make of anything any of them said.

It had just occurred to her that she might be able to understand Ben's cynicism after all when she heard his cell phone ring. The tones were straightforward, a series of electronic reverberations that revealed as much about him as would have the choice of classical music or something more trendy. The man was all business.

"Garrett," she heard him say as she watched a seagull land at the end of the little pier. "Yeah, Dad, I did. I gave the meeting to Kim Silverman. She's familiar with the whole campaign. This isn't a good—"

Time, she had the feeling he might have said, but he'd apparently been interrupted.

The beat of Italian leather on hardwood underscored a moment of heavy silence as he started pacing.

"That's covered, too," she heard him say. "It's a timing thing. I'll handle it. As long as you called, what about the message I left you a while ago? Will you be there?"

From the corner of her eye, Jillian caught a glimpse of Ben's profile. His head was lowered as he listened, still pacing, and his jaw had clenched tightly enough to shatter teeth. Whatever he was hearing wasn't making him happy. It also filled his tone with a careful and determined patience.

"I find it difficult to believe that the situation has changed that much since I saw him a few weeks ago. I don't think it's fair to judge Pops from a few phone calls. You haven't seen him in what…three months?"

She didn't mean to eavesdrop. It was just impossible not to overhear as he headed past the dining table to carry on his conversation away from her. It seemed just as impossible to ignore the tension she could practically feel radiating like sound waves from his long, lean body.

"Look," he said, stopping in the open patio door, "I have someone with me. I'll call you back in a while." His back expanded with a deep breath of frustration. Somehow, though, he managed to hold that frustration in check. "That's fine," he replied in response to whatever had just been said. "But I'm going to see him myself. I'll talk to you about the other later."

He said goodbye then. Though his tone had remained civil, his body fairly leaked the tension she saw when he turned and his glance caught hers.

"Sorry," he muttered, but offered nothing else as he dropped the phone in his slacks pocket.

He motioned across the room to the phone book on the island. "If pizza's okay with you, we should probably order dinner. If we stay in, there's no chance of you being recognized. We can figure out what to do about the requests for interviews while we eat."

Jillian turned from the deepening twilight beyond the window, watched him across the crane balanced on the coffee table. She could only marvel at how easily he'd seemed to switch gears. Moments ago there had been no mistaking the tension in his conversation with his father. Yet in the space of seconds, he'd all but buried the displeasure he'd so obviously felt and was ready to move on to dinner.

Wondering what else he suppressed, telling herself it was none of her business, she wished fervently for his ability to detach.

The thought of having to deal with anything else that evening put a knot in her stomach that simply didn't allow room for food.

"Please, order whatever you want for yourself. But I'm really not hungry," she confided, "and I'd appreciate it if we could wait until tomorrow to talk. Would you mind if I just go to bed?" she asked because his tension had somehow increased hers, too. "It's been kind of a long day."

Ben glanced at his watch. It was after seven-thirty. Considering what she'd been through since that morning, for her "long" was probably putting it mildly.

He conceded that he could use a little down time himself.

"Not at all. You're free do to whatever you want here."

He could practically see her relief as she eased her hold on herself. "Thank you," she murmured, and started toward the staircase. Two steps later, her forehead pulled into a frown and she glanced back to him.

"Does that mean I can go for a walk on the shore in the morning?"

"There's no reason you shouldn't. No one knows you're here. No one who's going to say anything, anyway," he qualified, thinking of his flight crew and the bodyguards. He trusted them as much as he did anyone. They had incentive, after all. If they ever divulged privileged information, they knew they'd lose their jobs. "This inlet is private, so you're not likely to run into anyone."

The knowledge that she had at least some freedom of movement back seemed to ease more of the strain in the fragile lines of her face. It also allowed for a hint of a smile when she murmured another quiet, "Thanks. I'll see you in the morning, then," she added and continued into the foyer.

She was halfway up the stairs before he shoved his hands into his pockets and eased out a long, strangely satisfied breath. He didn't question why it felt good to be able to give her that negligible bit of freedom. Or how the unfamiliar feeling seemed to ease the tension he still felt himself. For a few moments, anyway. His cell phone rang again. Pulling it from his pocket, he frowned at the number.

It was his dad again. J. C. Garrett, the founding father and senior of the four partners in the Garrett Group, didn't bother with a greeting when he answered. Robbing Ben of his momentary respite, he simply started off by saying he didn't think Kim Silverman was the right person to handle the client they'd spoken about minutes ago. The client, a four-term senator, had been found innocent of misusing campaign funds, but damage had still been done to his reputation and he needed a major image cleanup. Because Ben was a pro with politicians, his dad wanted him back in D.C. in the morning to take care of the client himself.

Ben had no intention of going back to Washington tomorrow. He was going to see Pops—which, Ben knew, was the only reason his father was pulling rank on the senator's account. Of the fourteen associates in their hire, the forty-something Kim, with her MBAs and fourteen years of stellar service, was one of the best. His father knew that, too. He just didn't want Ben where he could put ideas in Pop's head about possibly not selling his home.

Knowing that, Ben didn't address Ms. Silverman's competence. Concerned about his grandfather, he simply informed his dad that he was going to see Pops, whether he liked the idea or not. Ben honestly didn't know what his conclusion would be, or if he would to try to talk Pops into or out of anything. It probably wasn't his place to do either, he conceded. He just wanted to see for himself how the old guy was doing.

J.C. had nothing to say when he told him that. There was nothing he could say, which didn't please him at all. Both men loved the older one and both wanted what was best for him.

The problem was that they were polar opposites in their thinking of what the "best" might be.

Because Ben had left him no point to argue, J.C. reverted to using Kim as a scapegoat.

"I need you back here," his father insisted.

Ben clamped back months of growing frustration.

"No, Dad. You don't," he insisted, resenting his father's tactics. "In case you've forgotten, I'm still working the Kendrick affair. We agreed that would be my priority. Ms. Hadley still hasn't agreed to meet him, and every major media outlet in the country wants to talk to her."

He didn't mention that he currently had her under the protection of his own roof. His rationale for bringing her there wouldn't wash with his father, either, and the last thing he needed was another argument. But the fact that J.C. was willing to shortchange their most prestigious client spoke volumes about how determined he was to do what he saw fit for his father, no matter what his son thought. But then, they hadn't seen eye to eye on much of anything since Ben had divorced his now ex-wife. According to J.C., the beautiful and accomplished Brittany had been the perfect complement to him and he'd been hugely disappointed when Ben had let her go.

Disappointment didn't begin to describe what Ben had felt himself at the time. What he still felt, if he'd admit it, but he saw no point in taking the lid off that tightly sealed box of ugliness. When he hung up from his call, his only thought was to shake the irritation clawing at him so he could put in a call to William. With a little more information from him, he might well have the perfect approach for his client to take with the desirable and disturbing woman who would be spending the night two doors down from his own bedroom.

Chapter Five

The soft light of morning finally erased a night that had seemed forever long.

Jillian had spent hours tossing and turning in the down-soft bed and pacing the wood floor in her bare feet so she wouldn't disturb Ben. Had she been home, she would have baked. As it was, she didn't set foot in the kitchen until after she'd showered, pulled her well-worn University of Pennsylvania sweatshirt over a pale-yellow T-shirt and denim capris and headed down the stairs in her sneakers in search of coffee.

She found it already made and a clean mug sitting beside the stainless-steel coffeemaker on the counter. Beyond the dining area windows, she could see Ben on the patio wearing neatly pressed khakis and a pale-blue golf shirt. Looking entirely too male-in-control to her, he stood with one hip against a waist-high stone retaining wall. He sipped from a mug with one hand while he held the cell phone to his ear with the other.

He appeared very much to her like a man in charge of his world and everything around it. Feeling a definite lack of control over her own life, envying him the command of his, she poured herself a cup of the rich brew and turned to the island behind her. After four nights with little sleep, last night with about as much as the others, she felt a definite need for caffeine.

She managed two sips of the fabulous French roast before her glance skimmed to the newspaper on the far end of the island.

It had been her intention to avoid confronting her situation long enough to have her coffee and take a walk on the shore. But there it was right in front of her, captured in black, white and a dozen shades of gray.

The banner on the front page announced photos of William Kendrick's Lost Love Child in the Living Section.

She slid her mug onto the granite. All but holding her breath, she tore through the paper until she came to the page with the promised photographs. Most of them were of her in various stages of ducking. Two of them had been taken in front of her home yesterday. Another caught her through a car window, her hand up trying to block her profile.

Below those had been printed one of the infamous photos Tess Kendrick's ex-husband had apparently leaked of her looking undeniably upset and William, his hand on her shoulder, looking just as undeniably distressed.

Not nearly so dramatic, but by far the most flattering from her perspective, was the copy of the photograph on file with the state licensing board for teachers. At least she was smiling.

"I don't know who comes up with the brilliant captions, but you photograph very well."

Jillian's glance slid to where Ben crossed the dining room

toward her. She'd barely noticed the caution in his smile before she looked back to the article accompanying the photos.

> The quest to locate the illegitimate daughter of William Randall Kendrick ended yesterday with the identification of thirty-three-year-old Jillian Hadley of Hayden, PA. Hadley, a second-grade teacher at Thomas Jefferson Elementary School, spoke with reporters for the first time from her home in the Pittsburgh suburb, but failed to shed any light on her relationship with one of the country's wealthiest and most influential men.

"Are you all right?" he asked.

Her only response was the slow and inconclusive shake of her head.

Having pretty much expected that uncertainty, Ben set his mug beside hers and stopped an arm's length away. With her attention on what she was reading, he could only see her profile. Her hair was still slightly damp. The long dark waves and ringlets tumbled over her shoulders, the moisture in them temporarily taming the curls curtaining most of her face. She smelled of herbal body wash, something fresh, light and amazingly sensual, and the coconut shampoo he'd seen her grab from her bathroom.

Warmed by her body, the scents were like a tactical assault on his senses. But then, he was discovering that nearly everything about her had that effect on him.

He'd heard her pacing last night near midnight. Again nearer to 3:00 a.m. That was when he'd started for her room to ask if it would help to talk, only to stop himself before he could reach her door. He had no idea what she chose to sleep in. The casual, comfortable-looking clothes she wore suggested something cotton and practical with sleeves and a hem no shorter than midthigh. But he knew her enticingly feminine taste in undergarments. It was entirely possible that she preferred to sleep in a lace teddy that concealed next to nothing at all.

The thought of her long, lithe body covered with nothing more than a scrap of filmy fabric had pretty much ruined the more altruistic aspects of his mission. He'd already found himself reaching for her in broad daylight. In the dark, with her all sexy and vulnerable, he could easily be tempted to forget that he had no business touching her at all.

As disquieted as she looked when she turned to him, he was sorely tempted to forget it now.

He had thought he'd at least let her finish her coffee before they got down to business. With her worried brown eyes on his, her soft skin fairly begging to be touched, he figured he had two choices; reach for her and risk ruining the trust he needed to establish with her, or distract himself.

Thinking a swim in ice water might not be a bad idea, he casually nodded toward the dining table. Atop it lay a single manila file and his pocket notebook.

"There's more," he told her, opting to focus on the reason she was even there. "I went online first thing and printed off everything being said about you by the major papers. I didn't see anything that needs to be countered," he assured her, "so the first thing we need to address is the requests you've received for interviews." He picked up her mug, held it out to her. "Have you come up with a plan, or do you want me to propose one?"

Her thoughts last night had been too chaotic to form any sort of strategy. As the scene in her principal's office had played over and over in her head, she'd just kept thinking that all this couldn't possibly be happening. She would wake up in the morning and find it all had been nothing but a bad dream.

Taking her mug, she glanced back at the paper.

The nightmare continued.

"You're the expert," she conceded with far more calm than she felt.

"Then, come on. It's nice outside. Grab a muffin," he said, nodding to the package he'd left open on the counter. "We'll go out to the patio and work this through."

With a new appreciation for the dread a student felt being escorted to the principal's office, she watched Ben pick up the file and followed him with her breakfast to the curved flagstone patio.

The morning was lovely. A hint of a breeze that promised to warm tugged at her hair and nudged a scattering of leaves over the stones. In the distance, seagulls called as they circled the white dots of sailboats miles out on the bay. Considering how anxious she felt, the setting looked and sounded impossibly peaceful to her. Wasted as she feared the effort might be, she tried to absorb that peace, anyway.

The legs of a wrought-iron chair scraped against stone as Ben pulled one out for her at the blue-tiled table. "It's important that we respond to the networks soon," he told her, pulling out another for himself. "A celebrity is treated more kindly when they treat the press kindly themselves."

A celebrity.

She sank onto the chair angled to his. Had the odd weight of the label not suddenly felt so oppressive, she would have laughed at the absurdity of the word being applied to her.

Out of curiosity, or maybe it was a sense of self-preservation, she nodded to the file of news clips he'd laid beside his mug. "Tell me," she said, arranging her coffee and muffin, "what is William saying to the press? Do you have copies of his statements in there?"

"William isn't saying anything until he talks to you. Neither is any other Kendrick."

As if he hadn't intended to address this portion of the morning's agenda just yet, he hesitated. With his hands clasped around his mug, the look he gave her was quick, cautious. "They tend to go to ground when the press goes after a member of their family, Jillian. And they do consider you family," he warned her, "whether you consider them family or not. For what it's worth, the Kendricks are always loyal to their own."

That loyalty impressed Ben, too. It had been his experience that there were precious few people a person encountered in his life he could truly count on. Even fewer he could really believe in. But this woman wasn't going to believe she could trust William Kendrick just because a man he had hired said she could.

That doubt was written all over her lovely face.

"As long as we're on the subject," he said, before she could express that distrust, "one of the reasons he wants to talk with you is to help you understand his side of what happened. He said he doesn't know what your mom told you about them. All he knows is that when you asked to meet him, you said it was because you wanted him to know that your mother had remained faithful to him all these years.

"He knew you were grieving," he confided, needing her to know the man wasn't insensitive to what she'd gone through. "He also figured you were angry that it was your mother and not him that had died. It was that kind of pain he sensed in you when you met."

She was no longer looking at him. Yet, as resistant as he sensed she was to what he was saying, he knew from the way her brow furrowed that she was listening.

"He said he'd asked you about yourself during that meeting," he continued. He didn't want to think about how painful it had to be for his client and this woman to revisit that shared part of their past. He was only the intermediary here. He wasn't supposed to get personally involved. "He wanted to know where you lived, what you did for a living, if you were all right. He said you gave him very little, and that he came away knowing you wanted nothing else to do with him."

With her head still bent, Ben watched her tuck back the drying hair the breeze blew across her face and return to rolling the edge of her napkin. His ability to stay detached was what allowed him to see both sides of an argument, to offer solutions when the parties involved swore there were none. That ability seemed to have failed him with her, though. Right along with his usually keen sense of perception. He'd thought it was resentment holding her back from meeting with her father. Watching her uneasily lift her glance back to his, he realized it wasn't just resentment pulling at her. What he saw in her gold-flecked eyes was fear. And hurt. And an unexpected sort of confusion.

"Jillian?"

She shook her head, turned away from the concern in his voice as she rose. That concern only added to the turmoil she felt trying to know what was real and what was meant to persuade.

She hadn't expected William to acknowledge the pain she'd been dealing with that day. She hadn't thought that what she'd felt had mattered to him at all. At least, not beyond what he needed to consider to keep her from creating a scene. Not beyond what attention she had drawn, anyway, by starting to cry at the table in the hotel lounge where they'd met. She'd never intended to do that, to embarrass herself by losing control of her tears. All she'd wanted was for him to know how badly he had hurt her mother.

That meeting definitely hadn't been one of her finer moments.

"I didn't want him to know much about me," she admitted, pacing away two steps, turning back. "That wasn't why I went to see him. And I can't say that it even occurred to me to ask for his version of their relationship." What she remembered most was that he had expressed sympathy for her loss and said that her mother had been a good person. The words had sounded like meaningless platitudes at the time. Thinking about them now, they still did. "But he didn't ask what I'd been told about him," she defended. That she remembered for certain. "Not that I could have told him much."

Ben remained in his chair, his hands still wrapped around his mug. His expression intent, his deep voice quiet, he asked, "Can you tell me?"

She knew what he was doing. He wanted to know what she knew so he could help her frame any statement she might make to the press and help her deal with the questions they would inevitably ask. She was beyond denying the need for that help. In her desire to protect her mom, though, she hadn't considered the memories she'd have to resurrect to do that.

Refusing to give herself time to balk, she paced back to her chair absently rubbing her breastbone. A quick little ache had settled behind it.

"I don't know much beyond what she told me two days before she died. Mom had been drifting in and out of consciousness when she finally told me who my father was," she explained, "and a lot of what she said was pretty disjointed.

Before that, all she would say about him was that he wasn't from Pennsylvania and that he'd chosen to live with someone else.

"When I was younger," she continued, afraid she was going to sound disjointed herself, "I'd always thought his name was Robert Jones because that was the name on my birth certificate. Mom had told me he was a good man and that I could be proud to know he'd done great things, but that if he knew about me, he might try to take me from her and she couldn't bear that happening."

Her glance caught Ben's. "It made no sense to me that a 'good' man would do something like that," she told him, only to turn from the quiet way he seemed to absorb everything she said. "I was terrified to think that a total stranger could take me away from my mother, so I stopped asking about him after that. I actually pretty much forgot I even had a father until she told me who he was."

The breeze blew an oak leaf against the iron leg of the chair. Picking it up, she absently started shredding it.

"She wanted me to know in case I ever needed his medical history for myself or my children. It was difficult for her to talk. She was so weak," she confided, systematically tearing the edge of gold from the turning leaf. "But she managed to tell me that she'd been his secretary on Capitol Hill. He'd been a senator then, and she'd been madly in love with him. She would have done anything for him, she'd said, but he chose his wife over her, and their relationship ended before she discovered she was pregnant."

Jillian's voice dropped. The little ache in her chest increased as what she'd tried to forget drifted back; memories of those long, agonizing moments at her mom's bedside as her mom had struggled to speak.

"She said she never told him she was carrying his child.

She said she knew she could never compete with a princess, and that she feared that if he knew about me, he or his family would try to take her baby. She knew how strongly he felt about the sons he had then, and she figured he'd feel that way about me, too. That was why she'd refused to tell her parents who he was. She'd refused to tell anyone. With his money and influence she'd thought she wouldn't have stood a chance of keeping me."

Half of the leaf drifted from her hand. "It wasn't until then that I realized my mom had been involved with a married man. Or that my father was another woman's husband."

Ben watched the rest of the leaf fall as she tucked her arms around herself. He could see her struggling to keep the pain of those moments with her mom at bay. What he couldn't tell, though, was if she felt disillusioned by her mother or if she simply felt sorry for the woman. All he knew for certain was that he absolutely could not mishandle what he had just heard.

"After she'd told you his identity," he asked, his muscles tense with the effort to stay in his seat, "how did you feel about her keeping you from him?"

A reporter had shouted something similar at her yesterday.

Her chin came up. "The same way I always had," she insisted. "He was a name and a face. But he meant nothing to me. My mom loved me. Cared for me. She made us a family all on her own and I refuse to find fault with a woman who did what she felt she had to do to keep her child." She drew an agitated breath, released it. "But how I feel won't stop other people from finding fault with her, anyway."

That more than anything—more than her own disillusionment, her sudden lack of security, the loss of her privacy and loss of her job was what bothered her the most. There was no doubt of that in Ben's mind as he finally let himself rise and move to where she stood.

Considering the loss of her mom and the breakup with her fiancé, she'd dealt with a lot in the past eighteen months. She'd told him her friends had helped her through all that. But she hadn't told anyone what her mom had revealed to her about William, which meant she'd been left to cope with that knowledge and its aftermath alone.

Hating how alone she must feel now, he eased one hand to her shoulder.

The temptation to pull her into his arms was becoming harder to resist. But he only taunted himself with the thought of actually doing it before he offered what he knew would ultimately do her more good.

"You need to talk to William, Jillian. Not because he wants to see you," he insisted, feeling her muscles tense beneath his hand, "but because you're concerned about what people will think of your mom. If protecting her memory is truly what matters to you, then you need to hear him out. There's more you need to know."

"Like what?"

"It's not my information to relate. He didn't tell me the whole story. He's as private as you are when it comes to personal matters," he confided. "The only reason I know what I do is because he needed me to advise him on the best course of action. I'm sure there's a lot more."

Jillian closed her eyes, drew a deep breath. She didn't know if she admired his loyalty or simply felt thwarted by it. She did, however, know for a fact that she couldn't have imagined anything that would have made her want to meet with the man who had fathered her. Yet, what Ben had just told her made it impossible to deny the need she felt to meet with him now.

As she struggled with that discomfiting realization, she felt Ben's hand leave her shoulder. The warm weight of it had been more welcomed than was probably wise. Yet, the first tug of disappointment she'd felt at its withdrawal had barely registered when his hands cradled her face.

With his palms warm against her skin, he tipped up her head. "Talk to him, Jillian. You owe it to yourself as much as you do your mom. I promise, you won't regret it."

Jillian watched his blue eyes shift over her face. What he was searching for she had no idea. What he saw in her expression was beyond her just then, too. She knew only that she had never felt such tenderness as she did when he drew her closer and touched his lips to her forehead.

She didn't know which caught her more off guard, that gentleness or the sense of protectiveness behind it. She felt both in the seconds before he lifted his head and she caught the quick tightening of his jaw.

Ben had very nearly landed that kiss a few inches lower. For one totally irrational instant he thought to do just that. She had a way of looking at him that seemed to strip his defenses bare. He'd seen the need for comfort that she hadn't been able to hide and the next thing he knew he'd reached for her.

The last thing he wanted was the need he'd started to feel to be there for her. He didn't trust it, didn't want it. A relationship with a woman that went beyond dinner and bed didn't interest him. Emotional involvement led to expectations and expectations did nothing but set a person up for a fall.

His thumb brushed the soft skin of her cheek, slipped toward the corner of her inviting mouth. He'd have no problem at all with a purely physical relationship with her. Sex itself wasn't complicated. But sex with a woman looking for commitment and babies could lead to a minefield. Especially when that woman was the daughter of a client and in the unforgiving glare of the public spotlight.

Realizing that he'd gone from thoughts of kissing her to taking her to bed, and uncomfortably aware that in bed was exactly where he wanted her, he eased his hands away.

"Can I make the call?" he asked, resolving to keep on task.

With her focus on the middle of his chest, she gave a tight little nod. "Go ahead."

It would be totally impolitic to show how relieved he was by her capitulation. With that in mind, he motioned casually toward the table. "Have your breakfast. I'll be right back."

He'd left his cell phone in the kitchen. Snatching it up from the counter, he made the call he'd wanted to make four days ago and headed back to find her uneasily flipping through the list of press people they needed to get back to.

"He'll be at the airstrip at five o'clock," he said, checking his watch against the sun rising higher into the morning sky. "I'll pick him up and bring him here."

He didn't want to give her time to get any more nervous than he suspected she already was. He especially didn't want to give her time to back out or think too much about how close he'd come to kissing her the way he'd really wanted to do. In the interests of practicality and self-preservation, he took the notebook from her, closed it and picked up the file from the table.

"We'll be in a better position to decide what you want to do about the interviews after you and William have talked. Right now we need to leave. I want to get out to my grandfather's in case we have to cut the time here short."

The village of Taylor's Cove was little more than a collection of dilapidated, weather-grayed buildings that had withstood storm and sun for better than a century. Those homes and small shops lined the cove that protected the town's main focus: the marina with its long docks jutting into the deep gray water. Stacked with crab pots and coils of rope, those docks anchored the oyster skiffs and crab boats that were the life's blood of the community.

It took all of two minutes for Ben to drive them from his place past the cove, and another two to reach the inlet next to it where Pops lived. Considering the personal nature of the trip, Jillian strongly suspected that the only reason Ben had brought her with him was to keep her distracted. Since she knew she would just make herself crazy thinking about her meeting with William if left to her own devices, she was feeling rather grateful for the diversion when they pulled to a stop by a huge warehouselike building.

The structure practically hugged the shoreline. On the opposite side of the J-shaped inlet, a three-story, gray clapboard house faced the bay. In the distance, a lighthouse rose up from a half-mile-long sandbar.

She climbed out of the SUV, looked toward the house.

"We're going this way," Ben said with a nod toward the much-larger building.

Feeling a little confused, she hurried behind him, crushed shells crunching beneath her sneakers. From what she'd overheard of Ben's phone conversation with his father yesterday, Ben seemed to be concerned about the state of his grandfather's health. Mental or physical, she hadn't been sure. On the short drive, all Ben had said was that he hoped Pops remembered that he was coming. He said he'd left a message on his answering machine yesterday, but that the old guy didn't always hear the phone when it rang or remember to check his messages.

The comments and the fact that the man was turning

eighty-one, led her to expect an elderly, hard-of-hearing and forgetful gentleman in a rocking chair. As she moved from bright sunlight into the shade of the huge, gaping space and Ben hollered, "Hey, Pops!" she absolutely had not anticipated the weathered and tanned old salt with the neat white beard who turned to wave from atop a maze of scaffolding. That scaffolding supported a partially constructed thirty-foot-long sailboat.

Four other workers moved about the deck. Two lugged lumber from a crane hanging from the rafters. Another was on his knees hammering, his motions silent beneath the high-pitched buzz of a saw. She was thinking it no wonder the man couldn't hear a phone when the crew noticed her and Ben crossing the sawdust-strewn floor. With a quick wave of greeting for Ben, they gave her the same sort of incomprehensible glance she'd received from Mrs. Bingham and promptly returned to their tasks.

Looking from the hoists and pulleys attached to the ceiling beams, she watched Ben walk toward the tall, slender octogenarian hitching his way down a ladder.

"Come on," he coaxed with a glance back at her, then turned a grin to the man in a chambray shirt and worn jeans grinning back at him.

Ben's grandfather stood as tall as Ben himself. As straight as a mast pole, he looked just as sturdy. Except for a slight limp when he weighted his right leg, he moved with the energy of a man half his age.

"Got your message you were coming." His deep, raspy voice was as robust as the bear hug he wrapped Ben in the moment he got within reach. "Would have called you back, but it was near midnight when me and Skip Crammer finished playing gin."

Gripping him by his upper arms, he set Ben back. Behind

his silver-rimmed trifocals, sharp blue eyes assessed, judged and smiled again. "Glad you're here, Ben." With a clap to his shoulder that might have brought some men to their knees, he repeated, "Glad you're here."

"You're looking good, Pops."

"Feeling good, son." Giving him another pat on the shoulder, his glance darted to where the woman accompanying his grandson had stopped ten feet away.

The smile in his eyes turned to outright speculation.

"And who might this be?"

Looking as if he might be bracing himself, Ben motioned her forward. "Jillian, meet my grandfather, Josiah Garrett."

"It's Pops," the older man corrected, holding out his hand.

Her fingers disappeared into a grip that felt like warm sandpaper.

"Pops, this is Jillian," Ben continued, easing by her last name. "She's a client I'm hiding out from the press."

Heavy swaths of bushy white eyebrows jammed together. "Just a client?"

"Just a client," Ben echoed.

Clearly disappointed, or maybe it was resigned, he looked back to her.

"It's a pleasure, anyway, miss. Didn't mean to make it sound like it's not." Still holding her hand, he patted the back of it with his free one. "I should have known better than to hope he finally had himself a girlfriend. Far as I know, he's not even looking."

A note of discomfort entered Ben's voice. "Come on, Pops."

"Well, are you looking?" Finally releasing his grip, he anchored his thumb behind the loose waistband of his denims. Jillian noted that he didn't wear a belt. He wore suspenders.

"It's been two years now. You planning to stay single the rest of your life?"

"That's exactly the plan, Pops. Here." With that unequivocal response, he held up the dark-blue bag concealing the gift he'd brought with him. "Happy birthday."

Jillian's glance hit the floor as she bit back a smile. She couldn't have imagined anyone could ruffle Ben, but if the faint color pinking the tops of his ears was any indication, his grandfather just had.

It also seemed as obvious as Pops's unapologetic bluntness that he intended to put an end to any further queries about his love life. Or lack thereof. Especially in front of a client who probably looked a little more interested in the conversation than she should have.

Taking the hint, Pops pulled a tall, silver-labeled bottle from the bag.

The craggy lines bracketing his mouth deepened as he grinned at the hundred-year-old, single-malt scotch.

"You're a man of good taste, Ben. This sure beats the dickens out of birthday cake."

"I thought you might think so." As if to be sure he wouldn't return to the former subject, he nodded to the activity beyond them. "How's the boat coming? Is your new design still working?"

"So far. Come have a look." He set his gift on a table covered with blueprints. "You, too, miss."

"You *designed* this, too?"

Though flattered by her unrestrained awe at his skills, the old gentleman shrugged off the magnitude of his talent.

"Designing and building ships is what Garrett men have done for the past two hundred years. Look at these over here."

"Pops, Jillian didn't come here to—

"It's okay," she hurried to tell him. She couldn't tell if he was trying to spare her whatever his grandfather was about to say, or if he didn't feel comfortable having whatever it was shared. Suspecting it might be the latter, she shrugged. "I'd like to see them."

"See? She'd like to see them," Pops repeated, and took her by the elbow.

Totally sidetracked from his original destination, he left Ben frowning after them and led her to a wall hung with framed drawings and schematics of sloops, schooners and sailboats. Some of the drawings were so old the paper had yellowed. All of the boats, he told her, had been built in this very spot.

Sounding as proud as a father might of a favored child, the older man went on to tell her in gravelly tones that the first Garrett to arrive from Normandy before the Civil War started building boats that carried grains and other goods up and down Chesapeake Bay. Another generation of Garretts turned the focus from work to war. And still another from war to leisure. The company, still known simply as Garrett Shipbuilders, had turned to sailboats decades ago.

He only built one boat a year now, though, he confided, and that by special order. He had reservations for orders for the next twenty years. As prized as their boats were, some of those reservations had been handed down in wills.

The family crest held a place of honor in the center of the wall. On its shield, above what looked like a knight's helmet and a red cross, were etched "Garrett" and the Latin words "semper fidelis."

"Always faithful," she translated. "Isn't that the motto of the U.S. Marines?"

"It is. But it was ours long before they came up with it. Look down here," he continued, taking her arm to pull her with him. "This is a sloop we built for a retired Marine admiral in 1972. That's what he called her." With one crooked, arthritic finger, he pointed to the lettering on the stern of a sailboat. *Semper Fi.*

Jillian narrowed her glance at the photo, specifically at the young boy standing proudly by the tall keel of the dry-docked craft. There was something familiar about the dark-haired child, maybe the shape of his face or the impatient expression that seemed to say "hurry up and take the picture." "Is that Ben?"

"It is. He couldn't have been much more than five then. But he worked on her, too. That boy loved ships."

His wizened glance slid along the other photos, his voice going pensive with his recollections. Over the buzz of the table saw, he casually mentioned that he'd once hoped his son, Ben's father, would go into the business with him. But Ben's father had a yearning for the city, he confessed, and wanted to make his fortune there.

"J.C. didn't have the feel for boat building, anyway." Pulling an intricately carved pipe from his shirt pocket, he aimed its stem toward Ben. "He had it, though."

Pops looked straight at his grandson as Ben abandoned the inspection of his current project. "That boy worked hard, too. He used to stay with me and his grandmother every summer right through college. There wasn't a job here he couldn't do. Right down to the design work."

Brushing sawdust from his hands as he approached, Ben gave his grandfather an indulgent smile. "He exaggerates."

"I do not," came the offended reply. "You just had other footsteps to follow. Speaking of which," he muttered, "are you working today or can you stay awhile?"

"We don't have to be anywhere until later this afternoon."

"Then, how about helping me set the knees under the deck.

Jillian here can pack up that order I need to send back to the metal works company."

"Knees?" she asked.

A frown had creased Ben's brow.

"They're supports that reinforce the joints where the deck beams meet the frame." Though he spoke to her, he was looking at his grandfather. " I didn't bring her here to work, Pops. Jillian's a client," he reminded him. "I thought she could go for a walk out to your lighthouse. That's what she'd wanted to do this morning. Take a walk, I mean. I just didn't give her a chance."

It was as clear as the blue sky visible through the high rows of rain-stained windows that Pops had no qualms whatsoever about putting any available labor to use. As before, though, she couldn't tell if Ben didn't want his grandfather imposing on her, or if he was simply uncomfortable with her being so close to his personal life. Considering the guard she sensed behind his easygoing facade, and how little he'd actually told her about himself, her suspicions leaned heavily toward the personal factor.

The man had no reservations about poking into every facet of her existence, her sex life included. Having just been exposed to a side of him she never would have expected, the least he could do was allow her the chance to understand more about him.

She smiled at the man holding the unlit pipe. "What do you want me to do?"

"Rewrap fittings and pack them back up. Every single one they sent is anodized aluminum," Pops groused. "I ordered brass." He motioned toward a long table beyond the one holding blueprints and his birthday scotch. "They're right over here," he said, heading there himself. "I'll show you what I need for you to do."

She'd taken two steps when Ben caught her by the arm. With his big body blocking hers, her eyes darted from the hint of dark chest hair exposed by the open placket of his shirt to the guarded lines of his face.

"You don't have to do this," he told her, his deep voice low. "I really didn't bring you here to work, Jillian. Just give me a little while with him. Take your walk. Then we'll go."

Intent on ignoring the heat permeating her sleeve, she dropped her tone to match his. "It's his birthday. He'll be disappointed if you don't stay and work with him. I'm fine with this.

"Honest," she insisted, watching him wrestle with her conclusion while the scents of soap, citrus and warm male taunted her nerves. "I can see the lighthouse later."

He had pointed out the structure from the road, the tall, stocky column of white that sat empty and alone at the end of the spit forming the little inlet. She'd thought at the time how ironic it was that she could identify so completely with an inanimate object. "Right now I'd really like to do something useful."

She felt his thumb brush above her elbow, only to abruptly stop. As if realizing he shouldn't be touching her at all, his eased his hand away.

"You're sure?"

"Positive."

Still seeming torn, he murmured, "Don't let him bend your ear too much."

Afraid he'd tell stories about you? she wondered. "Actually, I like listening to him. He's an interesting man," she said with a smile and left him to see what Pops was scowling at.

The older man had set a large box full of tissue-like paper atop a table covered with metal hinges, cleats, pulls and knobs. Rubbing his thick beard, he told her he needed them all checked against the packing invoice and individually re-wrapped. He then bluntly confessed to having little patience anymore for work created by other people's mistakes. He said he could practically feel his blood pressure rise when he'd opened the order and discovered every piece was wrong. Because of that, he was truly grateful to her for saving him having to pack everything back up himself and being annoyed all over again.

She told him she was glad to help.

He asked if she really was just a client to Ben.

"Just a client," she assured him, echoing what Ben had said.

He gave a shake of his snow-white head. "That's too bad."

She watched him walk away then, absently rubbing the sore right knee that threw off his gait, and join his grandson and a short, compact barrel of a man to load pieces of smoothly carved lumber into a hoist.

He had given the impression of a man as concerned about his grandson as his grandson was about him—and of a man who rarely slowed down. She had the feeling that when he did stop to rest, it was only because his aging body couldn't keep up with the agenda of all he wanted—or felt he needed—to do.

Always faithful.

The elderly man's father had built boats before him, as had his father's father. Since Pops had mentioned nothing about having brothers of his own in the business, and since his son hadn't chosen to stay, she wondered if maybe Josiah Garrett was the end of the line.

The buzz of the saw quieted. Without its high-pitched scream, all she could hear in the cavernous room was the muffled pounding of a rubber mallet as wooden pegs were pounded into the boards forming the deck, the men's deep voices and the clank and clatter of chains as the hoist was raised.

Mostly, though, she was aware of Ben. She had the feeling he rarely slowed down himself. She wasn't sure what his own father was like. If she had to guess, she would suspect him to be fairly driven himself. But she could see hints of Ben's grandfather in Ben—along with a certain discontent the older man didn't seem to possess at all.

She watched Ben swing himself effortlessly from the ladder onto the deck and return the good-natured slaps on the shoulder of the men greeting him. She had been aware of a leashed tension in him pretty much since the moment they'd met. At first it had seemed to be a raw sort of energy, a force that radiated the impression of power and control he exuded so easily. But she'd come to sense restlessness in him, too. She'd just never been so aware of the grip that restiveness had on him until she saw it ease, right before her eyes.

She absently reached for the packing invoice, quickly glanced back up. Ben had crossed the deck with Pops to help lift the load from the hoist. He looked totally at home as he expertly grabbed the thick chain swinging toward him—and more relaxed than she would have imagined he ever could be as he worked alongside his wry and rather remarkable grandfather.

One hour led to another. At noon Pops's crew took their lunch pails and thermoses outside to the picnic table under a huge oak tree. As they did, Pops ushered her and Ben inside the spacious old house with the widow's walk atop the third floor to make sandwiches from cold cuts in his fridge.

They were only inside long enough to wash up and make the meal before carrying it down to the tree to join the men. But those few minutes surrounded by the family pictures on the walls and the old-fashioned doilies on the sofa and armchairs, were all she needed to understand why Ben had loved spending his childhood summers there. Even with his grandmother gone now for ten years, as she'd learned from Pops, the place seemed comfortable, welcoming and, she strongly suspected, filled with good memories for both men.

Pops's crew almost seemed like family, too.

A couple of the men had recognized her from their morning paper, but they didn't much care who she was beyond how accommodating they thought her for sparing Pops a stroke. It seemed the main concern for the people in Taylor's Cove was the effect of pollution and global warming on the oysters, crabs and fish in the bay, and who would be cooking the chowder at the church feed up in Beckley Saturday night.

Theo Bingham, Mrs. Bingham's wiry, sandy-haired nephew, seemed especially interested in that. Theo was the fortyish father of two who'd been pounding the pegs, which the men had fashioned themselves, into the deck. Like him, the others were all expert craftsmen whose fathers or uncles had practiced their particular skill here before them. They seemed a close-knit team, and all were quietly proud of the exceptional craft they produced.

As everyone returned to work, Jillian found herself wondering if Ben's passion and drive made him feel that same sort of pride for the work he did with his father.

She remembered Pops saying something about Ben having other footsteps to follow. His father's, presumably. But she didn't get a chance to wonder what it was about Pops's statement that bothered her. Having resumed her own task, she'd just rather absently looked from her worktable to the deck when she spotted Ben pulling off his shirt.

Her heart bumped her ribs. The day had warmed considerably. Despite the doors being open to allow in the breeze, it was eighty if it was a degree inside the building. She had long since pulled off the sweatshirt she'd worn over her yellow tee and scooped her hair into the scrunchee she found in her purse. The other men now worked in their white undershirts. Ben, though, hadn't been wearing one.

With his back to her, he tossed his blue golf shirt onto the side of the boat and bent to pick up a heavy length of wood. Hard, honed muscles bunched in his arms, shifted in his broad shoulders, along the indentation of his spine.

Shouldering the piece she assumed was another "knee," he turned to head for the hole in the deck he'd disappeared into before. As he did, she glimpsed a flare of dark hair dusting his beautifully formed pectorals. That dark shadow narrowed over the lean, rippling muscles of his abdomen and disappeared below his belt.

Something warm pooled low in her stomach. The man looked beautiful in a suit, totally amazing in casual clothes. Shirtless, he was downright dangerous to the health of a woman's nervous system.

Disconcerted by her reaction to him, and desperate not to get caught staring, she jerked her focus back to her task.

She'd yet to shake the thought of being held by him. That increasing need seemed to be a fair indication of how rattled she was by everything happening to her. She'd never in her life ached so badly for something from a man she'd known only four days. But all she'd wanted was the shelter she felt certain she would find in his strong arms. Just a few moments' sanctuary. Nothing more.

Now, though, the thought of being up close and personal with all that beautiful muscle dissolved any thought of finding a calming respite in his embrace. It also left her determined to distract herself as she finished packing the last of the parts, then occupied herself by sweeping what had to be an acre of floor.

Two o'clock came and went. With the hand on her watch approaching three, she was thinking of asking Ben how long she had for a walk before he would be ready to go when he crossed toward her, pulling his shirt back over his head.

Removing her gaze from the hard muscles of his stomach, she dumped the last dustpan load of sawdust into a tin trash can by a long workbench.

"You didn't have to sweep up," he said, plowing his fingers through his hair to comb it. "But, thanks. It saved Pops having to do it later. Are you ready to go?" Straightening his collar, he watched her prop the broom against the wall. She had sawdust in her hair. "I need to get cleaned up before I pick up your father. William, I mean," he said, correcting himself when the soft smile in her eyes died.

She had refused to call the senior Kendrick by anything other than his name.

"Any time you are," she murmured.

The quick change in her expression pretty much proved to Ben what he'd suspected: that she'd actually forgotten about her situation for a while. Or that it had at least moved to the back of her mind. Every time he'd glanced down to see how she was doing that afternoon, she'd either been checking parts against an invoice and rewrapping them, talking to the old gray tomcat that had adopted Pops years ago or checking out the drawings Pops had shown her on the wall.

Sorry he'd had to remind her of William now, he reached up and picked a bit of the sawdust from her hair. "Pops really appreciated your help. I did, too," he admitted, watching her pull out the fabric holding her hair back from her face. She shoved her fingers into the curls, ruffling them to shake out what he'd missed. "You were great with him."

"He's a great guy."

"Yeah," he murmured, stepping back. "He is." He just wished he could have worked a little longer with him as he nodded toward the open door of the building's little office. "We'll say goodbye and get out of here."

Pops was on the phone with a supplier, tracking down an order he'd placed for saw blades. The man was all but buried in the piles of papers and files that tottered on the edges of the old metal desk and filing cabinets crammed into the tiny space.

Looking up when they stopped in the doorway, he started to smile. Realizing they were leaving, his smile struggled behind his beard an instant before it appeared.

Jillian stepped forward, offered her hand. She didn't know when Ben planned to next see his grandfather. To give them a moment to themselves, she quickly said goodbye herself, wished him well and left the men with Pops stoically telling Ben he wished he'd stop worrying about him. He was just fine.

She didn't hear what else was said. It was none of her business. At least, she knew it shouldn't be. Still, she couldn't help feeling a little sad for the older man—for Ben, too, actually—as she waved to the crew waving to her from the deck and headed into the bright afternoon sunshine.

She wondered how Ben thought his grandfather was doing. From what she'd overheard him say to his father, seeing for himself how the man was getting along had been his purpose for visiting him. One of them, anyway.

Climbing into his SUV to wait for him, she settled herself into the passenger seat, stared at the huge old building through the windshield. Thinking about Ben's situation seemed infinitely preferable to thinking about her own. The moment Ben had mentioned her meeting with William, she could have sworn she knew exactly what men must have felt on their way to the gallows, or as they'd been escorted to the plank.

She dreaded that meeting. Because of that, she didn't want to think about it. Not yet. On the other hand, she didn't want to think about dealing with the press or not having a job, either. Since she also didn't want to think about how rugged Ben had looked working on the deck of the boat, that led her back to Ben's concern about his grandfather.

Since the old gentleman seemed perfectly fine to her, she was trying to figure out why that concern was there when Ben, looking a little preoccupied and a lot edgy, showed up two minutes later and climbed into the driver's seat.

Chapter Six

Within seconds of closing the driver's door, Ben silently started the SUV and looked behind him to back up. The preoccupation Jillian had noticed in him as he'd headed toward the vehicle seemed even more firmly etched in his face close up.

Over the refined hum of the engine, the tires crunched on the crushed shells.

"Is everything all right with Pops?" she asked.

Beneath his drawn brow, his glance caught hers an instant before it swung to the road ahead of them. "Everything's fine."

She was not convinced. Absently turning her attention to a knee of her capris, she picked off a bit of sawdust. "Will any of your other family come for Pops's birthday?"

"The only other family Pops has is my dad."

That didn't exactly answer her question.

"You're an only child?"

"I am."

"What about your mom? Will she be here?"

"She and Dad divorced years ago. She hasn't been back here since she remarried and moved to California."

"So your dad is too busy to come?"

The furrows in his brow deepened at her prodding. "Not exactly. He and Pops aren't talking." As if to save her the trouble of asking why, he added, "They disagree about whether or not Pops should sell the house and the business and retire."

"Why does your father want him to sell?" Incredulity colored her tone. "He loves what he's doing."

Seconds ago Ben had fully intended to change the subject. He wasn't in the habit of discussing family problems with anyone. Personal stuff was just that. Personal. Doing the work he did, he'd long ago learned that the more a person kept to himself, the less others had to use as leverage for their own purposes. Knowledge was power. Personal knowledge could be the most powerful of all. Not that he had anything to hide. The woman beside him, however, had immediately seen what he couldn't get his father to understand no matter how hard he tried.

Meeting her disbelieving expression, he easily read the concern in it.

"Pops had a heart attack six months ago." He felt that same concern in spades as he addressed one of the more valid reasons for his father's position. "He had a knee replaced six months before that. He needs to have the other one done, too, but he says he doesn't have time for it. Dad's afraid his leg will give out on him while he's on the scaffolding or a ladder and that he'll break a leg, or his back or his neck. If he doesn't have another heart attack first."

"Is his heart that bad?"

"His cardiologist said that it's not. The blockage was small and they put in a stent, but Dad is still afraid for him because of all the climbing around he does. He wants him to sell the business while it's still viable, retire and spend some time enjoying himself. What he doesn't seem to get is that Pops *is* enjoying himself."

He pulled onto the road that followed the shoreline. With one hand on the wheel, he drew a frustrated breath, blew it out. "I worry about him, too," he insisted, still irritated at his father for suggesting that he was in denial about his grandfather's limitations. "But I think Pops would die without his work."

"Have you told your dad that?

"I have. But he's as stubborn as his father. He's convinced that Pops needs to slow down. He wants him to sell everything and move to a retirement community in Chevy Chase where he can keep a closer eye on him. Pops's argument is that he's just fine the way he is. He has a business to run and he doesn't need looking after. Mrs. Bingham cleans his house and he takes care of everything else."

"And you're in the middle."

"Dead center," he muttered. "They both want me to convince the other that he's right. I can see some of Dad's logic and I understand Pops's. I just don't know whose side I'm supposed to be on."

For a moment Jillian said nothing. She just sat there, studying his profile and watching the muscle in his jaw twitch. Semper Fi. Always faithful. When she'd first noted their family motto, she'd thought only of the nobility of it. She hadn't considered its burdens.

"Maybe you should be on the side of the person who stands to lose the most."

Her quiet observation pulled his glance toward her. "My father stands to lose his dad if Pops doesn't slow down. Pops stands to lose what makes him happy if he does."

There could be no winners in this situation.

"Then maybe you should consider yourself in the equation," she quietly suggested, "and think about what would make you happiest, too."

The look he gave her made it clear he couldn't imagine why she'd suggest such a thing. "This isn't about me."

Maybe not directly, she thought but let it go, because she didn't want him clamming up on her before she could ask the question that had been on her mind most of the afternoon. She had the feeling he might, too, if she started poking into the discontent she'd come to sense in him. She had the feeling that the remarkable insights he possessed where his clients' problems were concerned could well be nothing but blind spots when it came to himself.

"Then about you," she said, thinking now as good a time as any to pose her query. "Will you answer something for me?"

He seemed to hesitate. "About what?"

"About what happened to your marriage. You told me you were divorced, but Pops mentioned that it's been a couple of years now."

"It has been."

"So what happened?"

A muscle in his jaw jumped. "That's personal."

"So is most of what you know about me," she pointed out easily, "but that hasn't stopped you from asking the questions."

Ben opened his mouth, closed it again. His first thought was that learning everything he possibly could about her was his job. It was what he was being paid to do so he'd know how to present her, package her or keep her quiet about what might cause larger problems than William Kendrick had already. Not that he had found anything to keep her quiet about. And, not, he had to admit, that he wouldn't have wanted to learn what he could about her anyway.

What he did know interested him far more than he should have allowed.

He knew she preferred pastel lace bras to the athletic variety, high-cut lace briefs to bikinis or thongs. He knew from having confronted her about what her ex-fiancé might reveal about her that she was probably shy about her body because she preferred sex in the dark. He knew having children was important to her.

As much as the sensual and nurturing sides of her intrigued him, there were traits about her that he found truly rare. Things that challenged his basic sense of distrust and left him with a vaguely uncomfortable sense of how jaded he had become. He hadn't met many people who wouldn't have taken full advantage of being a Kendrick, either by the affluence William could bestow or the million-dollar book deals and appearances available to her for the taking. When her life had turned into chaos, her first concerns hadn't been for herself. They had been for her neighbors, her students and her unwavering sense of duty and loyalty to her mom.

"Why do you want to know?" he asked.

"Because you implied that you planned to stay single the rest of your life. That's a long time to be alone."

His grandfather had said pretty much the same thing. He'd also asked outright why he wasn't interested in his pretty client. Pops had been totally charmed by her. He could hardly fault him that. She had a way of looking at a person and listening as if nothing and no one else mattered just then.

His totally lame response had been that he just wasn't and changed the subject before his grandfather could question the lie. He was interested in her. He just wasn't interested in complications. And that left him and the intriguing woman beside him with nothing—except for a certain shared understanding.

She knew exactly what it was like to have her future shift in a matter of seconds. It had happened with her ex-fiancé. She was in the midst of even more life-altering changes now. That was exactly what had happened to him, too. Nearly everything he had planned for, dreamed of and counted on had been there one moment and gone the next. For a long time it had felt as if his entire future had simply disappeared…

Maybe that was why he couldn't help the sympathy he felt for her. Maybe that was the reason he was having trouble separating the woman from the client. Whatever it was, it felt oddly natural to finally tell her what he'd told no one else.

"My family thinks Brittany and I split because we just didn't get along anymore." He would give her the basics. Keep it quick. Simple. "But I asked for a divorce because nothing we had together mattered to her. I just hadn't realized that until after…" He stopped, regrouped. He'd never said the words out loud before, never admitted what had been taken from him. "She hadn't told me she was pregnant. I didn't find out until after she'd had an abortion. She just got rid of the baby and went on as if nothing had happened.

"I wouldn't have known a thing about it if we hadn't been at a party and run into a friend of mine." He stuck to the facts, blocking the emotions he had finally managed to jam beneath a hard layer of bitterness. "Jace was dating a friend of hers who'd gone to the clinic with her. He asked how things were going with me and Britt. I told him I didn't know. I'd barely seen her since she'd been promoted to news director at the television station she worked for.

"Jace was on his third martini by then. Maybe it was his fourth. He was pretty wasted," he muttered, remembering, "but he told me there was something I needed to know."

To Jillian, Ben's voice sounded flat, totally devoid of emotion as he mentioned that Jace's girlfriend, Teri, had told Jace what Britt had done, and that his well-meaning friend had insisted he'd sure as hell want to know if a woman he was serious about had done something like that to him and their kid. Britt had told Teri there was no way she would risk her promotion by being pregnant. She'd known Ben would fight her about keeping the baby because he wanted a family someday. She just wasn't ready for one herself.

Ben went silent then. He didn't look left or right. He did nothing but stare straight ahead at the road, looking the same way he'd sounded—as if what he'd just revealed held little import anymore at all.

Jillian looked back to the road herself. She didn't believe for a moment that what he had told her no longer affected him. Though he might no longer think about what happened between him and his ex, he lived with the aftermath of that betrayal every day of his life.

It was no wonder he suspected people of self-centeredness and hidden agendas, she thought. He hadn't meant anywhere near as much to his ex-wife as her own goals had to her. The selfishness he apparently hadn't realized his Brittany had possessed had robbed him of the possibility of his child so she could get the promotion that clearly mattered more to her than their marriage.

Jillian had thought before that the cynicism she'd detected in him had been bred only by his work. Having dealt with the kind of animosity and hurt he'd undoubtedly suffered, she had no problem understanding why his faith in marriage had been shattered.

They had already passed the cove. As he turned onto the road leading into his place, she tried to think of something to say. Because there was nothing she could say that would matter, she simply offered what she felt.

"I'm sorry, Ben."

For a moment, he said nothing. He just looked at her as if the sympathy, while appreciated, was unnecessary.

"Thanks," he finally murmured. "But it was a long time ago. You've been there, too," he reminded her. "Wounds heal."

Some do, she thought. Others scar.

He pulled into the circle in front of the house, turned off the engine. Even as he did, she could practically see him switch mental gears. "We'd better get inside," he said, dismissing everything but the next item on his schedule. "I need to grab a shower. I have to leave for the airstrip in half an hour."

Jillian had needed a shower, too. A fine powder from the sawdust she'd swept had worked its way into her clothes and her hair. She didn't mind. Having to clean up and put herself back together had given her something to do other than pace, which was what she knew she would have started doing pretty much the moment Ben had closed his door down the hall.

She'd heard him leave over half an hour ago. Since she knew the airstrip was only fifteen minutes away, he could be returning any moment. That was why she stood at the open French doors in her room, slowly breathing in the fresh, salt air and trying valiantly to absorb the serenity of the view.

Serenity was a pipe dream. The muffled reports of vehicle

doors closing pierced the quiet solitude and told her Ben was back. With William.

Without giving herself time to enumerate all the reasons she resented William Kendrick, she pressed her hand to the nerves leaping in her stomach and headed for her bedroom door. Even as she pulled it back, she heard the front door downstairs open. Deep male voices joined heavy footfall on hardwood as Ben and the man she was absolutely not looking forward to seeing moved inside.

Wanting nothing more than to get the meeting over with, she headed down the stairs in her mocha-colored shell, matching capris and sandals. She would have preferred something more somber. Something without the tiny aqua flowers along the collarless neckline. Something more sophisticated. Something…black. But she wasn't a sophisticated person. Not in the urbane, refined sense the Kendricks were. Or that Ben was, she absently thought. And she wasn't going to present herself as something she was not.

What she wore also happened to be the only outfit she'd been able to pull together from the clothes she'd thrown into her suitcase that didn't involved khaki, denim or a T-shirt.

Her steps faltered as she reached the bottom of the stairs. Beyond the foyer, she could see the men in the wide space between the kitchen island and the living room. Their backs were to her. Ben stood at the built-in bar near the door to the powder room. With the sleeves of his white, open-collared dress shirt rolled to his elbows, he picked up a tumbler from the rows of glassware on the exposed shelves and opened the bar's small refrigerator.

William, tall, silver-haired and wearing a navy blazer and gray slacks, continued into the spacious living room. Passing the two blue, wing-back chairs flanking the model of a schooner, he came to a halt by the crane sculpture on the coffee table.

As if he sensed her presence, Ben turned. With the nerves in her stomach forming a neat little knot, she watched his glance move quickly from her freshly dried hair, down the length of her body and back to meet her eyes. His professional mask firmly in place, she had no idea what he was thinking in the moment before William turned, too.

William instantly pulled his hands from his slacks pockets. "Jillian," he said.

The man who had left politics to control an empire built on the fortunes of his carpetbagger ancestors was still undeniably attractive in his sixties. He looked as powerful and distinguished as he actually was, and totally uncertain about what to do next. Considering the bitterness she'd felt toward him the only other time they'd met, giving her a hug was clearly out of the question. Shaking her hand hardly seemed appropriate, given that she was his daughter.

With her making no attempt to move closer herself, he was left with nothing to do but say, "It's good to see you again."

Because she couldn't say the same, her response was to tighten her clasped hands and dart a glance toward the man who spoke into her silence.

"What can I get you, Jillian?" Ben asked. "William is having tonic and lime."

"Nothing for me. Thank you."

He motioned to the bottles of liquor in the cabinet and the wine cellar by the fridge. "If you change your mind, help yourself to whatever is here."

Turning to the bar, he quartered a lime he'd snagged from the fruit bowl and opened a small bottle of tonic water. "It's nice out on the patio if you'd like to talk out there," he said over the fizz of tonic hitting ice. A chunk of lime landed in the stubby glass. "Or you can stay in here if you prefer. Just make yourselves comfortable," he said to them both. Seeming the perfect host, he handing the drink and a cocktail napkin to the man whose image he'd been hired to protect. "I'll be in my study if you need anything else."

He was leaving them alone. The unease she felt realizing that must have been evident to Ben when he turned. For the space of heartbeat, something in his deep-blue eyes seemed to tell her everything would be all right. But with his main client standing right there, he looked away too quickly for her to do much more than wonder if she'd imagined that surreptitious reassurance.

Without another word, he moved past her, his footfall steady as he headed into the foyer and the short hallway beyond. As entwined as he had become in her life, she had wanted him to stay. But she understood that he really had no part in the meeting he had helped facilitate. He had done what he'd been asked to do by arranging it. His attendance was no longer required.

Without his stabilizing presence, an awkward strain crowded into the space between her and the man trying not to be obvious about studying her. Considering her level of disquiet, by the time she heard the door to Ben's study close, that tension had tightened around her like a rope.

For all his polish, William didn't appear too comfortable himself.

He lifted his glass toward the French doors. As he did, the overhead lights caught the glint of his gold wedding band. "Shall we go out to the patio? It look likes Ben has a nice view out there."

Jillian was not a rude person. Not normally, anyway. There

was just something about this man, who he was and what he'd done that made mincemeat of the manners that were normally second nature to her.

Having no desire to spend a second more than absolutely necessary with him, anything resembling small talk seemed utterly pointless.

"I'd rather just get right to the reason I agreed to see you." That detail was the only factor overriding her desire to pretend he didn't exist. "Ben said you'd tell me what happened between you and my mother."

With an appeasing nod, he murmured, "Of course." He motioned to the chairs. "Would you like to sit down?"

"I'm fine right here."

"I'd rather stand, too," he confided. Truly looking too tense to sit, his gray eyebrows pinched.

"Jillian," he said, conciliation in his tone. "I know this isn't easy. But you and I have more in common than you might realize. Like you," he continued despite her obvious doubt, "I would have much preferred that all this stay quiet. Not because I didn't want to acknowledge you as my daughter," he insisted. "I would never deny my own child. But because of exactly what has happened with the public.

"And, again, like you," he continued, before she could remind him that he was the one who'd told the public about her, "I want to keep damage to your mother's character to a minimum."

Because she offered nothing but distrusting silence, he paced toward the living room window, then turned to face her. "You'll have to forgive me, but I can't remember if you told me you knew your mother was my secretary."

Even if she hadn't felt so apprehensive and uneasy just then, Jillian knew she wouldn't be able to recall, either. To her eternal dismay, she'd been an emotional mess at their meeting. "I don't remember, either," she admitted, her arms protectively crossed. "But she'd told me she was."

"Did she tell you how much I valued her as an assistant? Or how much I relied on her to keep me on top of everything I needed to know to serve my constituency? Beth was truly indispensable to me," he claimed, his tone seeming sincere, his expression obviously uncomfortable. "I think we worked together for nearly three years before we became…involved. Our relationship was purely professional until then.

"You want to know what happened between us," he acknowledged. "Do you mind if I ask what she told you? I remember you saying how she'd felt about me," he reminded her, as if to save her from having to repeat herself, "and that she hadn't told me she was pregnant because she was afraid I'd take you from her. Did she tell you anything else?"

Jillian slowly shook her head. "That's basically it."

"She never told you about Katherine?"

Twin lines formed between her eyebrows as she shook her head once more.

"Then there is a lot you don't know," he murmured, and dropped his focus to the contents of his glass.

"Katherine had taken our sons and gone to her mother's in Luzandria. No one knew that she didn't plan to come back," he confided, starting to pace. "Not even Beth. Everyone thought she was just vacationing there because Washington was miserable that winter and I was in the middle of Senate sessions.

"I can't remember how long Katherine had been gone. Six weeks," he ventured. "Maybe longer. As I said, I'd never mentioned anything to Beth about what was going on. She just seemed to know something wasn't right. After she put through a call from Katherine while we were working one evening, I told her Katherine had left me.

"I don't know if Beth had asked if everything was okay or if I'd asked if I could talk to her. I just remember that I knew I could trust her." He glanced down at his heavy tumbler, ice clinking as he slowly swirled the liquid inside. "I told her Katherine wanted a divorce, and we wound up talking most of the night.

"One thing led to another." He offered the confession quietly, sparing her the details, if he even remembered them. Time and the desire to forget might well have erased most of the memories. "We were lovers for about a month when Katherine asked to see me."

From his pivot point near the stone fireplace, he glanced to where she'd remained silent at the end of the island. "You've heard of postpartum depression?"

Suddenly confused, Jillian murmured, "Of course."

"We didn't know much about it at the time. This was well over thirty years ago," he reminded her, "but we're sure now that Katherine was suffering from it when she left. Gabe was two and Cord wasn't even three months when the depression hit. When we finally sat down to talk, all we knew was that we wanted to make our marriage work. We had children. And we loved each other. I'd never stopped loving her."

As if realizing how that blunt bit of truth might sting, his glance faltered. Apology entered his tone.

"I cared about Beth, Jillian. She was a very special woman. Very special," he quietly emphasized. "I just had no idea how much I'd hurt her until you told me she'd never stopped loving me. I'd never realized she'd fallen in love with me to begin with."

He looked truly humbled by that. He looked terribly uncomfortable with the knowledge, too. He clearly had never felt about her mom the way he felt about his wife.

"Beth seemed to know that we were over when I came back from Luzandria," he defended. "I don't think we even talked about it. Or if we did, it was all very civil. She resigned the next day and was gone as soon as she'd trained her replacement. I hadn't heard a word about her until you called last year to meet me."

The defense in his tone moved into the mature lines of his face.

"I don't mean this the way it might sound," he qualified. "I obviously found your mother attractive and I thought of her as far more than my secretary or a friend, but I think you need to know that your mom and I would never have become involved had I not been separated. I honestly thought my marriage was over. So did Beth. She wasn't the sort of woman to get involved with a man still living with his wife. That doesn't excuse anything," he admitted, "but it does explain why we allowed ourselves to get intimate."

The man was too dignified to shove his fingers through his hair. Yet, it looked as if that was what he felt like doing, as recrimination, apology and discomfort with the entire situation had him drawing a deep breath.

He looked way, took a sip from his glass.

"As for what you said before," he continued a moment later, referring again to their first meeting, "about why she never told me she was pregnant. It's all supposition now, but I don't think I would have tried to get custody had I known about you. My marriage had all the pressure it could handle as it was. I'm inclined to think that what I would have done was ask for visitation and to support you." One corner of his mouth drew down as he gave his head a slow shake. "I'm really sorry Beth lived with that fear that I would take her child. She didn't deserve that."

When Jillian had first walked in, she'd been fully prepared to cling with both hands to the resentment she'd felt toward this man. Both for how he'd hurt her mother and for the mess he was now making of her own life. It hurt to know he hadn't even loved her mom. And she wasn't sure at all how she felt knowing she wouldn't even exist had his wife not left him for that short while. But she couldn't fault the man for not being forthcoming with her. Maybe it was that honesty, and his acknowledgment of the pain he had caused, that made outright resentment difficult to maintain.

Without that animosity pushing her, she didn't quite know what to say.

Looking from him to the grain in the polished floor, she heard William's footfall grow closer.

"For what it's worth," he said, the tips of his shiny black shoes entering her field of view. "I meant what I said about wanting to protect your mom." He stopped five feet away. "I don't want the media to disparage her. Neither does Katherine."

At the mention of his wife, St. Katherine as she'd come to not-so-kindly think of the woman, Jillian's mouth tightened.

"She knows everything," she heard him admit. "I told her about the affair when we were working things out years ago. That was part of our agreement when we got back together. That we would talk to each other," he explained as her head came up. "I'm sure there are psychologists out there who would argue that some things are better left unsaid, but for us it was necessary.

"Katherine understands the responsibility I feel to protect you," he confided, as if to defend the woman he'd chosen over her mom. "And your mother's reputation. She also wants you to know that she in no way believes that Beth came between her and me. I know the press is calling Beth 'the other woman.' But Katherine and I both know she was not. It's not like the press is saying. She didn't interfere in our marriage."

She was just there when you needed her, Jillian thought. Then probably forgotten with no small amount of relief when she didn't cause problems. He would not confess to that relief, though. He was being honest. Not brutal.

Her sense of fairness battled antipathy. She knew it could not have been easy for this man to confess what he had. Especially when he knew he couldn't profess an unrequited love for her mother, too. His heart had always belonged to his Katherine. But he seemed to have truly cared about her mom. He had respected her. He had even said he wanted to protect her now. She hadn't anticipated that.

Equally difficult to reconcile—given that she'd come to consider Katherine the reason her mother had been alone all those years—was that his wife apparently did have saintly leanings after all.

"Thank you." Aware that the knot behind her breastbone didn't feel quite so tight, she managed the first full breath she'd taken since she'd entered the room. "Ben was right. Seeing you did help."

"Ben is a good man."

He held his glass with the cocktail napkin beneath it. As he set both on the wet bar, he looked as if the scope of his guilt had just broadened.

"He told me what happened with your job." Sounding fully prepared to accept responsibility, he said, "I'm sorry about that, too. And for the way all this was sprung on you. That's the main reason I've wanted to see you," he explained. "I know I said it on the phone, but I want to make sure you understand I never would have broken my promise to say nothing about you if it hadn't been the only way to get Tess from under the thumb of that—"

"You don't need to explain again about your son-in-law. Ex-son-in-law," she qualified, sparing him the search for a term that didn't involve disparaging the man's mother. Scum surfaced in even the most polite of societies. "She was being abused. You did what you had to do."

She started to ask if Tess was okay, if this had all been worth it for her. She was afraid the question would sound catty, though. And that's not how she would have meant it at all.

Afraid anything else she said just then wouldn't come out right, either, she chose to stay silent.

"Thank you for that, Jillian. And don't worry about your employment situation. I'll take care of that. I don't want you to worry about anything else that's been disrupted because of all of this, either." He spoke the assurance with quiet authority, his manner infinitely more at ease as he moved from the past to deal with the present. "I'll assign you an assistant to take care of whatever it is you can't do being followed the way you are. If you'll—"

"Please." She held up her hand to stop him. He had clearly moved into take-charge mode. While he was obviously more at ease there, she most definitely was not. The last thing she wanted was for a man she barely knew to start making decisions for her. "That's not necessary. All I really want is direction in dealing with the press. I'll manage everything else." Somehow.

From the quick doubt in his expression, he looked fully prepared to point out how difficult that might be. Instead, faced with an adult daughter he'd only met twice, one he really didn't know any better than she knew him, he reluctantly backed down.

"As you wish," he conceded. "You have Ben to help you

with the press. He has an idea that I think will work well for all of us. I'd be grateful if you'd hear him out. Unless you have other questions," he carefully prefaced, "I'll get him and he can explain it to you."

He seemed to be doing what he could to accommodate her. Whether that willingness was borne of guilt or a sense of responsibility, she had no idea. She was just hugely grateful that he wasn't pushing her to let him step in and take control of the mess he'd made. What influence she had over her situation was becoming more precious to her by the second.

"I have no other questions," she murmured, torn enough by what she had already heard. "And of course I'll hear him out."

Relief moved through his patrician features. She wasn't sure if the expression was there because of her subtle shift in attitude or the fact that he didn't need to dig any further into his past. But there was no denying the sense of reprieve he felt as he gave her a nod and a restrained smile and left her to knock on the study door.

He must have stepped inside when Ben answered. As muffled as their voices were, she couldn't make out a thing they said in the moments before William walked back past the stairway and into the foyer.

"Ben is going to take me back to my plane." His forehead etched with concentration, he stopped by the front door as she moved toward it herself. "You need somewhere more appropriate to stay, Jillian. At least let me arrange that for you. I never intended for Ben to have to use his own property to hide you from the press."

Something about his phrasing gave her pause as heavy footsteps sounded in the hall.

"Please. I'm fine," she insisted, hoping the quick unease

she felt wasn't audible in her voice. "I can find somewhere on my own."

Again not willing to press, William let the matter go as their host walked up pulling keys from his slacks pocket.

As if remembering their last parting, or maybe just not wanting to risk ruining the truce they seemed to have drawn, William made no effort to move toward her. He simply told her to remember his offers, then turned to the man carefully watching them both.

Ben's eyes caught hers. "I'll be right back," he told her, then shifted his glance to the built-in bar as if he figured she might have reconsidered her desire for a drink by now. His expression otherwise inscrutable, he went to the front door and left her staring at its carved panels when he closed it behind him and his client moments later.

She'd barely heard the latch click shut when she sank on the nearest of the three stools at the island. She wasn't sure which had the firmer grip at the moment, relief that William was gone, or the sinking sensation she'd felt the moment he'd mentioned finding her somewhere else to stay.

She hadn't expected that the thought of leaving there would make her feel so unsettled. After the chaos of the past several days, she felt safe in this house and its protected little inlet, and as secure as she was likely to feel anywhere. What disturbed her even more was the thought that Ben might have said something to William about wanting his space back.

The sun was half an hour from setting. That left the back of the house with the view of the bay shaded, the air cooling with the breeze coming off the water. Because she couldn't stand being cooped up with her thoughts, she'd helped herself to a glass of wine and taken it and her cell phone out to the patio to pace the curving flagstones.

She'd finally connected with Stacy who'd been trying to reach her ever since she got her message and saw the footage about her on *Extra!* the night before last. Jillian had explained that she'd turned off her phone because some reporter had gotten hold of her number, and that things had been so hectic she hadn't thought to check messages.

Since she'd lost her job, couldn't go home just then and was somewhere on the Chesapeake hiding from the press, she'd thought her friend might offer a sympathetic ear. She got no sympathy. Stacy, whose inner-city experiences had bred a definite awareness of the inequities of the haves and have-nots, wanted to know why she sounded as if what had happened was a bad thing.

"You have a chance to make him pay," she insisted, speaking of William after Jillian had told her of their meeting. "He owes you and your mother big-time. Make him support you in the lap of luxury."

Jillian didn't want luxury, she informed her decidedly opinionated roommate from college. She wanted her life back. If she didn't get it back, she had the awful feeling she would lose her sense of who she was and what she was all about. She was a teacher. She needed to teach. Having stressed that point, she explained that what she really needed was advice on where she could move to escape the press and reclaim some semblance of the life she'd had. She told her friend she was considering some of the more remote places she'd taught children about in geography. The Alaskan tundra. Death Valley. Wyoming. She could live in Yellowstone Park and teach the children of the winter keepers and park rangers. With the cold and snow coming on there soon and all those moose and bison, reporters might lose interest in following her.

Stacy pointed out that her friends wouldn't go there, either. So unless she wanted to live alone with those bison, she should consider someplace tropical. She would be more than willing to use her guestroom if she would have William Kendrick buy her a house in Hawaii. Maui, preferably.

Her friend wasn't being any help at all. Jillian was about to point that out, too, when the sound of a vehicle engine drifted from the front of the house. Ben was back.

Telling Stacy she had to go, promising she'd stay in touch, she closed her cell phone and drew a long, deep breath.

Other than to say that she was being babysat by a Kendrick advisor, she hadn't mentioned Ben. Her intrepid friend would have wanted to know all about him, his marital status, what he looked like, what Jillian thought of him. Since Jillian was thinking of him far too much, she'd preferred to not subject herself to an interrogation that would have undoubtedly exposed just how drawn to him she was—and how quickly she'd come to depend on him and his advice.

Acknowledging that to herself was unsettling enough.

She'd just turned her back to the bay when she saw Ben emerge through the French doors.

In one hand he carried the bottle of wine she'd left open on the bar. In his other, he carried an empty goblet. Looking infinitely more at ease than she felt, he set the goblet on the table and poured himself some of the excellent, deep ruby pinot noir. Leaving the bottle on the table's blue tiles, he picked up the goblet and continued to where she'd stopped near the waist-high stone wall.

"How are you doing?" he asked, quickly scanning her face.

With the top two buttons of his shirt undone, a few dark hairs poked between the plackets of his starched white shirt. Beneath its rolled sleeves, dark hair dusted his sinewy forearms. Remembering the flare of dark hair on his chest, more specifically the narrow arrow of it that had darted over his six-pack abs and into his pants, she forced her attention to what was left of the wine in her own glass.

"I'm...okay."

"You're sure?" He ducked his head, trying to catch her eyes. "I know William thought it went fairly well, but you were more anxious about the meeting than he was."

He had obviously already debriefed William. Now, needing to finalize their course of action, he wanted her input. Yet, as he lifted her head back up with nothing more than the hold of his gaze, he seemed more concerned about *her* just then than he did her opinion of the encounter. That concern looked guarded. But there was no mistaking it. She heard it in his tone, could see it in the carved lines of his face.

She hated to admit how much that concern meant to her, how much it relieved her to know it existed. But she wasn't about to let herself forget why he was there for her. It seemed terribly important that she let him know she was aware of that, too. In case he was afraid she had forgotten.

"It went better than I'd thought it would."

She offered the admission with a small smile, dropped her glance back to her goblet.

"I know that getting me to meet with him was part of your job, Ben. And I know that helping him fulfill that goal was more important than providing me with answers about his relationship with my mom. But I'm glad you talked me into seeing him."

Her hair had fallen forward to brush her cheeks. With her

free hand, she snagged one side back. "Some of what he had to say was a little hard to hear," she confessed. "But to be fair, it had to be hard for him to say.

"He admitted that he'd never loved her," she told him, watching the shades of ruby shift as she slowly turned the crystal stem. "I really think he'd forgotten all about her until I showed up."

He had gone back to the woman he did love, she thought, and her mom had been left with little choice but to leave and start over somewhere else.

Knowing the details now, it seemed odd that the resentment she had once felt for William didn't seem quite so acute. Leaving her own upheaval out of it, antipathy still lingered at the inequity of it all for her mom. The edges just didn't feel quite so sharp.

She would never have become involved with me had I still been with Katherine. She wasn't that sort of woman.

His wife apparently knew that, too; that Beth Hadley had been honorable, decent.

"But I'm relieved by some of what he said, too."

For a moment Ben said nothing. He simply searched her tired features when she looked up. He couldn't—wouldn't—deny his goals with the Kendricks. The woman looking up at him with the weary brown eyes was too astute to believe they weren't his primary professional concern, anyway. But the part of him that she had touched when she'd first told him how much her mom meant to her wouldn't allow him to believe that everything he'd done had been for William and his wife. His commitment to them had nothing to do with the need he felt to reach for her, or with why he'd felt so torn when he'd left her alone with the man he knew she hadn't cared for at all.

Had he not known William to be an honest and honorable

man, he might well have overstepped himself with his firm's most prestigious client and asked if she'd wanted him to stay.

He set his goblet on the wide lip of the wall beside them. Taking hers, he did the same.

A long, spiraling curl clung to her cheek. As she looked up at what he'd done, he drew it behind her ear with the tip of his finger. "I'm sorry about the hard parts, Jillian." He'd never felt regret for any of his clients before. Never allowed himself to become invested in their problems beyond what it took to get them out of them. "I can't imagine there's much about any of this that's easy for you," he conceded. "But you're wrong about which was more important to me."

Her head moved ever so slightly into his touch. Drawn by that silent, almost unconscious invitation, he slipped his thumb over the incredible smoothness of her skin. "Helping you find those answers was just as important as what William wanted. Maybe even more so."

Her scent hooked him, drew him closer.

"That's just between us, though. Okay?"

Jillian felt her heart catch as he lowered his dark head. His lips hovered scant inches above hers, his breath warming her cheek, entering her lungs as she breathed in. With nothing more than the touch of his fingers to her jaw, he held her there while her pulse scrambled and he waited for her to respond.

"Okay," she whispered.

"Good," he murmured, and brushed his mouth to hers.

He did it once more.

And again.

His kiss was impossibly gentle. Part apology, it seemed, though for what she wasn't sure. It could have been anything. For the Pandora's box William had opened. For the turmoil her life was in. Yet, she felt assurance in it, too. The assurance that she could rely on him. That she could count on him to see her through whatever came next.

She needed his support as much as she needed his help. It should have distressed her that he so obviously knew that. Instead, the thought that she simply needed…him…had her clinging to his broad shoulders as he eased one arm across her back. She wasn't foolish enough to believe he would be there for her after this was all over. But as he drew her against the solid length of his hard, beautifully muscled body, she told herself that didn't matter. He was there for her now.

For the first time in days, she didn't feel the near-constant anxiety that had held her in its grip. All she felt as he coaxed her to open to him was his heat, the strength of his arms and a liquid ache low in her belly that deepened with the slow seduction of his tongue.

A tiny moan escaped from her throat.

Ben drank in that small aching sound, and bit back a groan of his own as he gathered her closer. His nerves were already tripwire tight. The feel of her stomach pressed to his, her breasts crushed to his chest, poured heat, swift and searing, through every muscle and vein in his body.

He hadn't intended to kiss her. Not like this. He'd meant only to let her know that she had him wrong. That he cared for her beyond his obligations. He'd meant to keep it chaste. Simple. Innocent. But there was nothing simple about the needs she aroused in him. *Innocent* no longer applied. And *chaste* had gone out the window the moment he'd tangled one hand in her hair, pressed his other to the small of her back and found himself wishing she were naked. All it had taken was one taste of her to know one kiss would never be enough.

Unprepared for the swiftness of the need she caused him to

feel, shaken by it, he made himself slip his fingers from the back of her head. Lifting his own, he eased his hand down to curve at the side of her neck and watched her eyes slowly open.

With her beautiful mouth damp from his moisture, she drew a deep, shuddery breath.

His thumb stole over the pulse hammering in her throat, his voice going oddly husky. "I think that should stay just between us, too."

The muscles in her slender neck convulsed as she swallowed. "Absolutely."

The temptation to pull her back was strong. The need to keep from crossing any farther over the line than he just had, felt stronger still.

He slowly eased his hold.

"So," he murmured, knowing he should move away completely, hating the idea. "Do you feel like talking about the press?"

Jillian managed a nod. Talking was good. Talking would keep her from thinking too much about why she so badly wanted him to repeat what he'd just done. And about why he was not. Her heart still hurt for what she'd learned about him today. Now knowing what she did about his ex, it was no wonder he didn't invite involvements. At least, not the kind that might lead a woman to think he'd be there for her in any permanent way. "William said you had a plan."

With his thumb and forefinger, he toyed with the softness of one long curl. Realizing what he was doing, how hard it was to not touch her, he reluctantly let his hand fall. He had more control than this.

As much to remove himself from temptation as to make it easier to think, he finally took a step back.

"Did he tell you anything about it?"

Determined to focus, she turned and picked up her goblet. "He said you'd explain it."

"You gave me the idea when I realized what mattered most to you in all this." Reaching for his own goblet, he put another foot of flagstone between them. "After William gave me a better idea of what his relationship had been with your mom, I knew it was the best way to go.

"You want to protect your mom's reputation. William said he told you he wants that, too. All I need to know now is if you still want nothing to do with him. I'm not asking if you're ready to start calling him Dad," he hurried to explain. "I just need to know if you could appear in public with him without being defensive."

"Appear in public?"

"I'll get to that," he promised. "I need you to answer my question first. Do you feel as adamant about him now as you did before?"

He had a way of studying her that made her feel as if she had no protective armor at all. He did that with everyone, she suspected. Those too-blue eyes simply lasered past the masks and practiced manners people used to protect their tender or touchy spots to be sure they were keeping nothing from him.

She doubted there was much he couldn't see.

Aware that she had already exposed far too much where he was concerned, she turned her attention back to a sailboat tacking a half-mile offshore. "Probably not so much. I still don't want anything more than absolutely necessary from him. But I'm not really sure how I feel about him now." He wanted to protect her mom, after all.

From an arm's length down the retaining wall, she saw Ben give a satisfied nod. "Then I think we can make this work."

"You still haven't said what 'this' is."

"An interview. The way I see it, all the speculation and second-guessing can be curtailed by you, William and Mrs. Kendrick appearing together. Their relationship is being torn apart in the press because of this," he reminded her as her eyebrows arched, "so we'd get everything on the table at once. The person your mother was. His relationship with her. Mrs. Kendrick's feelings about her.

"My preference is for an exclusive on *Good Morning, USA,*" he continued before she could offer a word of objection. "You know Nina Tyler has already asked for an interview with you. She's asked for interviews with the Kendricks, too. She handles her guests as well as anyone, and the three of you can get your story out there all at one time."

"You want me to go on television?"

"And tell Ms. Tyler whatever you're comfortable sharing," he replied, completely missing the disbelief in her voice. Or, more than likely, just ignoring it. "I think you should tell her just what you told me about Beth Hadley. About what a good mom she was. About how well she provided and cared for you. If you're not comfortable mentioning that your mom never loved anyone else, then don't. Same with her never having gone out with anyone else after William, either.

"Actually," he muttered, clearly in his element as he outlined her appearance with the press, "you'll be asked if she had other men in her life, so that will come out anyway.

"The main thing is to not come across touchy or defensive. That's like waving red meat in front of a starving jackal. She'll be on it in a heartbeat. If you're asked something you're not comfortable answering, just say so and don't answer it. Change the subject to a point you want to make. Or just smile and say 'next question.'

"I can see that you're not sold on this, Jillian. But not all of the focus will be on you. Only a third of it. And honestly," he said, looking as if he'd swear to it if he had to, "there's no quicker way to kill speculation and rumor than for the parties involved to appear together and let those rumors be addressed."

She couldn't deny his logic. But she couldn't deny her apprehension, either. "I've never been in front of a camera in my life. And the closest I've come to a microphone is the one in the school gym."

"I'll coach you through all of it. You'll be fine."

Skepticism shadowed the delicate lines of her face. "When would we do this?

"First thing in the morning. All I have to do is call Nina back and tell her we're a go. They're holding a spot for us."

"You already talked to her about it?"

"I told you that you have to play nice with the major media," he reminded her, his tone utterly calm. "All I did was acknowledge that you'd received her request so they'd know you weren't ignoring them. I told them you were considering your options. She knows it could go either way."

"But you really think this is the best way to go," she concluded.

Her reliance on his opinion wasn't lost on him. Reaching for her arm when he would have rather buried his fingers in her fabulous hair, he skimmed his hand to her shoulder. "If I could think of anything better, I promise, I'd tell you."

Indecision slowly faded as she drew a deep breath. He was right. There was no better way to protect her mom than to have the Kendricks defend her themselves. "Then, you should call her."

He gave her shoulder a sympathetic squeeze. "I can have the plane here in no time."

Chapter Seven

"Tip your head back for me, Miss Hadley? This will cut down shine. It gets hot under the lights and you don't want to look like you're perspiring."

A large makeup brush dusted beige powder over Jillian's forehead, cheeks and chin. Wielding it was a forty-something makeup artist who'd been introduced only as Jon before he'd proceeded to wax poetic about her fabulous bone structure and beautiful eyes. He wasn't so enamored of her mop of thick curls, though he never said so directly. When he got around to mentioning it after darkening her usual, spare eye makeup and lip gloss, he merely asked if she'd ever considered straightening it, thinning it and adding highlights.

She'd vaguely recalled that hair had been on the list of back-to-school resolutions she'd made what seemed a lifetime ago, when the studio page poked her head inside.

Amber Ames was in charge of making sure guests on *GM, USA* got where they needed to be. The perky blonde in her early twenties had already had way too much caffeine. In the time it took most people to draw a normal breath, she had glanced from her clipboard, to her watch, to Jillian, to Jon and announced, "Ten and counting."

She flashed a toothpaste-bright smile at Jillian. "How are you doing, Miss Hadley?"

"I'm fine," Jillian replied, lying through her teeth. She felt like throwing up.

"Can I get you more coffee?"

More acid in her stomach was the last thing she needed. "No. Thanks," she said, making herself smile. "I'm…good."

"Great." Another glance at her watch and Amber's eyes widened. "I'll be right back."

Backing up, she bumped into something solid and glanced away. Her smile promptly turned from beaming to flustered. Ben was right behind her. Looking impossibly attractive in a navy pinstriped suit, white dress shirt and burgundy tie, he appeared totally preoccupied and in a hurry himself.

"She needs to be in Greenroom B in two minutes," Amber informed him.

"I'll get her there."

"Thanks."

His vague smile for the cute, clearly enamored little blonde faded the instant he strode into the room.

Jillian thought she'd known all about schedules. Any given school day was pretty much programmed to the minute. Yet as she watched Ben push back his cuff and check his watch, she had the feeling the only thing timed with more accuracy than a live television show was a NASA space launch.

"How are we doing?" he asked Jon.

"Except for the hair, we're finished. I'd like to tame it a little."

Jillian quickly tucked a handful of curls behind one ear. The rest of it fell in a thick mass of ringlets and waves along the sides of her face and past her shoulders. "This is the way I usually wear it."

"Yes, well," the makeup artist hummed, "it overpowers you." His thin features narrowed in concentration as he ran an expert glance over her face. He'd worked with the guests and hosts of this program for ten years and had a great eye for what looked best on camera. He'd told her so himself. "I suggest that we pull it up and back in a French braid. Your features are too delicate to be overwhelmed by all those curls. You need something sleeker."

She felt her back stiffen. "I'd rather wear it down."

"You'd look more sophisticated—"

"Please," she asked, though she would insist if she had to. She wasn't the sleek sort. Never had been. Never would be. She'd tried to tell that to Ben's assistant, Sara Ables, last night when the woman had tried to get her to wear one of the suits she'd brought for her to try on. Ben had seen her pack, knew she had nothing he considered appropriate and had apparently sent Sara on a shopping spree.

She wasn't a tailored-suit person, either, which was why she'd pressed and now wore the mocha linen capris she'd worn when she'd met William yesterday. Her concession to Ben and his assistant was to add the short matching jacket and an aqua camisole Sara said she needed for color. Shades of blue apparently looked best on camera.

As for Jon, the only reason she hadn't balked more at the extra color he'd added to her face was because he'd told her that under the bright lights on the set, she'd look dead without it.

"Leave it."

Ben's decisive tone offered no room for further discussion. It also held the almost reticent protectiveness she'd sensed in him since he'd kissed her on his patio last evening. Other than for the most casual of contact, he had made no attempt to touch her again. But then, they hadn't been alone since the plane had arrived.

In many ways it was as if he didn't want them to be.

"It's her," Ben concluded. "She looks just fine.

"Remember what I told you about looking at Nina instead of the camera," he continued to her while Jon, having been summarily overruled, whipped away her black makeup cape. "Try to forget the cameras are there. And try not to fidget," he reminded her. "You might want to do a little less of this, too," he said, casually unfolding her crossed arms.

Taking her hand, he helped her from the chair. "Crossing your arms makes you look defensive or self-protective. I know you're feeling that way, but unless you want Nina to zero in on that, keep your hands folded in your lap."

His hand remained on her elbow, the feel of it supportive despite the odd distance she sensed in him as he moved her from the brightly lit mirror to the door. He had suggested on the plane last night that she let the staff that had met them at the hotel video tape her so she could see how she came across when answering the sort of questions that would be posed in a matter of minutes. But by the time they'd landed in New York, been whisked by limo to the Waldorf-Astoria and she'd been ushered up to a gorgeous suite, other demands had presented themselves.

There had been no time for a practice session. Not without cutting into the equally important time for a few hours of sleep. Having had precious little of the latter lately, her concentration was shot by the time she'd been introduced to Sara and to Andy, a voice-and-video coach, who outlined the schedule for the next ten hours.

Sara had told her that her wake-up call would come at four forty-five. Coffee would be delivered to her room. The limo would pick them up to take them to the studio at five-twenty. Andy had then asked if she knew what she was going to wear in the morning and suggested she lay it out before retiring for the night.

That was when Sara had produced the suits, and the discussion about which she would wear ensued. A person's first public appearance was hugely important, Sara had stressed. First impressions could never be undone.

She must have looked like a deer caught in headlights when she'd looked to where Ben had been on the phone arranging for her exit in the morning with hotel security. Seeing her expression, he seemed to realize that she had been pushed about as far as she could go. It was already midnight, Sara wasn't listening to her, and Andy was saying something about putting Vaseline on her front teeth so they wouldn't stick to her upper lip that wasn't making sense to her at all.

The moment Ben hung up, he'd cleared everyone out. With Sara and Andy waiting outside the door to talk to him, he'd written down his room number in case Jillian needed to call him, almost hesitantly brushed his finger over her cheek and left her with the promise that this would be over soon.

She could have sworn she'd barely pulled off her clothes and crawled under the covers when her wake-up call reminded her that she was definitely not in Kansas anymore. Like Dorothy and her little Toto, she'd been caught in some surreal tornado and dumped in a place where the familiar had been totally distorted and she had no idea how to get back to where she'd once belonged.

With Ben at her side, she now found herself being led past a plaque beside a door identifying the room as Greenroom B and on to one identified as Greenroom A.

"I thought we were supposed to go there," she said motioning behind her.

"I want you to meet Mrs. Kendrick first."

He must have felt her hesitate.

"Just remember who you're doing this for," he murmured, and opened the door.

The greenroom wasn't green. It was blue. So was most of the comfortably upholstered furniture. With all the activity inside, that incongruity barely registered.

A tall, slender ash blonde in a rose-colored suit stood with her back to the door. In front of her, a woman in black flicked powder over her face much as Jon had just done with her. Beside them, a short, round-cheeked woman in purple was reading aloud from a clipboard. Another lady paced nearby, speaking into a cell phone.

Seeing them in the doorway, the women suddenly went silent. The one in black stepped back. As she did, Katherine Kendrick turned.

"Oh, my," she murmured, immediately clasping her hands. Looking as regal as the queen she could have been, she looked to the others in the room. "I'm sorry. Will you excuse us, please?"

The little entourage had barely filed out when Amber poked her head inside. "Five minutes," she warned, only to have her efficient smile collapse when she saw Jillian standing there. Her glance darted accusingly to Ben.

"Miss Hadley was to wait next door."

"We decided not to."

"But Nina said they were to meet on the set."

"Tell her there was a mix-up in communication," he replied easily.

The anxious frown stayed in place as the page rushed to the next concern on her list. "Have you heard from Mr. Kendrick yet?"

"One of my associates is bringing him up. They should be getting off the elevator right about now."

The door closed without another word.

Clearly conscious of the time and logistics himself, Ben glanced between the women on either side of him.

"I don't know that introductions are really necessary," he said. "But I thought it better that you two meet here rather than on the set. Nina wanted the spontaneity. I told her you were all having your privacy invaded enough without doing reality television for her."

Katherine Kendrick was stunning. Tall, elegant, blond, she wore her pale hair in a shining French twist. The tasteful jewelry she wore, gold earrings and a wide gold necklace, were probably 24 karat. Her skin looked flawless. Despite her maturity, the faint lines fanning from the corners of her eyes seemed to speak more of strain than age.

"Thank you so much, Ben." Her voice held notes of culture, refinement. "We appreciate anything you can do to curb the sensationalism with this."

"We do our best." The seemingly easy smile he offered held as much charm as it did reassurance. "Miss Silverman will be here with William by now, so I'm going to leave you two and make sure we're good to go. I'll be right outside if you need me."

He glanced to Jillian. As if to keep from reaching toward her, he pushed one hand into his pocket. "You, too," he added, and left her alone with the woman who'd made it impossible for her father to ever love her mom.

In the awkward silence, the older woman's eyes skimmed her face. "You're lovely," she pronounced, only to have her glance flicker and fall.

Jillian looked just like her mother. People had told her that all her life. Since Beth had been William's secretary for so long, Katherine would have been aware of that resemblance when she'd seen the first pictures of her.

At the unexpected compliment, all Jillian could think to say was, "Thank you, Mrs. Kendrick."

"It's Katherine. Please. Come," she asked, taking her hand, "sit down with me. I've nearly paced a trench in this carpet. Are you as nervous as I am about all this?"

Nervous didn't begin to describe how anxious Jillian felt herself. But the thought that this elegant and idolized woman could be so apprehensive was unimaginable to her, until she felt the faint tremor in Katherine's beautifully manicured hand.

Not sure whether to be comforted or alarmed to know that this celebrated woman's internal composure was as shaken as her own, she sank onto the sofa beside her.

"Ms. Tyler seemed nice enough when I met her," Jillian prefaced, "and Ben gave me an idea of the kind of questions she would ask, but he said to be prepared for anything." Had it not been for Ben, she was sure she would have been even more of an internal wreck than she already was. "I'll just be so glad when this is over."

Katherine gave her an understanding smile. "You know this is really only the beginning for you, don't you? The questions and the interest in you won't stop here."

That was not what she needed to hear. Standing because

she couldn't just sit there, Jillian did what Ben had told her not to do and crossed her arms the moment she rose.

"Jillian." Katherine spoke quietly as she took in her self-protective stance. "I don't want to overstep myself with you. Quite honestly, I know this is awkward for both of us. But may I offer you something I learned a very long time ago?"

Sitting with her ankles crossed and tucked to one side, knees together, hands clasped, she patiently waited for a response.

A little surprised that she didn't intend to proceed without permission, Jillian asked, "What's that?"

"There are two ways to handle the public's interest in you. You can fight them and spend your time and energy trying to hide. Or you can use it to do something positive. If I didn't think positive things would come out of this for all of us and other women, I wouldn't be going out there now."

She watched Katherine's glance fall to her lap. Until that moment, trapped in her own crisis and concerned only about her own issues, Jillian hadn't bothered to consider that this woman had as much at stake in what they were about to do as she did. Her much-admired marriage had proven to be just as vulnerable as anyone else's. She was also about to publicly admit that her inability to cope following the birth of her second child pretty much drove her husband into the arms of another woman.

Jillian knew the Kendricks had made it a policy never to comment about anything personally controversial. That she and William were willing to break protocol to expose the details of something so private and, for Katherine, once very painful, told her how far they were willing to go to protect their good name, and to do right by her.

It also seemed that Katherine hoped that by exposing what

she'd kept to herself for so long, she would be able to help other women with the depression she'd suffered so long ago.

A sort of sympathy Jillian never would have expected to feel for this woman met with equally unanticipated admiration. Both bumped squarely into guilt. Respecting the woman her mom had never been able to compete with made her feel like a traitor. The last thing she ever wanted to do was betray her mom.

The door opened. William and Ben stood in the hallway, their hands in their pockets, their heads together as they spoke in low tones. In the doorway the page clasped her clipboard to her chest. "Ladies, if you'll come with me, please?"

The Kendricks and Jillian were a six-minute segment following the weather.

Ben stood beside Kim Silverman in the gray glow of the control room, his arms crossed, his mouth forming an upside down U as he watched the various monitors. Ahead of him technicians with headsets sat in front of tiny TV screens of their own, quietly punching buttons that switched cameras, regulated the audio for microphones and cued the teleprompter.

On the set to his right, Nina in her trademark red cat's-eye reading glasses sat with her guests in front of an expansive faux view of the New York skyline.

He had worked with Nina before with various clients and respected the grand dame of morning news shows as much as he did any journalist. Unless an interview was purely a promo piece, she often asked hard questions, especially those she knew the public wanted answered, but she wasn't without compassion. The bulk of his focus was on his clients, though. Specifically, the quietly attractive, admirably poised brunette he was dead certain felt totally out of her element.

Kim leaned toward him. "We need to do something with that hair," she whispered.

He regarded Kim as his next in command, the person he trusted most to know what was best for Garrett clients.

"Her hair is fine."

He caught the quick arch of Kim's eyebrow as she moved back. He hadn't meant to sound so protective. Or maybe it was possessive.

A muscle in his jaw tensed. It was probably both, but in another hour or so he wouldn't have to worry about whatever it was he felt about Jillian. In another hour, she would no longer be his direct responsibility.

He narrowed his focus on the set. Nina had led off the interview with William and Katherine. William's infidelity was The Big Story at the moment, with Jillian the intriguing, still mysterious by-product. Yet, rather than come off as a couple in trouble, William and Katherine appeared to be exactly what they were: a couple who had weathered a tough time in their marriage and come out stronger for it.

Katherine revealed the separation that had been her idea, what had led to it and acknowledged that learning of his relationship with Beth Hadley had hurt terribly. She went on to admit that she'd never blamed nor hated Beth or her husband for what had happened. In turn, William professed admiration for his wife's willingness to disclose the postpartum depression that had prompted their difficulties. They knew there were other advocates for young women suffering the awful symptoms. She just wanted to add her voice if she could be of help.

It got tougher for him when Nina asked about the woman everyone by now knew had been his secretary for three years. But he candidly told her pretty much what he'd told Ben he had disclosed to his daughter, which made Jillian's mom sound like a lovely, loyal young lady who'd been there for him when he'd thought his marriage was over, then had become the unintended injured party when he'd realized it was not.

"You must feel like another casualty, too," Nina said, turning to Jillian. "I understand your mother never married, so you grew up without a father figure. You weren't told who your biological father was until last year. Do you feel cheated by his identity being kept from you?"

Except for the quick tightening of her clasped hands, Jillian appeared admirably composed.

"It's hard to feel cheated when I had everything I felt I needed. I had a great childhood."

"But what about now? It's being reported that you lost your teaching position because security became a problem at your school. Paparazzi are now following you everywhere. How do you feel about your loss of privacy?"

Nina wasn't asking the questions she'd said she would.

Ben looked from the set to a monitor, watching the close-up of Jillian's face.

As straightforward as he knew she could be, he wouldn't have put it past her to say that it hadn't just been the paparazzi that had cost her her job. It had been the media in general, William Kendrick in particular and that, yes, she did feel like a casualty. But she clearly understood where a statement like that would lead.

"I hate it," she said. "But I welcomed this opportunity to put an end to the rumors about the sort of woman my mother was. She's being called everything from a gold digger and opportunist to a home wrecker. The Kendricks and I know she was none of those things."

"I know that protecting your mom's reputation was the only reason you agreed to this interview," Nina said for the benefit of her viewers. "Tell me, how would your mother have felt to know everyone knows about her affair with one of the world's most powerful men?"

"I can't answer that."

"Just knowing her as you did," she coaxed, "what do you think she would say now that her secret is out?"

"I can't answer that, either."

"Then how do you feel about it?" she asked, determined to get something more personal out of her.

With a tolerant look she might have given a particularly persistent student, Jillian slowly shook her head.

Getting nowhere, Nina changed topics. "Have you met your half siblings yet?"

The question about William's other children clearly caught her off guard. Not because she couldn't answer it, Ben thought, but because he doubted she'd given a whole lot of thought to the half brothers and sisters he happened to know very much wanted to meet her. That would not be his problem to deal with, though.

"No," she murmured, and was saved from anything more prying by the demands of a program schedule that called for a commercial break in five seconds, four, three…

Nina expertly segued to that break. A moment later the red light went off on the camera in front of them and the green On Air light across the set from them blacked out. Even as the show's host unplugged her earpiece, she graciously shook Katherine's hand, then William's, telling them both she'd love to have them back, then reached for Jillian's to thank her and ask if she could have her back, too. Alone. She'd like to do a follow-up in a month or so. Maybe sit down with her and her people and discuss documenting her life for the next year to see what changes she experienced as a Kendrick.

Jillian thought she'd rather have a root canal.

Fortunately, there was no time for a response, or for further discussion. An assistant producer rushed forward to coach Nina on the next segment while Amber, the page, escorted everyone else off the set and across the sea of television and electrical cables.

With the Kendricks ahead of her, Jillian saw Ben leave the control room. He was speaking intently with the striking, auburn-haired woman at his side.

She couldn't count the number of people she'd seen or been introduced to that morning. Part of them had been studio employees, some had been the Kendricks' assistants, others were security personnel. She knew for a fact, though, that she had not seen the woman with Ben now.

She had the look of a no-nonsense executive. Sleek, cropped hair, rimless glasses, trim black suit.

Jillian was wondering if she had something to do with the television network, and hoping rather desperately that Ben wasn't going to recommend a taped interview or some such now, when William fell back to walk with her.

"You indicated yesterday that you'd find your own place to stay," he began without preface. "Have you decided where you'll go from the hotel?"

Even Nina's question about William's other children hadn't caught her so unprepared.

She knew she was going back to the hotel because her things were still scattered all over the bed and bathroom. She'd given no thought, however, to where she would go—or be taken—from there.

She caught Ben watching her. Quick caution entered his expression an instant before he glanced away.

Without having to be told, she had the sudden and certain feeling that going back to his beach house was not an option.

"I'm...not sure," she conceded. All she knew for certain was where she couldn't go. She couldn't inflict the press on her friends by camping out with any of them. Even now, reporters and paparazzi were gathered outside the studio, waiting to catch shots of them leaving. She'd seen them on one of the television monitors. Media capitalizing on the media.

She didn't know where to go that they wouldn't follow. The only place she really had was her duplex, but if she returned, she'd disrupt her neighbors all over again. She had no idea what she'd do there, anyway. She couldn't work because she had no job and she'd be a prisoner because of the cameras.

"If you'd like," Katherine said, now walking with them, too, "you're welcome to use the apartment we keep in Richmond. It's on the top floor and quite secure. It has a small staff, so you wouldn't be there alone."

"It might be a good location for you," William continued, quietly because staffers kept bustling by. "Ben told me how much teaching means to you, Jillian. I know you don't want my help, but I am responsible for you losing your job. It's just something to think about, but we know the headmaster of a private school outside of Richmond. I'd be happy to arrange an interview for you."

The murmur of other voices faded as they stepped into the greenroom. Ben and a handful of others were already there.

"Just consider it," William requested, as someone asked if anyone had called for the cars.

There was no denying that William and his wife were doing what they could to help her deal with the upheaval she was going through. The fact that Ben had relayed her love for teaching to William wasn't lost on her, either. She just had no time to balk or respond to their offer, or to do much more than wonder why Ben was barely making eye contact with her now.

"Jillian." Ben walked up to her, the stylish lady executive at his elbow. "This is Kim Silverman." He nodded to the thirty-something woman who all but towered over her in her three-inch heels. "She'll help you arrange for the rest of your press appearances. Or help you avoid them," he added with a faint smile, "if that's what you decide. She's our top associate. You can trust her advice on just about anything."

"Just about?" Kim asked, her eyes smiling as she pretended offense. Turning that smile to Jillian, she held out her hand. "It's a pleasure, Miss Hadley. Ben said you didn't have time to practice in a front of camera, but you did beautifully out there. I'm going to enjoy working with you."

She went on to add something about images and how she enjoyed polishing them as Jillian shook the woman's hand. The words barely registered, though. As another voice announced that the drivers were waiting, she realized what was happening. She was being handed over to Ben's assistant. And Ben seemed to have no qualms about the transfer at all.

With all that had happened in the past week, Jillian thought she'd been prepared for just about anything.

She'd been wrong. She just wasn't sure how she felt about what Ben had done—and how he'd done it—as Sara and Jackson and Schroeder, who'd arrived early that morning, escorted her back to her hotel suite. She had no idea where Andy had gone, but Ben and Kim had stayed behind to talk with the Kendricks about another appearance. Sara had just told her they would join her shortly and left for her own room to pack.

Finally alone, Jillian turned her back to the closed door and leaned against it.

It seemed to her that Ben could have given her a little advance warning about what he'd planned to do. But then, she told herself, pressing her hand to the empty sensation growing beneath her breastbone, it was entirely possible he hadn't felt warning was necessary. He was probably just doing his job the way he always did. The fact that he'd come to know exactly which buttons to push and how much support and sympathy to add to accomplish his goals proved just how good at that job he was. She'd known who he was working for. So she had no business feeling betrayed.

She pushed herself from the door, crossed the expansive room with its view of Park Avenue, luxurious furnishings and its marble soaking tub in the bathroom. She could have lived in this suite. It had more square footage than her duplex.

The disappointment she felt didn't allow her to appreciate the fabulous surroundings, though. It was her own fault that disappointment was there. It wasn't as if he had ever led her to believe that anything could exist between them beyond what it took to get his job done. Knowing how badly he'd been burned, how totally cynical he'd become where people in general and women in particular were concerned, it had never occurred to her to believe there ever could be.

She pulled her suitcase from the closet, only to set it back down because she had no idea at that moment where she was going. Since she was now in immediate need of a plan, she was telling herself it was imperative that she focus and figure one out when a knock sounded on her door.

Taking a breath that smelled of the lavender potpourri in the bathroom, she closed the closet door. She figured that would be Ben and the woman whose stylish appearance had made her nearly as self-conscious as Katherine's.

It was Ben's dark head she saw through the peephole and his voice she heard talking to Jackson, who had remained in the hallway. But when she pulled open the door and found herself facing the platinum stick pin in his burgundy tie, she realized that Kim wasn't with him.

Reminding herself that she'd look defensive if she crossed her arms, she kept them at her sides as she invited him in and left him to close the door himself. That was when she discovered he wasn't exactly alone after all. As she watched him cut a guarded glance toward where she'd stopped by the bisque damask sofa, the tension that came in with him was almost palpable.

That tension seemed to follow in his wake, escalating her own and making it even more difficult to pretend the ease she was determined he would see.

"I thought Kim was coming, too."

"She'll be here in a while. I wanted to see you first."

It was apparent to Jillian that he knew how much she had started to count on him. And she knew he was walking away from her. She just didn't want him to know how much what he was doing mattered where she was concerned. Being totally realistic about the situation, it was obvious that she'd simply come to rely on him far more than anyone—herself, especially—had ever intended.

"Whose decision was it to hand me over to your associate?"

So much for not letting him know how much that bothered her.

The cuff of Ben's white shirt poked from the sleeve of his suit jacket as he rubbed his finger above the slash of one dark eyebrow.

"Mine." He wouldn't lie to her. There were, however, parts of the truth she didn't need to know. "Turning over the day-to-day responsibility of your PR was my idea."

His hand fell to his side before he shoved it into his slacks pocket.

"My job is crisis management, Jillian," he explained. "Your situation is no longer in that mode. I also think it will look better to the press if a woman is making your arrangements.

"This morning's paper has a shot of us on the patio last night," he told her, a hint of annoyance in his deep voice. "From the angle, it was taken from the water. I have no idea who tipped who off that we were there, but we're already being linked as more than client and advisor because of it. You have enough going on without having to deal with that kind of gossip."

The morning paper that had come with her coffee lay neatly folded on the mahogany desk in the corner of the room. There had been no time to look at it before she'd been hustled off to the studio.

Seeing where her glance had strayed, he walked over, opened it to page three.

Kendricks To Disclose Details capped three eight-inch columns on the upper left. The network had come forward with that information, undoubtedly within minutes of his call confirming their appearance last evening. His own office had supplied photos of William, Mrs. Kendrick and a shot of Jillian that Sara had obtained from a Thomas Jefferson Elementary yearbook of her talking to three students in a schoolyard. The kids' backs were to the camera.

Ben had previously selected the photo from those Sara had e-mailed him because it showed Jillian in her own element. Her smile lit up her whole face. He didn't doubt that half the little boys in her classes fell in love with her and that smile the very first day of school.

The paper had chosen to supplement those images, though, along with the press release they had been supplied. Beneath the photo of him and Jillian staring into each other's eyes with his hand tucked into the back of her hair was the comment that Ben Garrett, a partner in The Garrett Group, the exclusive Washington, D.C., PR firm retained by the Kendrick family, had been seen with her since the story of her paternity broke.

"That comment is benign," he conceded, not quite sure what was going through her mind as she stood beside him scanning the page. "But the text under the same picture in an L.A. paper suggested you were letting me orchestrate more than your debut as the latest Kendrick debutante."

As if finding it hard to believe her image was in papers coast-to-coast, she gave her head a slow shake. "I'm ten years too old to be a debutante."

"I'm sure they were going for the alliteration. And the scoop."

Except there wasn't a scoop, Jillian thought, looking up from the photograph that had been taken within moments of him kissing her. Not where a relationship between the two of them was concerned. He was making that as clear as the small crystal chandelier over the marble bathtub.

"The point is that it's still my job to make sure your press is favorable. I'd be letting you and William both down if I didn't do that job to the best of my ability."

He could admit he was stepping aside to protect her from unwanted publicity where he was concerned. What he wouldn't offer was the more critical reason he didn't want to remain personally involved with her. He'd never in his life met a woman who'd gotten under his skin so fast. She messed with his logic, caused him to think and do things that weren't like him at all.

Then there was the physical ache she'd created inside him. Even now, his fingers itched for the feel of her skin. He craved the taste of her mouth. He should never have kissed her. A man couldn't miss what he didn't know.

"You have to be careful these first few weeks," he insisted, easing his glance from her lush, peach-tinted mouth. "You really don't need suggestive or sensational headlines. Once those start, that's what will follow you. Kim's good. She'll keep that from happening."

Unlike him. He couldn't believe he'd been so careless with a client. Unfortunately, neither could his father. J.C. had been on his cell phone within minutes of seeing that photo himself that morning, giving him grief for not being more circumspect and wanting to know what in the hell he was doing with the daughter of their client.

Then there was William. If he'd seen the photo, he'd said nothing. But he could easily take exception to him being physically involved with the daughter he'd trusted him to take care of. Especially since Ben had no intention of getting serious about her.

Jillian cocked her head, studied him the way he had so often studied her. "What happens if I decided to let Kim go?"

"Then, I'll assign someone else."

"And if I decide I don't want The Garrett Group at all?"

The concern he didn't want to feel shadowed the carved lines of his face. "I'd recommend you to another firm. You don't want to go this alone." That, right there, was the best advice he could offer. "Anyone in your position will do better with someone who knows the ropes. It's like you and your bodyguards. You're going to need them for a long time."

"How long?"

"You're a mystery to everyone, Jillian." Then there was the fact that beautiful women tended to hold the public's interest longer than those with average looks. And she was definitely beautiful, in some impossibly natural, sexy and fresh sort of way. "You're a Kendrick."

You know this is only the beginning, don't you? Mrs. Kendrick had asked. *The questions and the interest in you won't stop here.*

Jillian snaked her fingers through her hair, turned to hide the distress she absolutely refused to let him see. It was only the beginning and the man who'd seen her through what she could have sworn was the worst of it was preparing to walk as far out of her life as he could.

In the space of a week, he had become her anchor. Even with all the arrangements waiting to be made for her if she wanted them, she couldn't help feeling as if she had suddenly been cut free and left to drift on her own.

The feeling was familiar. She'd felt it when Eric had walked away. She'd felt it when she'd lost her mom. She just hadn't expected to feel it because of Ben.

Grasping all the hints she'd been given about appearing composed when she most definitely was not, she managed to turn with an accepting smile.

"I understand," she insisted, giving back the reassurance he'd so often given her. "I'll work with Kim." She would work with her because the woman had become a necessity. Rather like her bodyguards. "I know you were brought in to make sure I wouldn't be a problem. Now that you know I won't be, your work here is done."

Discomfort at the truth jabbed Ben hard. So did the decision not to tell her it was far from that simple.

Deciding he should just be grateful that she hadn't allowed herself any illusions about him, he moved on to what concerned him most.

"William said he offered you their penthouse in Richmond," he told her, watching her eyebrows knit at the abrupt change of subject.

"Mrs. Kendrick said it was an apartment."

"That's what they call it. But it's a penthouse," he assured her. "He said he also mentioned arranging an interview for you at a private boarding school." He'd suggested the private school scenario himself. As much as he knew she wanted some of her privacy back, she stood the best chance of getting it there. "Have you thought about what you want to do?"

She blew a breath, turned away, turned back. "When's checkout?"

"Don't worry about it. You can stay here a couple more days if you need the time."

More time wouldn't change her options. Knowing that, knowing that accepting the Kendricks' offer had become a necessity, too, she crossed her arms over the knot in her stomach. She didn't care what her body language said just then. She could practically feel the last of the life she'd known slipping through her fingers.

"I'll take both."

That was what he'd hoped she would do.

"Do you want me to tell William?"

She barely met his eyes. "Please."

She wasn't comfortable with her decision. There was no doubt of that in his mind.

He was going to worry about her whether he wanted to or not.

The realization pulled his brow low as he took a step toward her. Without thinking, he lifted his hand, brushed his fingers over her cheek. He'd told himself he wouldn't touch her, but he hadn't realized how hard it would be to leave her. Had he not known he could keep track of her through his associate, he wondered vaguely if leaving her now might not have been impossible.

"You can always call me if things get really crazy."

Her head had turned ever so slightly toward his hand. As if catching that involuntary reaction, she went still an instant before she stepped away.

"Likewise," she murmured over the three quick knocks on her door. "With your dad and grandfather," she explained, seeing Ben's obvious incomprehension. "If you really think about it, that situation is probably more complicated than you realize."

Chapter Eight

Ben peeled another antacid tablet from the packet on his office desk and chewed it on his way to the window with its view of the Mall and the Tidal Basin in the distance. The trees were beginning to turn, bursts of orange and gold gaining on shades of green. Twelve stories down, at four o'clock on a Saturday afternoon, the wide streets were all but devoid of traffic.

Restless, he turned back to his desk to frown at the transcript of a congressional hearing he'd been wading through for the past two hours. No matter how many times he read his client's statements, there was no way to spin them to hide the fact that his client hadn't been up front with him. He had no idea how that client, a congressman, expected him to refurbish his reputation following a campaign finance scandal, if the man insisted on sabotaging Ben's efforts to help him. But he'd come up with something.

The thought made his stomach burn even more.

Preferring not to question why that was, he scanned the other projects demanding his attention.

Atop the two largest stacks of files were reports from assistants and associates on the status of active accounts, and an envelope of season tickets to the opera and Redskins games to be divided among certain clients. Use of The Garrett Group's box seats was a perk for a few of their longtime clients. Others received gifts of art, invitations to parties on his father's yacht or their annual holiday party at whatever venue the partnership decided would best impress their clients that year.

Yellow sticky notes reminded him that he needed to send birthday flowers to a reporter at the *Washington Post,* and a bottle of gin to one at NBC. Every good publicist had a select handful of press contacts he could call to get a story out in a hurry, or who could be counted on to give a head's-up for a story about to break on a client who would need immediate damage control.

Then there was the company's quarterly report. It was due Wednesday. He would have reviewed it last night, but he'd had to take a potential client to dinner.

He'd give anything for a day off. In the past two weeks, he'd managed exactly one evening to himself and he'd spent much of that on the phone with Pops.

His dad had been ticked off at him ever since.

He popped another antacid chew, washed it down with coffee from the mug on his desk. The combination probably wasn't ideal, but it was pretty much how he always fueled himself between meals.

His father had taken it upon himself last week to make an appointment with a real estate agent for Pops to list his home, land and business for sale. J.C. had insisted that if his father knew how much he could get for all of it, Pops would be inclined to think of all the things he could do with the money and see the appeal in a life of freedom and leisure.

Ben knew that his dad wanted his father where he didn't have to worry about the old guy. Tucked away in a retirement community, Pops wouldn't be living alone or climbing around all that scaffolding. But there was more to think about than what would put his dad's mind at ease.

Because Ben had come to no clear conclusion on his own, he had finally done what Jillian had suggested and considered who truly stood to lose the most if Pops sold his business. When he had, the answer had been far easier to reach than he would have thought.

His dad might have Pops longer if the older man slowed down, but J.C. would also still have his own active life and his career, which were the bulk of his daily focus. If Pops sold the home his parents had left him and the business that was more a way of life for him than actual work, then Pops would be left with nothing—with the possible exception of more time to miss what he no longer had.

He remembered Jillian suggesting that he figure himself into the equation, too, and consider what would make him happiest. Since he couldn't see himself coming out ahead either way, he had no idea why she'd seemed to think one had an advantage over the other where he was concerned. He wanted his grandfather around as long as possible, but not at the expense of the old guy's happiness. He was just grateful to her for helping him decide what to do.

What he had done was encourage Pops to cancel the appointment his dad had made with the real estate agent, which was exactly what his grandfather did. Now J.C. was treating him to the big chill in the office when others weren't around and with brusque formality when others were.

Plowing his fingers through his hair, he absently wondered what Jillian would do about a fifty-nine-year-old control freak who was acting like a seven-year-old. After all, seven-year-olds were her specialty.

The disquiet fueling his lack of concentration seemed to grow as he sat down and grabbed the nearest file. He was more than willing to blame his challenges with work and his father for part of that restiveness. But he knew as sure as he was breathing that much of the restlessness he felt existed because of the woman he couldn't seem to get out his of head.

He'd picked up the phone a half-dozen times to call her just to see how she was doing, maybe tell her what was going on with Pops. He'd just never finished punching out her number. He knew that hearing her voice wouldn't be enough. He wanted to see her and if he saw her, he'd want to take her to bed and he was already feeling frustrated enough as it was.

The electronic tones of his cell phone mercifully saved him from his thoughts. Reaching to where he'd left it by the digital phone on his desk, he glanced at the caller ID, flipped the phone opened and muttered, "Yeah, Kim."

"Can you talk?"

"I'm in the office," he told her, canceling her concern that he might be with a client or negotiating a traffic snarl. "What's the problem?"

"Jillian Hadley. She isn't cooperating with me at all, Ben. We got the misquote in that tabloid straightened out and I finally got her to agree to interview agents for the book offers she's received, but when I got here to go over my recommendations with her, the headmaster said she'd left the grounds for the weekend. She didn't tell anyone where she was going and she isn't answering her cell phone."

"Did she have any security with her?"

"The headmaster said she doesn't have a bodyguard here. There's no need for one on the grounds and this is the first time she's left."

"She didn't call you to cancel?"

"She did leave me a message," Kim conceded. "I was on another call when she tried to reach me. I called her right back, but all I got was her voice mail." The sound of a car door closing came over the line. Immediately following was the ding of a seat-belt reminder signal. "What do you suggest I do?"

"Did she ever agree to any of the other television interviews?"

There had been three on the table. Kim had reported that at the weekly staff meeting last Monday morning. Since Jillian's appearance on *GM, USA*, *Newsweek* and *Time* had both done cover stories on her. The Kendricks had separate stories of their own, but it was Jillian who'd captivated the press. The stories in the magazines pieced together the bulk of her life from public records, school newspapers, interviews with those who'd known her as a child and those who knew her now. There'd been a page in each about Beth Hadley assembled from the same sort of research.

Jillian had come across as a natural with children, a woman who'd once laughed and smiled easily, a loyal daughter and friend and someone more interested in maintaining her privacy than in seeking the spotlight. The fact that she'd gone to work at a private school where she'd become virtually inaccessible to the press had only heightened the public's interest in her.

Except for a couple of grainy tabloid photos of her walking on the campus, and an archive photo of her above an article about a paparazzi being arrested for trespassing on the grounds, photographic coverage of her had been at a minimum.

"She turned them all down," Kim replied, now that her car was started. "She said she saw no reason for more interviews. She said she did what she felt she had to do and she's not going to screw that up by saying something she shouldn't."

"What's she afraid of saying?"

"I think she's afraid she'll ask what's wrong with people that they don't have better things to do with their time than stick their collective noses in other people's business."

Ben almost smiled. Almost.

"Just back off on the agent and the book deals for a while. She's had a lot to deal with the past few weeks."

He could practically see Kim's carefully penciled eyebrows arch above her rimless glasses. It would be hard to miss the protectiveness in his instructions. She'd seen the photo of him and Jillian. He didn't doubt she'd picked up on his tension when he'd left Jillian at the hotel. But even if she suspected he had become more involved with her than had been wise, she would say nothing. They worked well together, he admired her tenacity and the drive that had her clawing for a partnership in the firm, but they were business colleagues, not friends.

"She's our client," he reminded her, wondering at how completely he'd stopped allowing anyone but family into his life. "If it's a low profile she wants, then that's what we give her."

"Of course," came the compliant reply.

He broke the connection, but he didn't set down the phone.

Jillian was a big girl. She could go where she wanted without having to account to anyone. The fact that she left under her own steam told Ben that nothing untoward had happened to her.

Still, he couldn't deny the quick need he felt to make sure she was all right.

As many times as he'd started to call her cell phone, he knew her number by heart.

Jillian ignored the ring of the phone on the seat beside her. She knew it had to be Kim, who seemed intent on subtly turning her into a Kendrick clone. Kim was the last person Jillian wanted to talk to just then. She didn't doubt that the woman excelled at her job. She just had the feeling that her goal was to turn her into someone constantly, deliberately in the public eye. Being the primary PR manager of a "Kendrick" and managing all that visibility would undoubtedly make her more valuable to her company than she already was.

On the highway ahead of her, a column of brake lights signaled yet another backup. She didn't much care. She wasn't entirely sure where she was headed—other than to the shore.

She had spent the morning doing her laundry in the small stacked unit in her modest accommodations in the teachers' wing of the girls' dormitory at Exeter Hall. She'd then graded the papers from her fourth-grade class, the only grade that had had an opening, and taken her shift in the dining hall for the students' lunch where she'd suffered the curious, reproving or reserved silence of the other teachers on staff. Still trying to shake the unpleasant feel of all those eyes on her, she'd canceled the appointment she never should have made with Kim and headed for the rental car she'd called her Kendrick aide last night to have delivered to her. The press knew her Volkswagen too well for her to drive it anywhere.

The phone stopped ringing. After changing lanes in the early-afternoon traffic, she flipped the phone open to see if Kim had left another message. It started ringing in her palm. The name glowing against the blue background wasn't Kim Silverman, though. It was Ben Garrett.

She felt certain to her bones that he was calling as Kim's boss. Still, she couldn't deny the quickening of her pulse as she allowed the connection.

Pathetic as it was, she needed to hear his voice. There had always been something in those deep, honeyed tones that had been like a balm to her.

Then there was the small, undeniable little fact that she missed him. More than she'd ever thought possible.

She swallowed. Hard. "Hi."

"Are you okay?" came his quick query. "Kim said you canceled your appointment and weren't answering her calls."

"That's because I know what she wants. I've told her every way I can think of that I'm not ready to attend a charity tea with two half sisters I've never met. I don't care if the appearance would give me a favorable image. I'd be on display with people I don't know, and I'm sick of being stared at."

A frown seemed to enter his tone. "I thought she said your appointment was to talk about literary agents."

"It was. But she's called me twice about the tea and I knew it would come up again. I don't want to think about a book deal right now, either. Maybe never," she concluded, because such things were so far out of the realm of what had once been familiar. She needed familiar. Desperately. "All I want is to go someplace for the rest of the weekend where I can be myself and do something ordinary. I don't want to be watched or patronized or avoided. I just want to…be."

Ben couldn't tell if it was frustration he heard in the tightness of her voice, or if she was actually near tears. It had been almost a month since her life as she'd known it had ceased to exist. He wouldn't be surprised if that stress was finally catching up with her.

"Where are you now?"

Jillian pulled a deep breath, let it shudder out. "On the 360 heading east. I figured I'd drive up the shore and look for a motel with a vacancy sign."

"Are you going to register under your own name?"

That was the little glitch she hadn't quite worked out. She'd thought about asking Mrs. Beck, her aide back in Richmond, to make the arrangements for her, but the woman would undoubtedly put her up someplace four-star where her clothes would be inappropriate and the other guests would be surreptitious about gawking, but she'd be recognized nonetheless. That meant paparazzi. She wanted simple. So she'd called Stacy to see if she could come with her, but one of her few links to the real world had a family thing she couldn't get out of attending.

"Not if I can get by without having to give them a credit card. If I can find something for under a hundred a night, I have enough cash for the weekend."

It sounded to Ben as if she needed a break as badly as he did. Without stopping to consider consequences, he glanced at his watch, closed the file on his desk. "Do you want to go to my place at the cove?"

After a moment's hesitation, she seemed to sigh. "I would love that."

It was his turn to hesitate. "Would you mind if I was there?"

For a moment he heard nothing but the faint crackle of a line about to break up.

Just when he thought she was going to change her mind about accepting his offer, he heard her say, "I'd love that, too."

Ben could make the drive from his row house in DuPont Circle to Taylor's Cove in an hour and forty minutes if the bridge across the upper bay wasn't backed up, less than that if he hit all the lights right heading out of town. Coming from outside Richmond, the trip would take twice as long for Jillian, but she'd already been on the road for over an hour when he'd given her directions.

He hadn't been back to the house where he'd once hoped to spend his weekends since he'd been there with Jillian a couple of weeks ago. That was actually something of a record. In the six years he'd owned the place, he had barely managed to make it there once every other month.

At first that had been because Brittany hated it. He'd bought it just before he'd met her and one trip was all it had taken to prove everything about the house and Taylor's Cove was far too quiet and quaint for her tastes.

He'd though little about her aversion to quiet at the time. The woman he'd made the mistake of marrying had thrived on the energy of the city, the hectic pace of it. Her idea of a quiet weekend was theater Friday night, dinner with friends Saturday evening and brunch with friends on Sunday. Caught up with her, his own ambitions and the plans they'd been making together, he'd given up the idea of weekends at the shore. There'd simply been no time for them. What he hadn't given up was the hope that there would someday *be* time, and that she would eventually grow to see the house the way he'd come to envision it. As a place to wind down with the family he'd once honestly believed she eventually wanted. That family had been a nebulous image in the back of his mind. Nothing concrete in terms of number or gender. Just…family. Someday.

That image had died and been buried right along with his marriage. Because he'd found that dreams did nothing but make a person vulnerable, he now saw the house only as he had when he'd first bought it. As four walls and a view of the bay that provided escape from the needs and demands of the people he worked with and for, and a convenient place to stay when he visited Pops.

It was the escape aspect that now sat front and center in his mind.

Because he knew Mrs. Bingham would have cleaned after he'd last left, he didn't call her to freshen up the rooms or run by the market for him. He stopped at the market in Beckley himself. Even with the stop, he'd been in his study nearly half an hour attempting to review the quarterly report while he had the time before he heard a car pull into the drive out front.

He didn't recognize the white, otherwise-nondescript sedan. He almost didn't recognize Jillian, either, when the door opened and she stepped out.

Her beautiful hair had been stuffed under a beige baseball cap. Despite the heavy clouds overhead, large, dark sunglasses covered her eyes. He knew she preferred subtle colors, but the zipped terry cloth hoodie she wore with matching sweat-style pants and sneakers was a shade of taupe that would have blended with just about anything.

If her goal had been to go as unnoticed as possible, she'd almost succeeded. Almost. A man would have to be dead not to notice the slender curves of her body, the elegant line of her throat, the lush, tempting curve of her unadorned mouth.

Reminding himself that he'd invited her there only to give her a place to hide out and himself a chance to see what had her so desperate to get away, he watched her slip off her glasses.

Her smile seemed decidedly cautious as he walked to where she stood closing the car's door.

"Bad week?" he asked, searching her gold-flecked eyes.

"Got wine?" she asked, searching back.

Despite the welcoming and easy smile he offered, he looked as stressed to Jillian as she felt. Beneath his black polo shirt and casual tan slacks, the muscles in his lean, broad-shouldered frame still radiated the latent tension she'd sensed in him before. Lines of weariness and fatigue were carved more deeply into his handsome features. But what she noticed most about him was the sense of solid strength and control that she wished she possessed but feared she never would.

For the past hour she'd tried not to imagine it, tried not to want it, but seeing him, she couldn't deny how badly she wanted him to reach for her. Just wrap her in his arms and hold her. That was all she needed. Just to be held for a few seconds. Okay, a minute, she thought, and felt her heartbeat skip when he took a step closer.

"We'll go find some. Where's your bag?"

"In the back seat."

He reached toward her, then past her and opened the door.

Disappointment lodged hard in her chest. Left to handle the agitation she was dealing with on her own, she made herself swallow that letdown when he grabbed her black travel bag instead of her, and moved with him into the house.

"You can use the same room," he told her, leaving her bag at the foot of the stairs. "Come on in. I'll get the wine."

The phenomenon was interesting, she thought. Even as anxious as she felt being with him again, she could almost feel a hint of the tension in her shoulders ease as she crossed the polished wood floor and stopped between the kitchen island and the blue and cream appointments of his comfortable living room. Except for the clouds that had rolled in and turned the bay and the sky a dozen shades of gray, the rooms and their expansive views looked just as she remembered them.

She had felt protected here before. She would give anything to feel that way now.

Leaving her purse on an end stool at the island, she watched him open the little wine cellar under the built-in bar.

"How is Pops?" she asked, trying to focus on something other than all she was trying to escape. "Has your dad changed his mind about wanting him to sell?"

A muscle in his jaw twitched as he slipped the cork from a bottle of merlot.

"You first. What made you go AWOL?"

She took the twitch to mean he had not.

"It was a lot of things. No," she immediately corrected, because she was so tired of having to jam back what she felt. "It's everything."

The bases of two crystal goblets clinked against the bar's granite top.

"Can you be more specific?" he asked, pouring.

"Only if you don't mind me dumping on you."

"Feel free. You know I'm not going to quote you."

At his offhand assurance, her glance darted to his profile.

In her silence, his head came up. "What?" he asked, seeing her frown.

"That's part of it right there."

"What is?"

"Saying something and having it come back to haunt me." What little of her agitation she'd managed to shake had totally reasserted itself. "I can't talk to anybody without wondering if I'm going to read about what I said the next day. I've had to change my cell number twice because reporters keep getting hold of it. The first time I changed it, I called the people I wanted to stay in touch with to give it to them." And to see how they were doing, she thought, because she'd badly wanted to talk about normal things.

"Carrie Teague, my teaching partner from Jefferson Elementary?" she prefaced, roaming into the kitchen because she couldn't stand still. "When I called her, we talked about the substitute she was working with and what it was like teaching at a private boarding school," she explained. They'd talked about Carrie's family and the changes made in the food in the school cafeteria, too, but that was beside the point.

"A remark I'd made about feeling isolated wound up in a Philadelphia newspaper. It then became a tabloid headline." Kim had traced its genesis. "So did a comment about the teachers I have to live and work with."

The quote had even been attributed to Carrie, by name and position. She hadn't spoken with her former colleague to find out why the woman had felt compelled to share their conversation with a reporter, but it was apparent she needed to be infinitely more cautious about what she said, and who she said it to.

"One of the teachers from Exeter Hall noticed the headline at a grocery store checkout and took the tabloid to Dr. Franklin," she told him, speaking of the school's headmaster as she absently inspected a pepper in the pile of fresh vegetables by the stainless steel sink.

"Dr. Franklin asked if I did, indeed, 'have problems with the department and decorum of the staff.'" That had only been one of several little nightmares she'd faced trying to fit into those hallowed, ivy-covered halls. "I told him I had spoken with the woman quoted and that I'd mentioned that the teachers there were all very proper. But I had never called them 'prim' or 'stuffy.'"

"Kim told me about the quote." Ben walked up beside her. Since she was washing her hands, he set the wine he'd poured for her on the white granite counter. "She said this Dr. Franklin told you he gave the article little credence, considering the nature of the publication printing it."

"He also said that since the staff was talking about it, it would be in my best interests to explain what it was I actually had said."

He handed her a towel. "How did that go?"

Vividly recalling her colleagues' response, she dried her hands, picked up her glass and took a sip of wine. Feeling its warmth slide down her throat, afraid she'd down the whole glass if she just stood there, she traded it for the potatoes beside the cutting board.

"Do you want these peeled?"

Digging in a drawer, he came up with a peeler. A moment later the gray view beyond the wide window disappeared when he flipped on the task light over the sink and lowered the blinds to thwart potentially prying eyes.

"They were all very polite," she finally said, turning back to the sink. "But I had obviously offended most of them. A few of the others just seem offended that I'm teaching there at all. There's nothing wrong with my credentials. Dr. Franklin made it clear he wouldn't have hired me if I hadn't been highly recommended by my former principal," she stressed, potato peels flying. "But some of them act like the position was bought for me.

"That's another thing," she continued. "Two of my old neighbors have called to see if I would loan them money. They got upset with me when I told them I didn't have any to lend them. It seems everyone thinks I now have a trust fund somewhere with a bazillion dollars in it and that I'm being selfish for not sharing with friends. They don't seem to get that I'm still supporting myself.

"Even Eric called," she muttered, rinsing that potato, grabbing another. "He said he'd reconsidered the idea of marriage and wanted to see if we couldn't work things out." She glanced to where Ben had leaned against the counter a few feet away. He had one ankle crossed over the other, his wine in one hand, his eyes on her. "You know as well as I do that he would never have made that call if he didn't think I'd come into money and he had a chance to get his hands on it." She turned back to attacking the tuber. "It's all about the money now. Even Stacy wants to know when I'm going to get my 'due' as she calls it."

"Stacy?"

"My best friend since college."

Ben took a sip of his wine. With her hair stuffed under the ball cap, her head bent to her task, his glance moved from her profile to the tense set of her shoulders. He could have told her that would happen; that the Kendrick fortune would affect her whether she possessed it or not. He hated that people she'd regarded as friends had become upset with her. He didn't doubt that she would lose a few of them in the future, either. What he found more regrettable for her, though, considering how trusting he knew she'd once been, was that from here on out she would never know if someone she'd just met was interested in her as a person or in what they thought she could somehow do for them.

He said nothing, though. It sounded to him as if she'd already figured that out.

"The good news," she continued, as if determined to find a silver lining in her little black cloud, "is that I don't have to worry so much about paparazzi at school. Security is excellent at Exeter Hall because so many of the students are children of wealthy and well-known people.

"But that's all so different, too," she admitted, over the rapid click of the metal peeler. "The children, I mean. The kids there don't need me the way some of my other students did. Those kids have absolutely everything. Some of the ones who board are picked up and dropped off for weekends by their family butlers. I've overheard day students talk about their cooks and nannies." She absolutely could not relate to that kind of pampering and privilege. "I'm so out of that loop that I even managed to offend the Kendricks' maid in the three days I stayed at their penthouse."

From the corner of her eye, she saw his eyebrows merge.

"How did you do that?"

"I'm a casual person," she explained, feeling as disjointed as her account of her life as she now knew it. She dropped her focus back to the sink. "I like doing things for myself. I had no idea Rita thought she wasn't doing her job to my satisfaction just because I tried to help her."

"How did you find out?"

"Mrs. Beck told me." Mrs. Beck, the Kendrick aide, had been with Kim when the two women had arrived at her hotel room just before Ben had left. "She said the poor woman was in tears and had asked if she should quit. After we got everything straightened out, I sent flowers and a note saying I was really sorry. Mrs. Beck said the note would have been enough." Just recalling the incident embarrassed her all over again.

Her voice dropped. "I had no idea there was protocol for apologizing to the 'help.'"

With both potatoes peeled, she picked up the foam container of mushrooms and turned to the man who, by now, had to think her pretty pathetic. He was far too easy to confide in. She wouldn't have dreamed of venting to Kim or anyone else the way she'd done with him from nearly the moment they'd met.

"What about these?"

"Go ahead," he said, and reached into a drawer near him for a knife.

"Sliced or chopped?"

"I thought we'd grill them with the steaks I bought."

"Sliced, then. You know," she muttered, dampening a paper towel, "that's another thing about living at the school. I can't cook or bake there. They only allow a coffeepot and a hot plate in our rooms, so when I can't sleep I don't have anything to do."

Ben watched the restive motions of her hands as she wiped a mushroom, reached for another. From what she'd just said, and what she was doing now, her chosen means of working off stress was in the kitchen. He preferred something more physical when restlessness hit: running himself into the ground on a jogging trail or working up a sweat at the gym. But he could appreciate how being denied the only release she had would only compound the stress she was already dealing with.

Everything else she'd mentioned sounded as if it would just take time to get accustomed to.

Telling her that would be of little use to her, though. As he resumed his position against the counter, he needed to offer her something more concrete. She needed help. Not platitudes.

"I know of others who had to deal with drastically altered lives for a while," he confided. "Tess was forced from the country by the scandal her ex created," he reminded her. "And Ashley wanted to escape the fishbowl she lives in so badly that she went into hiding for nearly a year. If you want, I can arrange for you to meet with them. Maybe they have advice that would help."

As if pulled by a string, Jillian spun to face him. From beneath the brim of her cap, her expression asked if he had lost his mind.

"You're not getting this, are you?" Disbelief collided with exasperation. The paper towel and mushroom landed in the sink. "I don't want to meet them. It's all I can do to handle the way I have to live now. Nothing, *nothing,*" she stressed, "is the same anymore. The last thing I want is to throw in something else to deal with. Meeting them is exactly what your colleague keeps pushing and the main reason I wanted to get *away* from her."

She moved past him. Throwing up her hands, she turned full circle. She'd thought he would understand. He'd seemed so understanding of everything else.

"I already feel as if I'm living someone else's life, Ben. I just don't know who that someone is. All I know for sure is that that family and that segment of society are things I can never truly be part of." She had no idea how anyone ever thought she could. "I even *look* different. The Kendrick women are all tall and blond and beautiful. They're all poised and polished and self-confident. I know which fork to use and not to drink from the finger bowl, but I'm short, brunette and so…not."

For one unbelievable moment she thought Ben was going to laugh at her. Caught between a plea and a glare as she watched his eyes glitter in the bright overhead lights, she had the feeling he was sorely tempted.

Reaching out, he snagged her by the wrist. Eyes still smiling, he drew her back with him to his spot against the counter.

Holding her in place with one hand, he handed her his wine with the other.

With her pulse pounding from irritation, she took the glass and a swallow and handed it back. If he was trying to calm her down, it wasn't working. He'd have to let go of her wrist to do that.

"No one wants you to conform to some kind of mold, Jillian."

"Your associate does."

"I'll talk to her," he promised. "You are who you are, and anyone who doesn't accept you that way," he said with a shrug, "that's their loss.

"As for how attractive you are…trust me," he insisted, as his eyes shifted from her mouth to the skin exposed by the V of her hoodie. "The last thing you ever need to worry about is how you compare to your half sisters."

Beneath his fingers circling her wrist, Jillian felt her pulse give a betraying little leap.

Too aware of his big body, more aware of its effect on hers, she took a step back, turned away.

"You don't need to humor me, Ben. That's not what I want from you."

He caught her arm, tugged her back. When she met his glance, his smile was gone.

"I'm not humoring you, Jillian. I meant exactly what I said." His blue eyes narrowed as he cautiously searched her face. "And now that you've mentioned it, what is it that you do want from me?"

With the heat of his hand seeping through the fabric covering her arm, she slowly shook her head. She'd thought before how easy it was to unload on him. She wasn't completely sure why that was, unless it was because he didn't minimize or dismiss her reactions or concerns the way others did. Or maybe it was because he'd made her feel she could trust him with just about anything she said. Whatever the reasons, she hadn't even realized how badly she had needed to talk to him until the events of the past weeks had started flooding out.

"I shouldn't have said that." Wishing he'd either let her go or pull her closer, she lifted her free hand to knead the knotted muscles in her shoulder. "I know I'm not your problem to deal with anymore. I have no business wanting anything from you."

"I didn't invite you here as someone I have to deal with." His thumb eased toward her elbow. "You're here for the same reason I am. We both needed to get away." And I needed to see you, he thought. To touch you. To figure out why I can't get you out of my mind. "So what is it you want?"

"Just for you to be honest with me," she admitted quietly. "And for you to listen." *And for you to hold me, but I don't have the nerve to tell you that,* she thought as her hand fell. "I think you're the only person I can talk to who comes even close to getting how frustrated I am with all of this."

The agitation crawling through her still pulled hard. "I'd give anything to be able to let it all go for a while, Ben. I'm just not sure how. There's no place I can go that some part of everything that's changed isn't right there in front of me."

"That's because you keep thinking about what's frustrating you."

"If I knew how to stop thinking about it, don't you think I would?"

"You just need something to help block it from your mind."

More than willing to accept any advice he had to offer on that score, pure indulgence entered her tone. "And that something would be…"

"How long an escape are you looking for?"

"I was hoping for the weekend. Right now, I'd settle for five minutes."

She had yet to move from his touch. Without asking why her trust in him mattered so much, the nature of what he'd thought to suggest underwent a not-so-subtle shift.

Moments ago he'd been about to propose that they take his skiff out to the oyster beds, but he could hear the rain coming down in earnest now. He'd thought of taking her to the Crab House in the Cove and having Charlene and the locals distract her with their stories for a few hours. But if five minutes was all she was after, he could offer that without even having to leave the house.

"Close your eyes."

In the shadow of her cap brim, he saw her glance narrow.

"Go ahead," he coaxed. "If this doesn't work, I'll stop."

Still seeming as tense as a bowstring and maybe a little curious, she did as he asked.

The moment her eyes closed, he lifted the cap from her head and set it on the counter. As he did, he caught the questioning furrow of her brow. Yet, she remained as she was while his glance skimmed the delicate lines of her face and settled on her dark and shining hair. He had no idea how she'd wound it all into such a compact knot, but the silky curls tumbled over her shoulders as he eased his fingers into their softness.

At the contact, her shoulders rose with a deep, indrawn breath. Her eyes remained closed, though, her lashes lush and dark against the creamy smoothness of her skin.

With his fingers buried in her hair, he slipped his thumbs over her temples.

"Don't think about anything but what I'm doing," he murmured, willing to bet his corner office that she hadn't relaxed for a moment in weeks. He knew he had problems unwinding himself. But he had this place as an escape. She had nowhere to go. She only had…him. "Okay?"

Jillian took another deep breath, slowly let it out. "Okay," she whispered.

She could feel the tips of his fingers drawing little circles at the back of her head. His thumbs mimicked the gentle motions. Like water slowly seeping down a drain, she could feel the tension leaking from the muscles at the back of her neck, from her shoulders, from her upper back.

The man was a magician. With his hands cradling her head, the rest of her body wanting to go limp, thinking about anything else seemed impossible.

"Good?" she heard him quietly ask.

"Mmm."

At her less than articulate confirmation, he eased his thumbs to her cheekbones. Moving slower still, he methodically stroked beneath her eyes, back to her temples, along her jaw. All the while his fingers worked the muscles at the back of her neck.

In the bright overhead lights, Ben could practically see the stress leave her face. The furrows in her brow smoothed, the skin across her cheekbones seemed to soften. He had hoped to give her a moment's respite. What he hadn't counted on was how much it meant to him to know that his touch could calm her. Or how impossible it would be to keep from moving closer.

With her hair brushing the back of his hands, her familiar scent taunting his nerves, he tipped her face to his.

Jillian felt his breath warm her temple.

"Stop?" he asked.

"No," she breathed.

His lips barely grazed her skin before she felt their warmth at the corner of her mouth. "How about now?"

With his lips hovering over hers, she felt something warm pool low in her belly. "No."

She'd barely managed to murmur the word before she felt his mouth settle over hers. He kissed her softly as his hands drifted from her hair, over her arms and down to settle on the sides of her hips. The touch of his tongue filled her with liquid heat, weakening her in some places, enlivening her in others. But when he leaned back against the counter and eased her between his legs, it was the feel of his hard body that threatened to completely rob the strength from her bones.

Digging his fingers into her hips, he drew her against the arousal straining behind his zipper. A groan rumbled deep in his chest at the intimate contact. Or maybe that needy sound had been her own as she'd lifted her arms around his neck and sagged against him.

Her breasts flattened against the solid wall of chest. Her heart beat hard against his.

She was finally where she'd wanted to be, where she'd needed to be since the moment she'd stepped from his arms what seemed a lifetime ago. She'd missed his strength, missed the sense of being protected she'd felt when he'd held her before. That protectiveness was there even now, along with something that might have felt like possessiveness had she believed for a moment that he would let himself stake a claim to any woman. Yet, that feeling remained as his hands skimmed under her top and grazed the skin of her bare back. It was in the kiss, which had her clinging to him simply to stay upright in the long moments before he brushed his lips against her throat and the soft skin behind her ear.

The rich tones of his voice had turned husky. "Stop?"

Wrapped in his heat, breathing in the comforting scents of citrus aftershave and warm male, she shook her head. He'd said five minutes. She wanted every second she could get. "How much longer do I have?"

His lips tugged her earlobe. "How much longer do you want?"

The thought of him letting her go at all was suddenly more than she could bear. She'd told him she felt as if she was living someone else's life, that she hadn't a clue who that someone was. Yet in his arms she didn't feel the fear of all those unfamiliar unknowns. She didn't feel the need to suppress her reactions or guard what she said. With him she felt the freedom to be exactly who she was, who she had always been. She'd just needed him to strip away thoughts of the changes in her life to realize how precious that freedom was—and how fleeting it would be.

"How much longer can I have?"

"You can have all night," she heard him say.

Desperate to keep those other thoughts at bay, she lifted her mouth to his.

"Then that's what I want."

A fist of need hit Ben at her admission. Or maybe it was the feel of her lips yielding against his that coiled white heat deep inside his gut. He didn't know where he'd gotten the idea that he could kiss this woman and not want more. He wasn't sure how he'd thought he could torture himself with the sweet taste of her mouth and the feel of her curvy little body against his, then simply let her go. All he'd known when he'd first reached for her was that he would stop if she asked. Yet as he backed her across the room and into the entry with their mouths clinging, she wasn't asking. And he wasn't paying any attention at all to the warnings clamoring in his head.

In one easy motion he tucked his arm under her knees and lifted her in his arms. He'd barely made it up the stairs and reached his bedroom at the end of the dimly lit hall before his mouth found hers again.

Thunder rumbled in the distance. Rain beat against the roof. Setting her on her feet, one arm around her waist, he reached with his other to throw back the thick navy comforter covering the king-size bed. He wanted to see her. All of her. But he'd never forgotten what she'd said about not liking to make love with the light on, so he ignored the lamp on the nightstand and drew her back to him instead.

There wasn't a doubt in his mind that he was complicating their relationship. And, no doubt, her life. He knew there would be consequences to face when the night was over. But those warnings were silenced by the needs she elicited in his brain and his body. The need to feel her bare flesh against his. The need to keep her from thinking about the very things that had driven her into his arms. The need to escape from the demands of his own life, even for a little while.

The need to take things slow.

They had all night.

He reached for the zipper on her top, slowly eased it down. "Tell me what you want."

Jillian's breath hitched at the feel of his knuckles sliding between her breasts. "I already did."

In the pale-gray glow from the night-light in the hallway, she saw his eyes glitter over her face. "Nothing more specific?'

Her heart knocked against her ribs as she gave a quick shake of her head.

His head dipped toward hers. "In that case," he murmured, lifting her hand to the only button he'd fastened on his dark polo shirt. "We'll just play it by ear."

He kissed her then, leaving her to fumble the button through its hole while he worked the zipper down on her top and eased the fabric over her shoulders.

He had told her downstairs not to think about anything but what he was doing. But within moments she wasn't really thinking at all. As their mouths mated while their hands pushed away cotton and lace and they tumbled onto his bed, she was simply feeling. And what he made her feel as he pulled her soft curves against his harder, rougher body went light-years beyond anything she had ever experienced before.

She had never known such gentleness as the feel of his hands exploring her breasts and her belly while he kissed her breathless.

She had never known such tenderness could lead to raw hunger until she felt his mouth trail moist heat along all the paths his hands had taken.

She'd never known hunger could spiral to an aching need to make *him* feel all the mind-numbing sensations he introduced her to.

Yet, it wasn't just the way he caressed her that had her reaching for him in an erotic game of follow the leader. It was the desire to let him know how very much she cared about the man he was, the man who protected his heart because he'd been so badly hurt, the man who worried about his grandfather, the man she shouldn't have been able to count on, but who, for now, was there for her, anyway.

A flash of lightning backlit the drapes over the French doors. Wind blew rain against the glass panes. The storm outside barely registered to Ben as Jillian's small, soft hands roamed his back and her legs tangled with his. The taste and feel of her had his nerves stretched about as far as they would go. Yet, he wanted to hold back. He wanted to give her this night. He wanted it for himself just as badly. Still, he knew he couldn't hold back much longer.

They lay on their sides, their hands now in each other's

hair, his mouth devouring hers. He hated to let her go, balked at the very thought of it, but some shred of common sense survived the red haze of sensual heat clouding his mind and reminded him of the need for protection. He didn't like the thought of there being anything between them, but as he eased to his back, he wouldn't indulge the primitive urge to spill himself inside her. He wouldn't even let himself wonder why such a thought was there. Fumbling open his nightstand drawer, he found the box he was looking for, rolled the condom in place and reached for her once more.

She was beautiful in her desire for him, exquisite in her need as her slender body flowed toward his. He wanted her with a fierceness that nearly stole his breath. Yet, as he rose over her, he bit back the urgent need to possess and made himself sink slowly into her heat.

She whimpered his name as he sucked in a harsh breath. With his head buried against her shoulder, he murmured her name back and thought he might die when she arched to meet him. But he wouldn't let her rush, either. At least, he didn't until the exquisite feel of her shattering in his arms long moments later broke the iron grip he'd had on his control and he felt himself follow her into that sweet oblivion.

The rain had gentled to a soft patter on the roof. The sound registered faintly to Ben as his heartbeat began to slow. He was sure that within the next minute he would feel the need to move. But all he felt at the moment was the need to stay right where he was.

Lifting himself on his elbow, he smoothed Jillian's hair from her forehead. Her features where in shadow, but he was aware of her eyes opening at his touch.

"You're beautiful," he whispered.

He felt her draw a deep breath. "So are you," she murmured, and cupped her palm to his cheek.

He caught her hand, turned her palm to press his lips against it. In the past couple of years, the aftermath of sex had left him feeling oddly discontent and alone. Yet what he felt with Jillian just then was more than just the relief of physical release. He felt complete somehow, not empty. He felt a part of something, rather than the solitary being he'd come to believe he was.

He gathered her to him, slowly stroking her back while he listened to her breathing quiet. He didn't believe for a moment that what he felt with her could last. Moments were fleeting. But he wasn't going to ruin their temporary respite by thinking of anything beyond the unfamiliar peace he'd found holding her in his arms. For now, with her, he would just…be.

Chapter Nine

Jillian awoke, stretched and went totally still the instant she realized where she was. Specifically, in Ben's bed.

She looked toward his pillow.

Ben wasn't there.

Shoving her hair back from her eyes, she raised on one elbow to look toward his bathroom. The door was open, the light off, but as she drew a deep breath, she caught hints of soap-scented humidity lingering from the shower he'd apparently taken while she'd slept in.

The digital clock on his nightstand indicated it was 9:47.

She couldn't remember the last time she'd slept that late. Or slept so soundly once deep sleep had finally come.

Memories of the night flooded back. She had awakened a little after ten o'clock and slipped downstairs in his shirt to get a glass of water. She'd barely made it into the kitchen when he'd come in behind her, kissed the back of her neck and told her he was starving. Since they'd missed dinner, they'd scrambled eggs with the potatoes and mushrooms she'd left in the sink, then made love all over again when he'd caught her to him at the top of the stairs and, kissing her breathless, backed her down the hall and into his bed.

The last thing she remembered was being curled up in his arms, his legs tangled with hers and wishing for the impossible.

Since his black polo shirt provided the most and quickest cover, she pulled it on again, picked up her clothes from where they were scattered over his blue-and-burgundy rug and hurried toward the room she was supposed to have slept in.

Apparently knowing she would need it, Ben had already set her suitcase outside its door. Grabbing the handle, she dragged it inside, closed herself in and set the suitcase on her bed.

When she had thrown her bag into her rental car yesterday afternoon, her only goal had been to seek escape from all the changes and uncertainty currently plaguing her life. All she had succeeded in doing was adding to the emotional chaos. She was falling in love with Ben. Had fallen, if she wanted to be perfectly honest with herself. Body, mind and soul. She saw no point in fighting that unfortunate little fact.

Unfortunate because, even though there was no doubt in her mind how much she cared about him, he operated on an entirely different and more sophisticated plane than she did. Even more significant than that fundamental disparity was the fact that, physical desire aside, he wouldn't—or couldn't—care that way about her.

She would be a fool to let herself build dreams around a man who would only pull those dreams right out from under her. She'd been there. Done that. Only this time, it would be her own fault because he had warned her from the beginning that he wanted nothing to do with a committed relationship. She was not about to let him know how much of her heart had been involved in what they'd shared last night and have him remind her of that.

Gathering clean underwear and her toiletries, she headed for the shower. She knew what she couldn't expect from him. But that didn't stop her from being grateful for all that he had given her. Specifically, the ability to look the world in the eye and hide the worst of how shaken she was inside.

The skills he had taught her were firmly in place when she walked into the kitchen half an hour later wearing what she hoped was an easy smile and the sweater and slacks she'd packed so she wouldn't have to change to meet the dress code when she returned to Exeter Hall.

The smile was wasted. Ben was on his haunches by the open French doors in the dining room, doing something with a screwdriver at the threshold. The view beyond was the same gunmetal gray of the toolbox beside him. The air he let in held a damp chill.

"Problems?" she asked, eyeing the brewed coffee waiting in the coffeemaker as she walked past the kitchen.

"This is just something I meant to do the last time I was here." He gave the screw in the metal band one last twist. "The weather stripping needed replacing."

She'd never seen him in jeans before, wasn't even sure he owned a pair. As he rose, her glance moved from the well-worn fabric hugging his long legs and lean hips to the Annapolis Yacht Club logo on his navy pullover.

The moment he closed the door, his eyes settled on hers.

Hers promptly darted away.

Two short pieces of the shiny stripping material lay on the floor beside the toolbox.

"I'm sorry I slept so late," she said, apology—or maybe it was embarrassment—heavy in her tone as she picked them up. "I never sleep in like that."

Sleep had been a problem for her. Ben had realized that last night when she'd mentioned how not having a kitchen bothered her. Recalling how he'd heard her pacing in the wee hours the last time she'd slept under his roof, he would have taken her comment now as compliment, had she not been so busy avoiding his eyes.

He caught her chin, tipped her head up. "You needed the rest."

"Could be," she murmured. Offering a small smile to the shaving nick on his neck, she stepped back and handed him the bits of thin metal and foam. She'd rather not stand there thinking about how long she'd been in his bed. She especially didn't want to think about how susceptible she was to his touch. "You're doing repairs today?"

"I've done a few." There were more to be done. Minor things he would have enjoyed tackling had he not been more interested in being with Jillian now that she was up. He just wasn't quite sure how to read her this morning. "But I was thinking we could go see Pops. Then maybe pick up some crabs and come back here. Build a fire. Watch a movie." See where that leads, he thought. "Unless you need to be back to school before seven or so, I figure we don't need to leave until around four."

Jillian turned away. She needed to not be so close to him. She needed to not be so tempted by the day he had planned. What he wanted to do sounded wonderful. It also promised a day of memories she would undoubtedly have to work very hard to forget.

Needing caffeine, she asked if she could get a cup of coffee. He told her to help herself and left her with the feel of his eyes on her back as she headed for the pot on the counter.

Behind her, she heard metal rattle and clank as he put the screwdriver away and closed the toolbox. By the time she'd poured her coffee and taken a couple of fortifying sips, Ben was back from having put the tools away.

He also seemed to have figured out that she wasn't as unaffected by what had happened between them as she was pretending to be. But then, he was good at that.

"You're not staying." He offered the observation quietly as he casually refilled his own mug.

With the slow shake of her head, she offered the deceptively calm smile he'd missed earlier. "I probably shouldn't have come here at all," she confided. "And I shouldn't have unloaded on you like that. Managing my life postupheaval isn't what you were hired to do," she quietly reminded him. "I should have just found myself a hotel the way I'd first planned to."

"You didn't have a plan."

"You know what I mean."

"Yeah," he murmured, lifting his mug. He took a sip. "I do."

He knew exactly what she meant. It was as clear as the vulnerability she didn't want him to see in her eyes that she thought sleeping with him had been a mistake. He hadn't been prepared for that. Not yet. The thought of spending what was left of the weekend with her held more appeal to him than anything had in longer than he could remember. But he'd warned himself last night that there would be consequences for complicating the situation between them.

Now that he knew the feel of her, knew how beautifully she responded to his touch, he couldn't be with her without wanting her. There was no going back, but no going forward, either. He'd known all along that a casual sexual relationship with her simply wasn't possible. Not without her or her reputation getting hurt in some way.

Faced with those consequences now, he knew he had no choice but to let her go.

Something uneasy settled in his chest. Regret, possibly. Guilt, definitely.

"I don't mind that you unloaded on me." He bit back the odd sensation of loss. She was making what he would have had to do himself that much easier. "I just wish there was something I could do to help you fix all that's changed."

She actually managed to look forgiving when she said, "That's not your job, either."

Regret tugged harder. "Even if it were, there isn't a lot I could do."

Knowing he would soon not be able to touch her, he nudged her hair back from her cheek. He could too easily recall the sweet taste of her skin, her mouth, the tender flesh of her breasts. Aware of the tightening low in his gut, he wasn't sure what felt more dangerous about her just then: the thought that he didn't want to let her go or the sense of responsibility for her that he'd never been able to shake.

Dismissing the alien and impractical notion, responsibility took priority.

"You're the only one who can change anything now."

Her head came up, her dark eyes wary.

"How?"

"Start looking at the bigger picture." She was new to the game. Still a neophyte participant. The least he could do for her was help her play the hand she had been dealt. "I think all you can see is what you no longer have…and that you feel trapped by the way you're having to live now."

The man had a gift, Jillian thought. For understanding. For making her want when she knew she should not.

He was too close again. Ducking her head, she slipped

from his reach. She refused to torture herself with his touch. She wouldn't refuse his insights, though. He had just totally summarized her life as it presently existed.

"So what do you suggest I do?"

Behind her, the refrigerator kicked on. Its low hum joined the muffled clink of ceramic on granite when he set his mug on the island.

"Stop fighting so hard," he said simply. "Your life at Exeter Hall isn't all you have. I know it may seem like that right now, but the sooner you accept that you actually possess a lot more, the easier everything will be."

Needing to know what he could see that she couldn't, she looked up with a plea in her eyes. "What else is it that I have?"

Reluctance suddenly shadowed his face. Even before he spoke, something about that hesitant expression seemed to warn her that she wasn't going to like what she was about to hear.

"You have a support system just waiting for you to accept them, Jillian. Tess and Ashley would be more—"

"Don't." Confusion jerked to resistance. "I told you last night—"

"I know what you told me. Just hear me out," he insisted, when she would have continued to protest. "You asked me to be honest with you. So I will be. All you've done so far is focus on how you won't fit in. You'll never know whether you will or not until you give them a chance to prove they're not perfect or snobs or whatever else you've imagined them to be. You've made up your mind about them without giving them a chance to prove that you might very well be wrong."

She looked from the unmistakable challenge in his eyes. He was only halfway right. She had met their mother. If Ashley and Tess were anything like Katherine, then she would think them gracious and kind and she'd have to feel guilty about admiring them, too.

"You're not in my shoes," she reminded him. "You have no idea how disloyal I'd feel associating with the people it probably hurt my mother to even think about. And you don't know what it's like to go from being an only child to suddenly being the odd man out in a whole family who have known each other all their lives."

Ben could not mistake the growing defensiveness in her voice. He felt that same defense himself. Or maybe what he felt was resentment. Or jealousy. At the moment, wishing to heaven that he had the support she could have for the asking, he couldn't be sure. All he knew was that he would give up everything he owned for what her stubborn independence wouldn't allow her to accept.

"You have no idea how fortunate you are, do you?" He stepped closer, shaking his head at what held her back. "Forget the obvious. Forget the opportunity for wealth or fame or whatever else it is being a Kendrick could get you. You keep thinking of how everything has changed for you. And it has. No question. But have you once stopped to see how some of those changes might be for the better?"

With him searching her face for an answer, the feeling of being manipulated hit her all over again. "Is meeting his children something William wants?"

Frustration stripped another layer from his patience.

"This isn't about what William or any other Kendrick wants, Jillian. It's about what you're denying yourself. You talk about feeling disloyal. If your mother was half the woman I think she was, there is no way she'd want you to be as alone as you're choosing to be now. You said she never stopped loving him," he reminded her. "If she'd cared about him that much, then I don't think she could find fault with you for caring a little about him, too. As for his other children," he continued, systematically addressing her arguments, "they were no more responsible than you are for everything that happened. She would have known that, too.

"You have a whole family just waiting for you to accept them," he muttered, pacing now. "I'm not saying fitting in will be without challenges. And it's not like you have to live with any of them," he pointed out. "But you have a chance for a relationship with siblings you can share with, or dump on, or turn to when things feel like they're falling down around your head."

He pushed his fingers through his hair, trying to find a way to make her appreciate the gift she'd been given. "I talked my grandfather into canceling an appointment with a real estate agent this week," he offered, " because I'm afraid if he does what Dad wants him to do, he'll be miserable. I have no backup plan that will help him out over there. I have no one I trust and no brother or sister to help me come up with one, or to run interference with my dad...who is royally pissed at me, by the way, for not taking his side. The Kendricks have no agenda with you. You could trust them. And you wouldn't have to make decisions like that totally on your own unless that was the way you wanted it.

"I'd give anything to be in your shoes right now," he admitted, as the weight of his own concerns pressed harder. "And you're not even willing to give the opportunity you have a decent chance."

He hadn't raised his voice, but his words seemed to echo off the walls as she looked from where he'd come to a halt ten feet away. Even feeling chastised, torn and defensive, she couldn't escape his doubts and fears about his own situation. His frustration with it was a tangible thing, a silent force that snaked around her, coiling in her stomach, knotting her nerves.

He was an only child, too, and alone in the battle for his grandfather's independence. Yet as much as she could appreciate his need for support with his grandfather, she couldn't help but think him every bit as blind as he was accusing her of being.

"Then, I'll gladly trade you places," she said with a calm she truly didn't feel. "You don't need siblings to do what you need to do with your grandfather, Ben. All you need to do is stop living the life that's made you so unhappy. At least I'm fighting. You've given up."

Confusion deepened his scowl. "What are you talking about?"

"I'm talking about what you just said about not having a plan to help your grandfather. Have you ever considered how much what he does matters to you?" Her hand swept toward the living room. Ships were in his blood. His living room held a three-foot-long model of a schooner. A massive painting of a Yankee clipper hung over his fireplace. He could look out nearly any window in the back of this house and see boats on the same bay visible from his grandfather's place. "You've completely surrounded yourself with what you loved when you spent summers with him."

His broad shoulders lifted in an uncomprehending shrug. "So I like boats."

"So help him build them. At least think about it," she insisted, when he blew a breath that summarily dismissed the idea. "Pops told me how much you enjoyed working with him, Ben." She herself had seen how much he still did. He had seemed a different person. At ease. Relaxed. She'd actually heard him laugh.

"It seems to me that what he does was once a huge part of

you. I imagine it still would be if others hadn't overtaken your dreams," she ventured, thinking of his father. Pops had mentioned those other footsteps he'd had to follow. "I don't know what all those dreams were," she admitted, though she strongly suspected a few. He'd once wanted a wife and family himself. The wife he'd had. The family had been denied him. "But I do know you weren't born as cynical as you are. You let others make you that way."

Ben felt the tension in his body undergo a subtle shift as he looked from where she'd motioned to where she stood looking as self-protective as he suddenly felt.

"You're talking about my ex," he muttered. He was dead certain of that. Though how she'd made the leap from his wish that he had someone else to help with his grandfather to his cynicism and distrust had him totally baffled. Unless, he thought, she was upset because he wasn't fighting to pursue a relationship with her. He'd yet to understand how the female mind worked, but he wouldn't be surprised if this somehow had become all about last night.

His defenses had risen like missiles in a silo. Yet he spoke with deceptive calm.

"You know I never intended for us to get serious, Jillian."

For a moment she said nothing. She simply stared at him, her mouth open, unable to believe what she had just heard.

Her voice went suddenly, utterly flat. "You are so…so…male," she accused. The man was as dense as a medieval forest. "This isn't about me, Ben. This isn't about 'us.' And I think your ex-wife is only part of the problem. The manipulation you have to do in your work is probably just as responsible for killing your faith in people as she was. I'm talking about the choices you've made where your father and grandfather are concerned and the choices you could make now."

She no longer sounded upset. She no longer even felt annoyed with him for bringing up her half sisters again. At his heavy silence, she felt nothing so much as the need to shut her mouth before he told her he was just fine with his choices and she really needed to butt out. It was that kind of closed resolve carved in the unyielding lines of his face.

"I'm sorry," she murmured into the unnerving stillness. "This obviously isn't getting either of us anywhere."

"No," he agreed. "It isn't."

She lifted her chin, fought for a smile that refused to appear. This was hardly the civilized and gracious way she'd planned to say goodbye. "I think I'd better go now."

With her arms locked around her, she hurried past where he stood, hands on hips, his expression a study in stone.

Ben didn't try to stop her. He didn't try to stop her a few minutes later, either, when he heard her come down the stairs and hesitate in the foyer. Not until he heard her close the door behind her did he even move from where he'd stood, jaw working, staring at nothing.

Jillian was clueless about him. She had no idea what he wanted, needed or cared about. Convinced of that, he picked up the phone to let Pops know he was in the cove.

Being annoyed with her was far easier than considering the regret tearing at him when he finally heard her car pull out of the drive. But that protective annoyance refused to hold as he made the familiar drive past Taylor's Cove to his grandfather's inlet. Once it subsided, the regret he didn't want to feel surfaced like a buoy rising from beneath the bay.

He killed the engine, then sat with his wrists draped over the steering wheel, staring at the wide swath of gray water visible between the dark and silent shipyard and his grandfather's weathered-but-solid old house.

He tried again to tell himself that Jillian was wrong about him. He wanted to believe that he had his life firmly on track and that he neither wanted nor needed anything he didn't already have. He knew how to present convincing arguments. He did it for a living, after all. The only problem was that he couldn't come up with a single point to convince himself that he liked the track his life was on. All he could see ahead of him was more of the same; more of what he'd left Washington yesterday to escape. It had only been when he was with her—talking with her, holding her, just *being* with her—that he hadn't felt the restiveness he'd been living with for the past two years. At least, he hadn't until she'd accused him of being as blind as he'd accused her of being about their respective lives and families.

You need to stop living the life that's made you so unhappy.

Leaning back, he drew his hands down his face, wanting to shake the echo of her voice in his head.

All he needed to do right now was to go see Pops. The old guy probably already had the cribbage board set up and another pot of coffee on. Since he didn't have to be back in Washington until that evening, he'd spend the day catching up on the local gossip, getting an update on the boat's progress and maybe work on it awhile himself.

Have you ever considered how much what he does matters to you?

With a frown, he shoved open the door. Of course what Pops did mattered to him. He wouldn't be so upset with his own father for trying to take the business away from the old guy if he wasn't.

Broken shells and gravel crunched beneath his feet as he headed for the house, dismissing the discussion, argument or whatever it was that he'd had with Jillian back in his kitchen.

He knew he was deliberately overlooking some of the finer points she'd made, but he wasn't ready to question what he'd done with the changes and disappointments life had handed him. If he did that, he'd have to admit that she might well be right after all.

The sitting room down the hall from the headmaster's office was used mostly for formal staff teas and as a quiet, private place for staff to meet with students' parents or other callers where a certain correctness and decorum were required.

Jillian figured that Ashley Regina Kendrick Calloway and Theresa Amelia Kendrick-formerly-Ashworth-soon-to-be-Parker qualified in the latter category. So had Dr. Franklin, who had directed her to Mrs. Harris, his secretary, to arrange for the tea and finger sandwiches that the very proper older woman had just carried in. Neither of them knew that Jillian hadn't met the women before. Both thought Ashley and Tess were just paying their half sister a visit.

"The guard just called from the main gate," Mrs. Harris advised. With the faint clink of fine china, she carefully placed the tray of refreshments on the tea table anchoring a Queen Anne sofa and two wing-back chairs. "The limousine is on its way in."

She stepped back. Clasping her hands in front of her, she glanced around the heavily draped, book-lined room as if to make sure everything was still in order from her last inspection. "If you need more hot water, please call me. I'll be in my office."

"Thank you, Mrs. Harris."

"It's my pleasure, Miss Hadley. I'll tell Dr. Franklin your guests will be here momentarily. Being that he's an acquaintance of their father, he wants to escort them in himself."

Jillian had no idea why she felt relieved when the amazingly efficient and organized woman left and closed the tall, carved door behind her. Unless it was because she had just been saved from potentially embarrassing herself by going down to meet her guests herself. Apparently, she was supposed to wait and have them brought to her.

Smoothing her hair for the dozenth time, she glanced down at the brown tweed skirt she wore with a chocolate turtleneck, matching tights and flats and smoothed it, too. The only jewelry she had on was a pair of small bronze hoop earrings, which were pretty much hidden by the curls and ringlets tumbling over her shoulders.

Because she was feeling more insecure than she wanted to admit, about what they might think of her, she checked her earrings' clasps, too, as she moved past the tea tray with its rose-print porcelain pot, cups and saucers and stopped by one of the tall, mullioned windows. In another minute she should be able to see the limousine coming up the tree- and lawn-lined drive.

It had taken her well over a week to admit that Ben was right. Another to actually do something about it.

She had rebelled at and fought nearly every change that had taken place in her life over the past weeks. She had accepted access to Mrs. Beck only because she'd needed someone on the outside, as she'd come to think of the world beyond Exeter Hall, to handle packing up and storing what possessions hadn't been delivered to her. And she would use the services of Jackson or Schroeder or both if she needed to venture out again. Having been recognized at a gas station on her way back from Taylor's Cove two weeks ago had pretty much cured her of striking out on her own again.

She'd been paying for her purchases of twelve gallons of

regular and a diet cola when a busload of tourists checking out the gift shop next door had started snapping pictures of her and asking for her autograph. A guy at the pump had gotten angry with her because she wasn't moving her car so he could gas up himself. He didn't seem to understand that she couldn't get to her car because she was being mobbed. Growing more impatient by the second, the by-then-irate customer had started yelling at the kid behind the counter, who had promptly called the police. Her name had apparently been mentioned on the police scanner. Two squad cars had barely arrived when the press had shown up.

All she'd wanted was gas and a cola. The incident, however, had reinforced her decision to allow William to pay for her personal protection. She had drawn the line at accepting assistance beyond Mrs. Beck, bodyguards and his introduction to Dr. Franklin, though. And while that line remained firmly in place, she had, finally, stopped fighting the idea of meeting Ashley and Tess.

In the distance a black limousine came into view. Pressing her hand over the nerves coiled in her stomach, she turned from the window.

In the back of her mind she had known all along that the only way to cope with a situation that couldn't be changed was to change her attitude toward it. Since fighting the public's interest in her and her mom had gotten her nowhere—and remembering what Ben had said about getting her own story out there about her mother—she had signed a contract three days ago with *Vanity Fair* for an exclusive. What they were paying her for the article and the photos she had from her childhood was more than she would have earned from now until she retired teaching.

She'd also asked Kim to arrange for her to meet the women who would be entering the room any minute.

So much of her life still felt unsettled. So much felt either dead-end or directionless. Even surrounded by her students, she still felt alone. Ben had said she was choosing to be that way.

His words had jarred her. So had his insistence that her mother would want this family for her. The emptiness she'd felt had only compounded itself when he'd said nothing to her before she'd left. With him still possessing her heart, it seemed all she'd been left with was his assurance that her mom wouldn't think less of her for accepting the friendship of kin.

A knock sounded on the door an instant before it swung open. From the hall, she heard Dr. Franklin's deep, well-modulated tones as he asked that his regards be given to William. Two female voices assured him they would be talking with their father soon.

A heartbeat later Jillian heard their thanks for the escort, and both women walked into the room.

The door closed discreetly behind them.

For one awkward instant Jillian's glance darted between them as theirs fixed on her. Both were as classically beautiful as their mother. Both had sleek, shining hair in a dozen shades of wheat. Ashley, with her clear blue eyes and wearing a beautifully tailored caramel silk pantsuit, wore hers clipped at her nape. Tess, her deep-brown eyes so remarkably like Jillian's own, wore hers skimmed back with a silver headband that matched the buttons on her slim charcoal jersey dress.

"Jillian," they both said at once.

"Hi," she murmured, and met them in the middle of the room to offer her hand.

Opening her arms, Ashley smiled. "We can do better than that," she said and gave her a designer-scented hug.

The moment she stepped back, Tess, taller by a good four inches, smiled her lovely smile and hugged her, too.

Setting her back, she left her hands on Jillian's upper arms. "I'll confess, we have a dozen questions to ask. But first, how are you holding up under all this?"

"We managed to get out of town without paparazzi following us, but we ran the gauntlet of yours down by the main gate," Ashley explained. "I just hate it when they hang around like that waiting to pounce when you leave," she confided, touching Jillian's forearm. "You're using a decoy when you have to go somewhere, aren't you?"

"A decoy?"

"Someone who looks like you in a similar car. Your bodyguards haven't suggested it to put them off your track?"

"My bodyguards are back in Washington right now. I really haven't been going anywhere."

"By choice?" Tess asked. "Or because it's too scary out there?"

Jillian looked from one sister to the other. She had no idea what she'd expected from these undeniably poised and polished women, but immediate concern—and understanding—hadn't been it.

Feeling the knot in her stomach begin to unravel, she offered a smile of her own. "*Scary* pretty much sums it up."

"Oh, Jillian," Tess murmured. "We're sorry. We know how unsettling it is to be bait for those sharks. We've grown up with it and I'm still appalled at the lengths some will go to get a shot." Her hands fell. "We're sort of under siege ourselves at the moment."

"It goes in cycles," Ashley told her. "It's worse right now for Mom, Dad and Tess because of the scandals. And for you," she said, including her in the misery. "As claustrophobic as I know it must be, I'm sure you do feel safer out here in the country than you would if you were still staying at the apartment. We heard you couldn't set foot out the door there without being blinded by flashes." Her coral-tinted mouth pinched. "That always makes for such a lovely photograph."

Tess matched her faint sarcasm. "Almost as charming as the reaction shots. I just love it when they jump out and startle you so they can get something truly unflattering. Those invariably get blown up to cover the front page of a tabloid and plastered all over the inside."

Ashley frowned at her sister. "I thought you didn't read those things."

"I don't. I don't read anything about any of us that doesn't have to do with our foundation work or one of Mom's charities. I even avoid all the political stuff about Gabe. Especially that," she murmured, referring to their oldest brother, the governor of the state. "And I never read what was printed about Cord before he finally settled down." She gave an elegant shrug. "Somebody inevitably mentions a lot of it to me, though."

She stepped back, a diamond in the two-carat range winking from her left hand.

She'd just become engaged to her bodyguard. Kim had mentioned that she'd handled Tess's press announcement herself.

Ashley's own wedding set flashed as she toyed with the strands of cream seed pearls at her throat. "I try to avoid the worst of it, too," she confessed, making it sound as if it was easier to keep her sanity that way, "and let Ben Garrett or his people handle anything controversial." She smiled at Jillian. "They've been a godsend haven't they?"

The unexpected mention of Ben's name brought an odd pang beneath her breastbone. Doing her best to ignore it, Jillian backed toward the sofa, motioned them to join her.

"I don't know what I would have done without Ben when this all started," she admitted, being as candid with them as they were being with her. She had never considered that the imprisoned feeling she was living with was something they had experienced all their lives. "I'm working with Kim Silverman now, but it was Ben who kept me focused and guided me through that first week." His advice still guided her. It was why she was with them now.

Understanding entered both women's expressions as they lowered themselves into the wing-back chairs.

"You can tell him anything and he'll only use what he knows will help you." Tess crossed her legs, her tone growing confidential as she leaned toward where Jillian settled in the middle of the sofa. "Dad swears he's the absolute best at crisis management."

"After this thing with Bradley," Ashley said, speaking of Tess's ex-husband, "there probably isn't much about any of us that he doesn't know."

"Isn't that the truth." Looking as relieved as she did chagrined at having had her dirty laundry so publicly aired, Tess gave a small sigh. "I'm really sorry he left the firm."

Jillian's hand stilled as she reached for the teapot. "He left?"

"To go into boat building, I heard," said Ashley, reaching to help.

"With his grandfather," Tess added. "That's what Kim said when I talked with her the other day.

"By the way," she continued, as Jillian quickly covered her shock, "we know Kim wants you to attend a fund-raising tea with us. The one next week," she reminded her. "It's for our foundation, but please don't feel it's something you have to do."

"Would you like me to pour?" Ashley asked as casually as if they'd had tea together a hundred times before.

"Please." Relieved by the request, Jillian edged back on the cushion. She wasn't totally sure what she was supposed to do, anyway. She'd never served tea. She was also hugely grateful that whatever had been in her tone and expression had raised no questions as the conversation had moved to, then past, the man she'd give anything to stop thinking about.

"We have a scholarship program we raise funds for…and we'd love for you to be part of that," Tess continued, "but there's something related to it we'd like to talk with you about."

Ashley's perfectly arched eyebrows pinched ever so slightly as she placed a small silver strainer over a delicate pink cup. "We said we'd give her a chance to get to know us before you start recruiting her, Tess.

"We want to know how you're doing. Aside from the press," Ashley continued to Jillian, watching the strainer catch loose leaves as she poured the steaming gold liquid. "Are you settling into your new position here? Do you like your students and the rest of the staff?

"Because if you don't," Tess piped in, "we have a proposition."

Ashley all but rolled her eyes. "Not now," she whispered.

"I can't help it if I'm excited about her," her sister defended, taking the first cup. She handed it to Jillian on its saucer. "Sorry. I didn't mean to talk as if you weren't here. It's just that we've heard so much from Dad about how important teaching is to you, and you have something we really need."

Both of her half sisters were younger than she was. Ashley, by a couple of years. Tess by another two more. At her youngest sister's enthusiasm, and her other sibling's protectiveness of her, Jillian couldn't help the smile that settled next to the void in her heart. She just couldn't imagine what she had that they could possibly need.

Since she couldn't imagine it, she asked. "What's that?"

"Expertise." Apparently having been just as anxious to get to the subject but far more reserved about broaching it than her sister, Ashley jumped in with both expensively-shod feet. "Our scholarship program is for underprivileged moms," she explained, forgetting her own tea in her concern for their program. "I'm in charge of administering the scholarship portion, and Tess is overseeing building and staffing day care centers for the recipients' children. She's just in the planning stages for the centers now."

"I have a teaching degree," Tess told her, her passion for her project bright in her expression, "but I need the expertise of someone with actual classroom experience to develop and oversee the programs. Or just develop and advise, if you wouldn't have time for more than that. And you wouldn't have to do anything public unless you wanted to. It could all be behind the scenes."

Their enthusiasm was infectious. But then, as they went on to describe what they hoped to achieve for the moms and children in their programs, they were speaking about subjects already near and dear to her heart. After-school tutoring. Programs for struggling students. But what hooked her was Ashley's absolute dedication to providing education for women who would never get any without their help, and Tess's wish to develop a program for their centers that would allow those women's children to acquire basic reading and math skills before they entered first grade.

Ben had implied that she had more in common with her sisters than she thought. It had just never occurred to her that within half an hour of meeting them she would feel almost as if she'd known them forever.

For the first time since she'd lost her job, she felt as if she might have actually found her niche. Tess wasn't talking about opening just one center. She was talking about a half-dozen in cities all over the state of Virginia.

The more they talked, the more her own excitement grew, and the more animated she became. By the time they left, two hours later, with everyone promising to check their schedules for the earliest date to get together again for her to meet their children, she realized she'd even managed to forget about Ben.

He was front and center in her mind, though, from the moment Ashley and Tess passed between the Greco-Roman pillars flanking the administration building's front door and their chauffeur closed them into their limo.

He'd left the firm, they'd said. To build boats.

She didn't know which felt stronger just then, the need to protect herself or the need to tell him how happy she was for him and his grandfather.

Chapter Ten

Jillian listened for the buzz of the saw that had greeted her the last time she'd entered the warehouselike shop overlooking Pops's little inlet. As she approached the open door, though, all she could hear was the crunch of crushed shells and stones beneath her feet and the cry of gulls wheeling in the blue October sky.

Had it not been for the industrial lights she could see lit through the upper windows, she might have thought no one was there. It was Sunday, after all. But the BMW Ben had driven from D.C. when she'd last been to his place was parked not far from where Schroeder watched out for her from the black SUV he'd been chauffeuring her in all weekend.

Hugging a gold gift bag to her cream cable-knit sweater, she stopped in the doorway and drew off her sunglasses.

Across the high, open space, the boat under construction

still rose amidst its scaffolding. A cockpit and the framing of a cabin now rose where there had only been deck before. The scents of resin and solvent mingled faintly with the crisp fall air coming through the large open doors that let in the lap of deep water against rocks. The floor needed sweeping again.

She'd barely noticed how quiet the space was without the clank of cranes, saws, hammering and male voices when her glance moved to the long workbench on the wall. Ben stood at one of the worktables in front of it. His back was to her. Charcoal cargo pants hugged his lean hips. A gray fleece shirt stretched across his shoulders as he bent over the table, his arms braced on either side of him while he studied the blueprints covering its surface.

It seemed no one else was there.

She'd barely drawn the breath of the courage she needed to step in when she saw his head come up. He couldn't have heard her. She hadn't made a sound. It was more as if he'd sensed someone was there as he straightened and turned toward the door.

Pushing back the dark hair that had fallen over his forehead, his eyes narrowed. With the bright light at her back, she thought it might take him a few seconds to recognize her.

It took two.

"Jillian?"

"Hi."

"Hi, yourself."

Curiosity and something that looked almost like pleasure moved into the lean, masculine lines of his face as he walked toward her. She'd had no idea how he would react to seeing her. But there was no denying the relief she felt at his guarded smile.

She moved closer herself, met him halfway across the concrete floor. "Where's Pops?"

"Watching a football game over at the Binghams'."

"You didn't want to go?"

"I wanted to figure out a wiring problem." He tipped his head, his blue eyes on hers. "What are you doing here?" he asked.

"I was on my way home, so I thought I'd drop by. I went to your house first, but your car wasn't there."

"On your way home?" Confusion joined curiosity. "From where?"

"Ashley's. I spent yesterday and last night with her. And Matt and Amelia," she added, speaking of Ashley's husband and daughter—her brother-in-law and niece, she mentally corrected. Tess had been there, too, with her fiancé, Jeff Parker, and her three-year-old son, Mikey. Gabe and his very pregnant wife, Addie, had come by for a while. As had Cord and his wife, Madison. She had more relatives than she'd thought.

"Doesn't she live in northern Virginia?"

"She does." On a fabulous two-hundred-acre estate in a gorgeous home that her contractor husband built for her so they could have their privacy. "I'm just taking the long way back to Exeter Hall. Actually, Schroeder is driving. I've given up going out on my own for a while."

"Because of the incident at the gas station," he concluded.

"You read about that."

"It was sort of hard to miss. It made the front page of every paper in the state and was an item in all the rest."

"Yeah, well, live and learn, huh?" She offered a smile, gave a small shrug that totally belied the anxiety she felt seeing him again. "That's sort of the reason I'm here. Life lessons," she explained. "I need to thank you for talking me…badgering me," she corrected, because the term was infinitely more accurate, "into meeting my sisters.

"You were right, Ben." She offered the concession as she toyed with the little gold rope handles on the gift bag. "I fought pretty much everything that had happened. I'd probably still be doing it if it I hadn't listened to you. But then," she admitted, because she wanted him to know this, too, "your advice for me had always been pretty sound."

He didn't seem interested in taking credit. "Most of it was just logical."

"To you, maybe. It wasn't at first to me." She held out the bag to him. "This is for you."

It seemed he felt as cautious with her as she did with him. As if to avoid brushing her hand, he took the narrow sack she offered by the bottom. The furrows in his forehead deepened as he lifted out the bottle inside. He'd barely exposed its gold foil-wrapped neck when one dark eyebrow arched.

"You're giving me champagne?"

"I wanted to bring you something to christen your first project with."

Her visit—and a two-hundred-mile detour—now seemed to make sense. He lifted his chin, gave a little nod.

"You heard that I'd come to work with Pops."

"And that you'd left the firm." She could still hardly believe he'd done that. "Tess told me last week. I'd been afraid you might still be angry with me over some of the things I said," she quietly confided. "I guess I'm hoping now that what you've done means we can end on a better note than we did."

For a moment Ben said nothing. He just looked from the bottle to the woman he'd missed more than he had thought humanly possible. He hadn't intended to talk to her about what he'd done. Not just yet, anyway. There was too much he wanted to have settled before he approached her with his proposition. With as much change as she'd had to cope with already, he hadn't wanted to hit her up with a plan where so many things were still up in the air.

From what she'd just said, though, he wondered if he'd sensed a connection between them that hadn't really been there.

"Do you want us to end?" he asked.

Jillian's heart bumped. Desperate not to sound…desperate, she made herself smile. "Do I have a choice?"

She was getting better at masking what she felt, Ben realized, the moment he saw the quick shadow of anxiety vanish with the soft curving of her mouth. When he'd first met her, he'd doubted she could have hidden what she felt had her life depended on it. Nearly every emotion she experienced had been visible in her lovely golden-brown eyes.

Now it seemed she'd all but mastered the composed facade he'd helped her build. He'd feared she would be too vulnerable in public without it. But she wasn't in public now. And he didn't want her hiding what she felt from him. He needed to know just how much of a chance he had.

He stepped closer. With the bottle in one hand, he lifted his other to her cheek. Relieved to be touching her, more relieved that she wasn't pulling away, he skimmed his knuckles over the curve of her jaw.

"You do," he assured her. "It's just not the choice I'd wanted to offer."

The mask was still a work in progress. At his touch, or maybe at what he said, she drew an unsteady breath. "What do you mean?"

He glanced toward the door. "How long can you stay?"

"Until I'm ready to go. Schroeder reads when he doesn't have to be driving or looking out for me. He's out there working on *War and Peace*."

"Then, come on." Dropping his hand, he turned to set the

bottle on the workbench. "There's something I want to show you."

Leading her around the scaffolding, he headed to the huge door that opened to the deep grays and blues of the bay. Moving along the back of the high, weathered building, he pointed to the lighthouse at the end of the long spit a half-mile away.

"When my dad grew up here, this inlet and Taylor's Cove over there," he said, indicating the promontory of rocky land jutting into the water behind them, "was pretty much the extent of his world. Except for this business and a few mom-and-pop operations serving the crabbers and fishermen, there wasn't anything for a man to do here but work the water himself. It's a hard life. A good one," he qualified, "for those with the bay in their blood. But I think Dad was born missing that gene.

"I think it really bothered Pops," he continued. "But Dad couldn't live the life his father wanted for him. Dad told me once that he'd decided when he was fourteen that he was getting out of here no matter what it took. He was a big kid, big guy now. And smart. He managed to earn both football and academic scholarships. He got his MBA from Yale, went to work as a press secretary and married the daughter of a diplomat. Within ten years he'd started his own PR firm and was signing A-list clients.

"That's the environment I grew up in," he said.

With his hands in his pockets Ben walked slowly along the path two centuries worth of Garretts had trod along their little piece of the Chesapeake. A dozen feet away the water gently lapped the rocky shoreline, creating little pools between the bigger boulders.

Jillian walked beside him, snatching back her hair from the crisp breeze as she studied the pensive lines of his profile.

"My parents' friends were either in politics or CEOs of major corporations. We belonged to the country club and the yacht club and there was never any question that I'd go to Yale, too. Even when I spent summers here, I'd never believed I had the option of making it my life. The only time I ever mentioned it, Dad said I'd suffocate in what he'd escaped.

"It wasn't as if I didn't like what I had in the city," he explained. "As I got older, I realized I liked having money. I liked being the best at what I did. I liked winning," he concluded, summing up what had probably driven him to the success he'd demanded of himself in everything he'd attempted.

Except his marriage, he thought. He'd truly been his father's son. "I honestly thought that was how I'd live the rest of my life," he said over the distant ring of a bell buoy, "until you made me see that my life was sucking me dry."

You need to stop living the life that made you so unhappy.

Jillian's words had kept coming back to him. Every time they had, he'd dismissed them as summarily as he had the idea of leaving what he had to go and work with Pops—until he realized he was hearing her soft voice every time he reached for an antacid, which seemed to be every other hour.

When he'd finally stopped insisting to himself that she had no idea what she was talking about, he began to admit how truly unhappy he was.

She had clearly known him better than he'd realized. Socially and in business he'd always sought out high-powered, single-minded and driven people like himself. He'd even married one, then felt utterly betrayed when her ruthless ambition had allowed nothing and no one to derail her from the fast track. He should have realized then that the price of staying in the game was too high. But, unlike the woman walking quietly beside him, he'd blamed only his ex-wife for the bitterness and distrust that threatened to consume him.

"Are you okay?" he heard Jillian ask.

"Never better," he said, meaning it. "I have a new plan," he told her, "it's just going take a while to iron out the kinks."

"Kinks?"

"I'm not exactly sure how I'll manage my time between working with Pops and working in D.C. I've kept a couple of clients who said they'd leave the firm if I didn't stay," he told her. "And I don't want to do that to Dad. I've told him I'll handle them until their current contracts expire. They're promotional PR mostly." And not at all likely to create problems that they expect others to fix for them. The Kendricks had never been in that category. He'd felt good about what he'd accomplished for them, too. Especially now that he knew Jillian had let them into her life. The Kendricks were good people. Clients like that, he had no problem working with at all.

"I'll have to travel once in a while," he continued, still mulling logistics. He'd keep his town house in Washington. He'd need a base there. But he'd need a way to make better time between there and Taylor's Cove. He knew how to fly. Maybe he'd buy a small plane. "But I'll spend most of my time working with Pops here. I figure I'll work the business with him until he's gone. Then I'll decide whether to continue with it or sell it." Unless I have sons who want to continue the legacy, he thought, but he was getting light-years ahead of himself.

"What would you do if you sold it?"

"I'm not sure." In his mind that decision was twenty years down the road. And the idea of selling what had been in the family so long just didn't seem right. "All I know for certain is that I won't go back to the firm. Dad and I have realized we get along better when we're not working together."

"Because you were living his dream?"

A smile kicked up one corner of his mouth. "Something like that."

"How is he with what you're doing for Pops?"

"He doesn't understand it and he's not crazy about me not wanting to take on his company when he retires, but *he* didn't want to take on his father's business, either. There wasn't much he could say.

"How about you?" he asked, needing to know where she was in her new life. Mostly, needing to know if there was room for him. "It sounds as if you're okay with the Kendricks now."

He watched her lift her face to the breeze, letting the cool wind push the hair from her face.

"I am," she quietly admitted.

The glimmer of hope she'd felt when he'd caressed her cheek had flickered out. She wasn't sure why he'd told her all that he just had—unless he was setting up ground rules. He'd implied that they didn't have to end, but knowing how he felt about relationships, it was entirely possible he was letting her know that if they continued, it wouldn't be for a while. Even though she was no longer his client, he had too much going on right now to spend any real time together.

"How about with everything else?" he asked as gravel and shells gave way to stones embedded in hard-packed dirt.

It would have been so much easier not to be hurt by her apparent lack of importance to him had she not already been in love with the guy.

"I've resigned myself to accepting that nearly everything has changed, if that's what you mean. And some of it is for the better," she conceded, because he'd told her it would be. "I'm just not sure how long I'll stay at Exeter Hall. I will through next May because I signed on for the school year and it's providing me a place to live right now. But I'll also be working in Richmond with Ashley and Tess a couple of days a week for this scholarship program they run.

"For underprivileged mothers and their children," she explained, though she suspected he was fairly well acquainted with the work the two sisters did. Ashley had told her that Ben had done the foundation's promo work for free. "In the meantime, we'll work by phone and e-mail, and anything we have to do in person, we'll do on weekends."

"Things sound as unsettled for you as they are right now for me."

She looked over to see his features clouded in thought. She wanted to feel pleased for him for what he'd done for himself. And she did. She could only imagine how he must feel to be free of what had been draining the spirit from his soul. For that and the satisfaction he had to feel knowing he was there for his grandfather, she was hugely grateful. She just didn't want him to feel he needed to point out again how crowded his life already was.

"The voice of experience here," she said with a sympathetic smile. "You'll get used to it. It's all a matter of figuring out your priorities." She'd needed to protect her mom's reputation, accept bodyguards and find a safe place to live. Pretty much in that order. He'd helped her see that. What he needed first, she had no idea.

"I have them figured out," he assured her. He just wasn't nearly as prepared as he would have liked to be to talk to her about them. But now that he'd started…

"I'm just wondering if your life is still too unsettled to add to the chaos."

He felt her hesitate.

"What do you mean?"

Coming to a halt, he caught her arm, turned her to look at him. With the breeze now at her back, her hair blew in a cloud of sable curls around her head. But it was her eyes that held his focus.

"I have everything in my life that I need now, Jillian. Except you."

Looking straight ahead, all she could see as she caught her hair back from her face was the soft gray fleece covering his chest. Looking up, past his chin and the carved line of his mouth, she met the absolute conviction in his eyes—and an odd sort of hesitation.

The conviction looked just like him. The hesitation did not.

She felt as if she were barely breathing. "Me?"

"Yeah, you," he murmured, and watched the thin veil of her guard fall.

She wasn't masking anything from him now. A sense of reprieve washed over him. Or maybe it was relief he felt as he slipped his hand around the back of her neck and her vulnerability to him pulled him closer.

"I fell in love with you," he said, grazing her jaw with his thumb. "It's just that when I realized it, I was in the middle of telling Dad I was leaving and Pops that I wanted to work with him…and I wasn't sure that I hadn't totally blown it with you.

"I'd planned to call you from D.C. next week," he admitted, following his glance as his thumb edged toward the corner of her mouth. "I figured you'd either tell me to drop dead or come on down. If you thought we could pick up where we'd left off, then I planned to just take it slow for a while. See each other when we could. As much as has changed for you already, I didn't think you'd want to rush into anything."

Jillian wasn't quite sure what "anything" meant to him. At

the moment, she didn't even think to ask. He had just told her he loved her. Of everything he possibly could have said, she couldn't imagine anything she'd been less prepared to hear.

"I'm fine with…picking up."

A smile tugged at his mouth. "Yeah?"

"Yeah," she murmured, touching her hand to his chest. "Because I love you back."

The smile in his eyes faltered, then gave way to something far more sober as his glance held hers. With his heart beating heavily beneath her palm, he slowly cupped her face with his hands.

Her breath hitched, then escaped in a sigh as his head lowered and his mouth covered hers.

Ben drank in that small, sweet sound, savoring it, meeting it with a more guttural groan of his own. She felt the same need he could taste on her lips as she returned the kiss that started tenderly, then edged toward hunger as he buried his fingers in her hair, her long tresses billowing around their heads.

He had feared he might never again know the warmth and peace that had touched him as he'd lain with her in his arms. With her warmth flowing through him as she curved her arms around his neck, he could almost feel the void inside his heart slowly close, then quietly disappear.

Having done a fair job of altering his heart rate and her breathing, he turned his back to the wind to block her from it and eased her head to his chest.

"So," he said into her hair, "no pressure. But considering the changes you've already been through, how much more would you be okay with now?"

At the cautious note in his voice she lifted her head. "I've become a pro at it. What did you have in mind?"

"Eventually?" he asked, smoothing his moisture from her mouth with the pad of his thumb. "Or for now?"

Hope reared its head again. "Eventually."

"Marriage. Kids."

She blinked at his surprisingly relaxed expression.

"You asked," he reminded her. "I answered." He tugged her closer. "Or we could forget the slow plan and go for broke by getting married whenever we can find a spare weekend."

She now fully understood what he'd meant a while ago about adding to the chaos of her life. Yet, as she stood there with his arms wrapped around her, the sounds of the gulls and the ring of the distant buoy surrounding them, she felt no concern at all about merging their respective worlds. The logistics might be a challenge, but they'd met challenges together before.

She lifted her arms back around his neck, raised up on tiptoe. "I think I've actually grown rather fond of change," she said, smiling into his eyes. Both of their lives had taken turns in totally unexpected directions. But those turns had led them straight to each other. "Life actually might be rather boring without it."

"You think so?"

"Within reason," she qualified. "I'm rather fond of stability, too."

He gathered her closer. "Then, anytime you're ready," he murmured, and lowered his head to hers once more.

Epilogue

"How about over Thanksgiving?"

"That's only three weeks away, Ben. That's not nearly enough time to plan a wedding. Besides, I told the headmaster I'd stay on campus for the students who won't be going home."

"Christmas, then. That would give you another month and you won't have school for a couple of weeks. That would even give us time to get away for a while."

"I can't do it then, either. I told them I'd stay at the school then, too."

"Why did you do that?"

"Because when the schedule came out, I didn't think I'd have anyplace else to go myself."

Jillian felt Ben's hand on her shoulder give a little squeeze. He stood behind her at the kitchen island at his shore house, where she sat with her day planner open and feathered with sticky notes. His day planner, larger and with fewer doodles on the pages, sat open next to hers.

"How about over spring break?" she asked. "I scheduled myself to stay at school then, too, but that would give me enough time to work something out with one of the other teachers."

"When is it?"

She flipped pages. "The first week in April."

Ben leaned forward, his big, solid body brushing her back as he flipped pages himself.

"Not good," he muttered. "We're handling Gabe Kendrick's PR for his re-election next year. That first weekend is the kickoff banquet."

"You have to be there?"

"That's one of the accounts I told my dad I'd keep working for a while. Since the Kendrick name is so important to the firm, it would be politically incorrect not to be. Especially since the Kendricks are my future in-laws."

He handed her his pen, mentioned that she should probably attend, too. If she could arrange the time off, he clearly wanted her there himself. "Anyway," he murmured, easing back as she wrote, "William and Katherine will be there, too. And Cord, Ashley, Tess and their spouses."

"Which means that date wouldn't work for them, either," she concluded, and set the pen down. Turning on the backless stool, she glanced up at the carved lines of Ben's handsome face. In the past few weeks, they'd managed to meet every weekend. Twice at his brownstone in Washington because he'd been there attending meetings. Twice now at his shore house, because that was where he now spent most of his time and where they both wanted most to be.

"I forgot to tell you," she said, "Ashley offered yesterday

to let us have the ceremony and reception at her and Matt's estate. She said she has a great caterer and florist and that they're quite discreet. That would minimize chances of a date being leaked to the press."

"Do you want to get married there?"

"It's a beautiful place. And it's about as private as we can get without hiring the entire staff of Bennington's to keep paparazzi out of a church and hotel. But having it there would make it difficult for the people here that you want to invite to attend. I don't know what kind of accommodations there are nearby. Or how affordable they'd be."

Ben's brow pinched thoughtfully as he gently nudged her hair back from her face. "We can always have a party for everyone around here later. The only person I want to have there for sure is Pops."

"And Jace."

Jace Hunter would be his best man. She'd met the affable, still-single, high-powered corporate attorney in Washington last week. Ben's racquetball buddy—who also happened to be the man who'd broken to Ben the news of his ex-wife's deceit—had seen him through what Jace called Ben's "black period." He'd seemed genuinely grateful to her to have his old friend back.

"What about your father?"

"Of course, I'll ask him to come."

"And your mom?"

Ben blew a breath. "I'd rather just have people I'm close to there. I'll ask her, but I know she won't come if Dad attends, anyway. The last time they saw each other was at my college graduation. Dad kept trying to pick a fight with her and her husband. Mom did a great reenactment of the first Ice Age."

Lovely, Jillian thought.

"How about you?" Ben asked, absently stroking her cheek with his finger. "Other than Stacy—" who he knew would be her maid of honor "—who do you want to have there?"

If someone had asked her that question a couple of years ago, back before her life had started to change so radically, she would have come up with a list of neighbors, people she worked with, her students. She'd always thought that when she married, she'd want it all. The fabulous gown, the huge cake, acres of flowers.

She could have that, too. All of it. And on a grander scale than she would have once dreamed possible. When William had learned from Ashley that she and Ben were engaged, he had called to tell her that, as the father of the bride, he'd be happy to foot the bill for whatever she and Ben wanted. Katherine, whose kindness never failed to touch Jillian, had come on the phone then to offer use of the estate at Camelot, if she'd feel comfortable being married there.

"Ashley and Tess," she replied, because the women had so quickly become wonderful friends as well as siblings. "All the Kendricks," she admitted, thinking of how easily her brothers and their wives had drawn her into their rarified little circles. "And Pops."

"That's it? You don't want something bigger?"

Laying her hand on his chest, looking into his eyes, she slowly shook her head. "Not unless you do."

"Then if we're only having a handful of people why do we need time to plan a wedding? There's only a two-day waiting period from the application date until a license is issued in Maryland. In Virginia, there's no waiting period at all. We could get one and use it the same day."

Her heart was doing the little bumping thing against her breastbone again. "How do you know that?"

"I checked. So," he continued, pulling her up to gather her in his arms, "what are you doing the weekend after Thanksgiving?"

Smiling, she eased her arms around his neck. She knew they both had that weekend free. They'd planned to spend it together. "If that date's okay with Ashley, it looks like I'm getting married." She tipped her head, watched his eyes lower to her mouth. "Do you want to call her now?"

"In a minute," he said. "There's something I need to do first."

He kissed her then, leaving her a little breathless, just as he always did, then set her back with a grin and handed her his cell phone.

According to Ashley, the weekend after Thanksgiving would be absolutely perfect.

And it was.

* * * * *

THE ROYAL HOUSE OF NIROLI

Always passionate, always proud

The richest royal family in the world—
united by blood and passion,
torn apart by deceit and desire

Nestled in the azure blue of the Mediterranean Sea, the majestic island of Niroli has prospered for centuries. The Fierezza men have worn the crown with passion and pride since ancient times. But now, as the king's health declines, and his two sons have been tragically killed, the crown is in jeopardy.

The clock is ticking—a new heir must be found before the king is forced to abdicate. By royal decree the internationally scattered members of the Fierezza family are summoned to claim their destiny. But any person who takes the throne must do so according to The Rules of the Royal House of Niroli. Soon secrets and rivalries emerge as the descendants of this ancient royal line vie for position and power. Only a true Fierezza can become ruler—a person dedicated to their country, their people...and their eternal love!

Each month starting in July 2007,
Harlequin Presents is delighted to bring you
an exciting installment from
THE ROYAL HOUSE OF NIROLI,
in which you can follow the epic search
for the true Nirolian king.
Eight heirs, eight romances, eight fantastic stories!

Here's your chance to enjoy a sneak preview of the first book delivered to you by royal decree...

Five minutes later she was standing immobile in front of the study's window, her original purpose of coming in forgotten, as she stared in shocked horror at the envelope she was holding. Waves of heat followed by icy chill surged through her body. She could hardly see the address now through her blurred vision, but the crest on its left-hand front corner stood out, its royal crest, followed by the address: HRH Prince Marco of Niroli…

She didn't hear Marco's key in the apartment door, she didn't even hear him calling out her name. Her shock was so great that nothing could penetrate it. It encased her in a kind of bubble, which only concentrated the torment of what she was suffering and branded it on her brain so that it could never be forgotten. It was only finally pierced by the sudden opening of the study door as Marco walked in.

"Welcome home, *Your Highness.* I suppose I ought to curtsy." She waited, praying that he would laugh and tell her that she had got it all wrong, that the envelope she was holding, addressing him as Prince Marco of Niroli, was some silly mistake. But like a tiny candle flame shivering vulnerably in the dark, her hope trembled fearfully. And then the look in Marco's eyes extinguished it as cruelly as a hand placed callously over a dying person's face to stem their last breath.

"Give that to me," he demanded, taking the envelope from her.

"It's too late, Marco," Emily told him brokenly. "I know the truth now…." She dug her teeth in her lower lip to try to force back her own pain.

"You had no right to go through my desk," Marco shot back at her furiously, full of loathing at being caught off guard and forced into a position in which he was in the wrong, making him determined to find something he could accuse Emily of. "I trusted you…."

Emily could hardly believe what she was hearing. "No, you didn't trust me, Marco, and you didn't trust me because you knew that I couldn't trust you. And you knew that because you're a liar, and liars don't trust people because they know that they themselves cannot be trusted." She not only felt sick, she also felt as though she could hardly breathe. "You are Prince Marco of Niroli…. How could you not tell me who you are and still live with me as intimately as we have lived together?" she demanded brokenly.

"Stop being so ridiculously dramatic," Marco demanded fiercely. "You are making too much of the situation."

"*Too much?*" Emily almost screamed the words at him. "When were you going to tell me, Marco? Perhaps you just planned to walk away without telling me anything? After all, what do my feelings matter to you?"

"Of course they matter." Marco stopped her sharply. "And it was in part to protect them, and you, that I decided not to inform you when my grandfather first announced that he intended to step down from the throne and hand it on to me."

"To protect me?" Emily nearly choked on her fury. "Hand on the throne? No wonder you told me when you first took me to bed that all you wanted was sex. You *knew* that was the only kind of relationship there could ever be between us! You *knew* that one day you would be Niroli's king. No doubt you are expected to marry a princess. Is she picked out for you already, your *royal* bride?"

* * * * *

Look for
THE FUTURE KING'S PREGNANT MISTRESS
by Penny Jordan
in July 2007,
from Harlequin Presents,
available wherever books are sold.

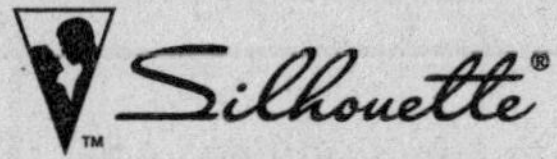

Romantic

SUSPENSE

Sparked by Danger, Fueled by Passion.

Mission: Impassioned

A brand-new miniseries begins with

My Spy

By *USA TODAY* bestselling author

Marie Ferrarella

She had to trust him with her life....
It was the most daring mission of Joshua Lazlo's career: rescuing the prime minister of England's daughter from a gang of cold-blooded kidnappers. But nothing prepared the shadowy secret agent for a fiery woman whose touch ignited something far more dangerous.

My Spy

#1472

Available July 2007 wherever you buy books!

Visit Silhouette Books at www.eHarlequin.com SRS27542

Do you know a real-life heroine?

Nominate her for the Harlequin More Than Words award.

Each year Harlequin Enterprises honors five ordinary women for their extraordinary commitment to their community.

Each recipient of the Harlequin More Than Words award receives a $10,000 donation from Harlequin to advance the work of her chosen charity. And five of Harlequin's most acclaimed authors donate their time and creative talents to writing a novella inspired by the award recipients. The More Than Words anthology is published annually in October and all proceeds benefit causes of concern to women.

HARLEQUIN

More Than Words™

For more details or to nominate a woman you know please visit

www.HarlequinMoreThanWords.com

MTW2007

REQUEST YOUR FREE BOOKS!

2 FREE NOVELS PLUS 2 FREE GIFTS!

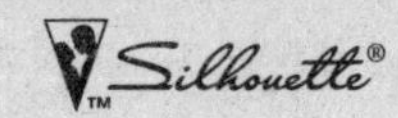

SPECIAL EDITION®

Life, Love and Family!

YES! Please send me 2 FREE Silhouette Special Edition® novels and my 2 FREE gifts. After receiving them, if I don't wish to receive any more books, I can return the shipping statement marked "cancel." If I don't cancel, I will receive 6 brand-new novels every month and be billed just $4.24 per book in the U.S., or $4.99 per book in Canada, plus 25¢ shipping and handling per book and applicable taxes, if any*. That's a savings of at least 15% off the cover price! I understand that accepting the 2 free books and gifts places me under no obligation to buy anything. I can always return a shipment and cancel at any time. Even if I never buy another book from Silhouette, the two free books and gifts are mine to keep forever. 235 SDN EEYU 335 SDN EEY6

Name (PLEASE PRINT)

Address Apt.

City State/Prov. Zip/Postal Code

Signature (if under 18, a parent or guardian must sign)

Mail to the **Silhouette Reader Service™:**
IN U.S.A.: P.O. Box 1867, Buffalo, NY 14240-1867
IN CANADA: P.O. Box 609, Fort Erie, Ontario L2A 5X3

Not valid to current Silhouette Special Edition subscribers.

Want to try two free books from another line?
Call 1-800-873-8635 or visit www.morefreebooks.com.

* Terms and prices subject to change without notice. NY residents add applicable sales tax. Canadian residents will be charged applicable provincial taxes and GST. This offer is limited to one order per household. All orders subject to approval. Credit or debit balances in a customer's account(s) may be offset by any other outstanding balance owed by or to the customer. Please allow 4 to 6 weeks for delivery.

Your Privacy: Silhouette is committed to protecting your privacy. Our Privacy Policy is available online at www.eHarlequin.com or upon request from the Reader Service. From time to time we make our lists of customers available to reputable firms who may have a product or service of interest to you. If you would prefer we not share your name and address, please check here. ☐

SSE07

**The richest royal family in the world—
a family united by blood and passion,
torn apart by deceit and desire.**

Step into the glamorous, enticing world of the Nirolian Royal Family. As the king ails he must find an heir…each month an exciting new installment follows the epic search for the true Nirolian king. Eight heirs, eight romances, eight fantastic stories!

It's time for playboy prince Marco Fierezza to claim his rightful place…on the throne of Niroli! Emily loves Marco, but she has no idea he's a royal prince! What will this king-in-waiting do when he discovers his mistress is pregnant?

THE FUTURE KING'S PREGNANT MISTRESS

by Penny Jordan

(#2643)

On sale July 2007.

www.eHarlequin.com

HP12643

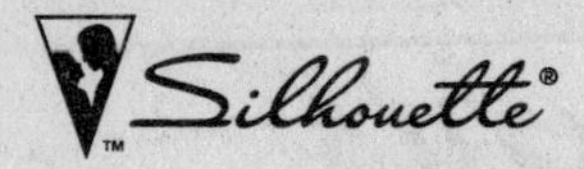

SPECIAL EDITION®

COMING NEXT MONTH

#1837 THE MAN WHO HAD EVERYTHING—
Christine Rimmer
Montana Mavericks: Striking It Rich
When Grant Clifton decided to sell the family ranch, how would he tell Stephanie Julen, the caretaker who'd always been like a little sister to him, that she and her mother would have to leave…especially now that he was head-over-heels in love with her? Was the man who had everything about to lose it all in a betrayal of the woman he was falling for?

#1838 THE PLAYBOY TAKES A WIFE—Crystal Green
As the new CEO of his family's corporation, scandal-sheet regular Lucas Chandler needed an image makeover fast. Visiting a Mexican orphanage seemed like the perfect PR ploy for the playboy—until volunteer and ultimate good girl Alicia Sanchez taught him a lesson in living the good life through good works…and lasting love.

#1839 A BARGAIN CALLED MARRIAGE—Kate Welsh
Her mother's troubled relationships had always cast a pall over Samantha Hopewell's own hunt for Mr. Perfect. Then Italian race-boat driver Niccolo Verdini came to recover from an accident at her family manor, and the healing began…in Samantha's heart.

#1840 HIS BROTHER'S GIFT—Mary J. Forbes
Alaskan bush pilot Will Rubens had carved out a carefree life for himself—until Savanna Stowe showed up on his doorstep with Will's orphaned nephew in tow. Will now found himself the guardian of a young autistic boy…but it was earth mother Savanna who quickly took custody of Will's affections.

#1841 THE RANCHER'S SECOND CHANCE—Nicole Foster
As childhood sweethearts, dirt-poor Rafe Garrett and wealthy Julene Santiago had let their differences tear them apart. Now, years later, Julene returned to town to help her ailing father—and ran smack dab into Rafe. Would the old, unbridgeable gulf reopen between them… or would the love of a lifetime get a second chance?

#1842 THE BABY BIND—Nikki Benjamin
After several unsuccessful attempts at conceiving left her marriage in tatters, Charlotte Fagan had one last hope—to adopt a foreign child. For the application to be approved, though, she and her estranged husband, Sean, would have to pretend to still be together. He agreed to go along with the plan—on one condition….

SSECNM0607